THE
FOSTER
DAUGHTER

BOOKS BY LAURA WOLFE

Two Widows

She Lies Alone

Her Best Friend's Lie

We Live Next Door

The Girl Before Me

The In-Laws

Prom Queen

Laura Wolfe

THE
FOSTER
DAUGHTER

bookouture

Published by Bookouture in 2024

An imprint of Storyfire Ltd.
Carmelite House
50 Victoria Embankment
London EC4Y 0DZ

www.bookouture.com

Storyfire Ltd's authorised representative in the EEA is Hachette Ireland
8 Castlecourt Centre
Castleknock Road
Castleknock
Dublin 15 D15 YF6A
Ireland

ISBN: 978-1-83618-038-8
eBook ISBN: 978-1-83618-037-1

For my family

PROLOGUE

He'd left me no choice but to steal the money. The gloves made my hands sweat as I crouched beneath the desk, ducking into the shadows. I aimed my phone's flashlight at the low-budget safe, focusing on hitting one number at a time. The drawer beeped open, and I tipped my head back, breathing in shallow gulps. I'd gotten the code right. I told myself to calm down and get a grip. No one would be at the office of Toven Brothers Construction at 10 p.m. on a Wednesday night.

A handle rattled opposite me, the noise stopping my heart. *Shit! Shit!* Someone was here. The door swung open, and harsh lights blinded my eyes. I toppled backward, knocking my elbow against the desk.

"Sandra? What the hell?" My boss, Drew Toven, tilted his head in confusion as he looked at the open safe, clearly shocked to find me lurking in the shadows. "What do you think you're doing?" His eyes were strange and possessed as his feet hit the floor in heavy thuds. He grabbed my arm, pinning me between him and the desk.

A nightmarish vision of what would happen next tore through me. This man would overpower me and take what he thought I owed him. I yanked my arm away and kneed him in the groin. Drew snatched a handful of my shirt, the collar digging into my windpipe. I couldn't breathe. Black spots hovered before my eyes as I envisioned my little son, Noah, asleep in the break room across the hall. One arm stretched behind me, straining to locate the hard handle of the knife I'd slipped into my back pocket on the off chance I'd have to defend myself. The blade swung forward, plunging into Drew's flesh. My grip on the knife loosened as I stumbled backward, gulping for air.

Drew lay at my feet, clutching his stomach and gasping.

No. This couldn't be happening again. I leaped toward the light switch, returning the room to darkness.

My mind spun, thoughts tangling as the beam of light from my phone bounced around the cluttered office. *Quickly. Quickly.* My plan was spiraling, but I couldn't panic. Noah and I needed money before we ran. I returned to the safe where Toven Brothers stashed their piles of cash, stuffing the loot into my bag with trembling hands.

Drew moaned. I flashed my light toward him as he touched the knife's handle. Blood bloomed across the fabric of his shirt.

"Don't pull it out," I whispered before using the office phone to call for an ambulance. Although I hated the man, I had never planned to injure him, much less cause his death.

Drew gurgled, but I was already halfway out the door, ducking into the break room to retrieve Noah. We'd be long gone by the time my boss was coherent enough to tell the authorities who stabbed him.

My foot hit the accelerator as I followed the highway out of Las Vegas, checking for flashing lights in my rearview mirror. All traces of Sandra Matthews would disappear when I shed the fake Southern accent and the dyed blonde hair. Once we reached Michigan, I could hide in plain sight and make a fresh start with Noah. It was the place I'd grown up in what felt like another life. Shame crept up my neck at the horrible thing I'd done back then—the way I'd run away and the mess I'd left behind. But the house on Marigold Street was the closest thing I had to roots. Returning was risky, but I was tired of running.

It was time to face my past.

ONE

We hovered on the doorstep of 1189 Marigold Street, Noah's clammy hand in mine. It had been over fifteen years since I'd stood in this spot on the Eckharts' front step. The two-story red-brick house looked the same as the last time I'd seen it, except a little worse for wear—a shingle missing from the roof and a few greenish stains on the white siding. But the lawn was freshly cut, and an attractive wooden gate led to a manicured backyard, where the hedges bordering the fence had grown taller, and snapdragons bloomed from well-tended flower beds. I craned my neck, spotting the detached garage in the back and what used to be a small apartment above it.

It took us over two weeks to get to Berkley, a small, middle-class suburb just north of Detroit with tidy lots and bustling shops and restaurants. It was the kind of tight-knit community that many never left, or if they did, often returned after other adventures took them somewhere else. Noah and I had stayed at a few low-budget motels along our cross-country drive, where I'd dyed my hair from blonde to black, cut it to shoulder length, and added bangs. After the stabbing in Nevada, I needed some time to lie low, shed my previous identity, and clear my head. As I waited on the doorstep, I reminded myself again that I was no longer Sandra. Or Bethany. Or Ginny. Or Kayla. Or any of the other names I'd used over the last fifteen years. I was Riley Wakefield, as I'd explained to Noah a few days earlier, and I had the original birth certificate to prove it. With a deep breath, I stepped forward and pressed the doorbell.

A few seconds passed in silence. Only a dog barking from a neighbor's yard and the rumble of a distant lawnmower cut through the suburban air. Noah stomped his foot, clutching his stuffed monkey. I looked down at him, offering a reassuring smile. "Mommy used to live here."

His saucer eyes gleamed in the midday sun as he pointed to the house. "Right here?"

I nodded, and he did a little hop.

Just then, the lock on the door clicked, and a bear of a woman filled the opening, eyeing us. "Yes?"

"Hi, Mrs. Eckhart." I heard the quiver in my voice, unsure how my sudden and unannounced arrival would be received or if she would even recognize her runaway foster daughter from so many years ago. I'd been second-guessing my plan, imagining a thousand different scenarios, the worst case being a slap across my cheek followed by a police escort off the property. I swallowed, my throat suddenly parched. "I know it's been a long time. But I hope you remember me."

The woman studied me. Her lips were pinned, her eyes narrow and wary. She looked at Noah, then back at me. Her hands dropped to her sides, and her mouth fell open. "Sorry. Who are you?"

"I'm your former foster daughter. I lived here for almost a year." I hoped she'd see something familiar in my face, in the curve of my nose or the shape of my eyes. But I was fifteen years older—a curvy woman in my early thirties, not the malnourished sixteen-year-old she likely remembered. "It's me... Riley Wakefield." I pulled out the birth certificate I'd kept in a box for years and held it out to her.

She took it, looking at the document and back to me with a flicker of emotion. Her eyes raked over me again as she took a minute to process the sight before her. "Oh my God. It can't be." Her hand flew to her mouth.

"I know it's been a long time. I'm sure this doesn't seem real after the way I left. And I'm sorry for all the pain I must have caused. But it's me. Riley." I stretched my collar down around my shoulder, exposing a tattoo of a black dove about the size of a silver dollar. "Remember when I got this? You were so mad."

Mrs. Eckhart gasped, shaking her head. "What in the—?" She stopped mid-sentence, the color draining from her face. "I can see it's you, but I still don't believe it. How on earth?"

I stepped closer, softening my voice. "I'm sorry I ran off on you and disappeared. I have a son now. We've fallen on hard times." I glanced over at Noah, and toward my battered Honda Accord parked near the curb; the plates recently changed. "But I understand if you want us to leave."

"Oh, for heaven's sake." The woman lunged forward and enveloped me in a hug, squeezing so hard I thought she might crush my ribs. "Oh, Riley. Riley. Riley. We thought we'd lost you to the streets. I didn't even know if you were still alive. Everyone was looking for you." She backed off, and I was surprised to see tears pooling in Mrs. Eckhart's eyes. "This is nothing short of a miracle. George will be ecstatic when he gets home. I'm so glad you're safe."

My shoulders relaxed at her sudden show of warmth. "Thank you, Mrs. Eckhart. I'm sorry about the money I took when I left. I can pay you back now that—"

She waved me off. "Please. The money was never important. And call me Wendy." She pulled her chin into her neck, appraising me. "Look at you! You're a grown woman now. I remember that beautiful black hair and those eyes like the ocean." She aimed her smile at Noah. "And who is this cute little fellow?"

"This is Noah. He just turned four."

"Well, I'll be. This is truly a miracle." She beamed at him like a proud grandma. "He has your eyes, doesn't he?" Wendy looked toward the street and then at the neighbor's house. "I feel like I'm dreaming. Or like someone is playing a prank on me." A dazed look fell over her face. She seemed to get lost inside herself for a moment before refocusing on me. "Have you stopped by the police station?"

"No. I really don't want to get the police involved. I've done desperate things over the past few years. Some of them weren't exactly legal." I blinked away an image of the money I'd stolen and the knife in Drew's gut. And that wasn't the worst thing I'd done. Not by any stretch. I placed my hand on Noah's head. "I can't risk going to jail."

Her mouth twisted to the side as if she was struggling to see my side of things. "Hmm. You know, there was a lot of trouble after you left. We were all so worried. The agency blamed us. They questioned everyone. And there were so many horrible rumors swirling around. No one could find even a clue to where you'd gone. Many of us feared the worst."

"I'm so sorry. I was a dumb teenager... so selfish. I should have been more grateful for everything you did for me."

She shook her head as if I were from another planet. "Riley Wakefield. Where in the world have you been for the last fifteen years?"

I turned away from her eager stare as memories of the previous years rushed through me. I could never reveal too much of the truth for fear of her handing me over to the police. "I'll tell you the whole story later. It's been a long few days, and I'm so tired."

"Of course. That's fine." She patted my shoulder. "We'll talk later."

Disappointment swam in her eyes, causing guilt to ripple through my gut. Of course, she wanted answers after not knowing what had happened for so long. I offered a little more.

"The short version is that I got mixed up with the wrong people and addicted to drugs. But I've turned things around since Noah was born. I'm determined to give him a better life."

Wendy reached out and squeezed my hand. "I'm not surprised you came out on top. You were always so strong-willed." She smiled down at Noah. "And what a lucky boy you have."

"I'm clean now—going on five years—and looking for a fresh start. I have experience in the restaurant business and plan to get a job here while I earn my real estate license." I paused, not wanting to ask for too much. "But Noah and I are homeless at the moment."

Wendy rested her hands on her hips, her face brightening. "Well, this might be your lucky day. We have a vacant apartment above the garage, the one where Cody used to live. I've been meaning to list it again, but I didn't want a stranger on our property over the summer. It's nothing fancy, but it would be a roof over your head."

"Really?" I asked, raising my heels off the ground.

"Yes," she replied without hesitating.

"How much is the rent?"

"Four hundred and fifty a month. It's cheaper than lots of similar places nearby."

I looked toward the sky, knowing she was correct. I'd searched the online rental listings, and this place was a deal. Still, my money would be gone before I knew it. "That's a lot."

Wendy angled her face as she considered something. "Tell you what. I'll throw in the first month free, so you have a minute to get back on your feet. But starting September first, you'll have to either pay or move somewhere else." She shrugged. "George and I have to eat, after all."

Today was July 25th. Wendy was offering almost five weeks of rent-free living, and it felt like I'd won the lottery. "That sounds great. Thank you so much." I could almost feel my feet levitating off the ground. Noah and I had a safe place to stay, a home base to start fresh. I wouldn't have to waste more of our savings on rooms at seedy motels. Sandra Matthews was gone, vanished into thin air. And Riley Wakefield had returned. I wiped my palms together, realizing I was sweating. "Do you still have foster kids living with you?" I asked, wondering about our personal space.

Wendy shifted her weight, turning her head back toward the house for a second. A shadow passed over her face despite the sunny day. "No. After you disappeared, the agency wouldn't allow us to take in more kids. Said we didn't watch you close enough."

"I'm really sorry." My fingers found Noah's shoulder as shame swelled through me. "I made so many bad decisions. I wasn't thinking."

Wendy shook her head, holding up her hand. "Stop right there. You were just a kid. You had a rough childhood, and we never blamed you. We were more upset at the agency than you, but they had to pass the buck to someone, I guess. And we've managed just fine. George sells used cars at the Chevy dealership, and I started renting out the apartment on occasion. Our previous tenant moved out six months ago, so I'll be happy to see you in there."

I took in Wendy's warm voice and sunny expression. She was generous to a fault, more forgiving than I would have been in her shoes. But people were resilient. That was something I knew for sure.

"This will be just like the old days when you and Cody lived here. You remember Cody, right?" she asked.

"Yes. Of course. He was always nice to me." In truth, my memory of Cody was vague. He was another foster kid the Eckharts had taken under their wings. He'd been about the same age. Quiet. Kept to himself. A nerdy computer kid. They allowed him to live in the apartment, an arrangement that must have been approved by the social worker overseeing him. I recalled peering through the bedroom window at the back of the house, spying the lights on in the apartment above the garage, the movement inside. I'd been jealous of Cody's semi-independent living arrangement. He'd been granted the freedoms of an adult but none of the responsibility.

Wendy grunted. "Cody was so troubled after you disappeared. Barely said two words. I think it was hard on him." She crossed her arms. "He's done well for himself though. Graduated from college. He lives in Birmingham," she said, naming a more fashionable suburb just north of Berkley. "But he works at a computer repair business in town. He probably runs the whole place by now. He comes around once in a while to say hello. He'll be thrilled to hear you're back."

I said I was excited to see Cody too. Then Wendy invited us into her living room, which smelled like musty books and day-old coffee. Noah began to squirm, and she offered him some lemonade and pretzels, and gave me a glass of water. As the cold drink slid down my throat, Wendy chattered away about updates to the house and a few trendy restaurants and high-end boutiques downtown that might have job opportunities. She pointed up the narrow staircase. "I turned your old bedroom into a home office, but you're welcome to take a look."

"That's okay. Maybe tomorrow."

"Of course. You must be exhausted. How about we get you into the apartment so you can unpack? It's already furnished, so you shouldn't have to do much."

I looked at Noah's drooping eyelids, which mirrored my own. "We'd love to get settled."

We headed out the back door onto a small patio. A few pots with red geraniums lined the perimeter of the cement slab, adding to the array of flowers along the fence and giving the space a welcoming feel.

"Your backyard is beautiful."

"I've gotten into gardening the last few years. I just love planting things and watching them grow. I even joined the local gardening club at the Y."

"That sounds nice. I bet it's so relaxing." I looked up at the passing clouds, realizing I had no enjoyable pastimes besides reading or occasionally concocting a new recipe. My lifestyle had never allowed for many hobbies, but maybe things would be different now.

Wendy held up a key ring as we cut across the grass. The garage stood on the far side of the small backyard, with a wooden staircase running up to a platform and a door on the second level. "I've got the key right here. I keep a spare in the laundry room in case you ever lock yourself out."

"Thanks. I'd love to say I've never done that before, but it happens."

"Ha. I spent ten minutes looking for my phone the other day, and it was in my hand."

I giggled along with her as I climbed the stairs, helping Noah up each step. Wendy unlocked the door and entered the apartment as I paused outside to take in the grid of surrounding homes. From my elevated position, I had a clear view of the alley running behind the garage. Something out of place caught my eye: a man in a baseball cap and sunglasses creeping slowly between the garbage bins and garages. He stopped when we locked eyes. *Was he watching me?*

"Ruby! You coming?" the man yelled toward the backyard of a nearby house.

A girl about eight years old burst through a gate diagonally across the alley, taking the hand of the man I now realized was her dad. "Can we get ice cream too?" the girl asked.

I squeezed my eyelids closed, annoyed with myself for being so paranoid. He was only a neighbor. Still, it hadn't even been three weeks since I'd stabbed my former boss and stolen thousands of dollars, and people were likely searching for me. I had to stay on alert and keep my head down.

I ducked inside the apartment, pulling Noah behind me.

TWO

I pressed my spine against the door as I took in the small apartment.

Wendy turned around. "You okay?"

"Yeah. It's just those stairs," I said, shaking thoughts of Drew Toven from my head. "I'm not used to them."

"They're steep, that's for sure." Wendy waved toward a sink, refrigerator, and stove lining the far wall. "Here's the kitchen. We made some updates a few years back. I did this floor myself, and George installed some more cabinets for storage."

I took in the cramped kitchen, the square of linoleum flooring, the Formica countertop peeling in the corners, mismatched cabinets, and a table big enough for two. She nodded to an open space with a ratty, plaid couch and a dated TV. "And there's the living room. No cable TV, but you get a few channels with the antennae. And the Wi-Fi signal reaches this room from our house." She gave me the password.

I told her it looked great, although the apartment felt hot and dark and appeared to be a mishmash of styles—a decade's worth of Wendy and George's DIY projects.

"There's no washer and dryer, but there's a laundromat in town." She winked and moved five steps to a single bedroom and bathroom that Noah and I would share. She promised to deliver a couple of fans for the windows and some toys for Noah that she had in storage. "I can't wait to call George and tell him the good news!"

I thanked her again, collapsing into the wall when she finally left us alone.

As Noah zoomed his matchbox car across the wooden floor, the man from the alley crept back into my mind. I stepped out to the landing, peeking toward the narrow side street, relieved to find it empty. I reminded myself I'd been careful, abiding by my own protocols: I had left Vegas quickly, ditched my phone and replaced it with a new one, swapped the plates on my car as soon as I got to the next city, and only used cash. The chance of thick-headed Drew Toven tracking me down was slim. The money I'd taken from the safe had totaled just over $15,000. It was a jackpot for me but measly pocket change for them. I hoped Toven Brothers wouldn't report the theft for fear of exposing their crooked business dealings and payouts to government officials, not to mention my boss's progressing sexual harassment of me.

For three months, I'd ignored Drew's not-so-subtle advances —the compliments on my body, the uninvited shoulder massages, the inappropriate jokes. But things had come to a head two days before I stabbed him when he discovered that the social security number I printed on my paperwork didn't match government records. Drew had cornered me in his office, something evil dancing behind his small eyes as he chomped on a piece of spearmint gum. "I'll have to withhold your pay," he'd said with a creepy smile. "Or there's another way we can resolve this." From behind his mop of wiery hair and leathery skin, he told me I could sleep with him a few times a week, and he'd brush the discrepancy under the rug and pay me in cash. Time had stopped as I took in the sweat beading on his forehead, the leather belt cinched around his polo shirt, and the disgusting way he chewed his gum. I made a date with him for that Friday night, knowing I'd never keep it.

But my scheme to steal the money and flee hadn't gone as planned. The stabbing would have been reported to the police as soon as Drew arrived at the hospital. Thankfully, he had survived. I'd googled his name two days ago, locating an article about a local hero who'd walked in on a robbery at his construction company and survived a brutal attack. Police were looking for a woman going by the name Sandra Matthews, possibly an alias, who may have ties to San Antonio, Texas. The piece included a photo of me, flowing blonde hair and overdone makeup, taken at a company picnic five weeks earlier. The article reassured me that the police were on the wrong track, but a deadweight in my gut knew I wouldn't get off that easily.

Noah slammed a closet door, drawing my attention back to him and our new apartment. Despite its piecemeal feel, I was grateful for the landing pad and the comfort of a familiar place. We returned to the car and unloaded our things. A trip to Target followed, where I picked up a twin air mattress, a sheet of puffy dinosaur stickers for Noah, and some food staples. Tired and sweaty, I unpacked the groceries, handing Noah a box of raisins. As I plopped on the couch, ready to relax with a cold glass of water, several light knocks sounded at the door.

"Riley! It's us." It was Wendy's voice, slightly muted by the closed door and the drone of a hedge trimmer from somewhere outside.

I raised myself from the couch. There was a chance George wouldn't be as forgiving as his wife, and the thought sent a spike of anxiety through me. I cracked the door as Wendy and her husband filled the opening, George looking a little broader and grayer than the last time I'd seen him. He lifted a bunch of daisies wrapped in cellophane, but his stony expression told me

Wendy had likely been responsible for the flowers. "Riley. Isn't this a surprise?"

"Hi, George." I accepted the flowers, the palpitations in my chest increasing in speed. "It's nice to see you again. Thank you for these."

I waited for the same type of hug Wendy had given me, but none came. George's eyes moved from my face to my toes and back up again. "Look at you."

I peered down at my legs, unsure how to respond.

George raised his chin. "You really upended our lives by taking off like that. Left us in a bind with the agency." His voice was tinged with the anger that must have been lingering for years.

Forcing myself to own up to him, I lifted my gaze to meet his. "I'm so sorry about that. As I told Wendy, I was young and wasn't thinking. I should have been more grateful for what you did for me. I've changed a lot since then, and I hope you can forgive me." I'd been carrying the guilt of my reckless teenage decisions for years, but I reminded myself that I'd grown up without parents to guide me. Running away had seemed like the best option.

George scratched his ear, glancing at something in the distance. "You never had it easy growing up without a mom or a dad. I can appreciate that. And I'm glad you're okay."

I sensed that was as close as I would get to George offering me immediate forgiveness, so I simply said, "Thank you. I'm happy to be back." I placed my hand on Noah's shoulder, encouraging him to step in front of me. "This is my son, Noah."

"Well, I'll be. Hi, Noah." A sparkle appeared in George's eye as he stooped down and gave Noah a fist bump. Noah smiled.

Wendy held out two fans and scooted past me, placing them in the apartment. "I brought the fans. They'll help keep you cool. And there are a few boxes of toys for Noah," she added, pointing toward the landing.

"Look, Legos! And trains!" Noah scooped up a box, dropped it to the floor, and immediately started sorting through the pieces.

"Thanks so much. That's so thoughtful of you."

Wendy smiled as she watched Noah. "George and I would love it if you two had dinner with us tonight. We can sit on the patio. I'm making pasta alfredo. I remember how much you enjoyed that dish."

"That's so nice, but I don't want you to go to any more trouble for me."

Wendy shook her head. "It's no trouble at all. I insist. We've been waiting fifteen years for this."

"Yes, please join us," George said, although with slightly less conviction.

The long road trip had worn me out, and I didn't necessarily feel up to dinner and small talk with Wendy and George. In truth, my weariness had been growing for years, my energy eroded by more than just my travels. Living on the edge for so long had been exhausting, moving from location to location, changing my identity in each place so the authorities couldn't track me down after the illegal things I'd done. And now I'd dug my hole deeper by stabbing Drew. But Wendy's eyes brimmed with hope, and I didn't want to be rude. They had received me with open arms and given me free housing, which was more than I could have wished for. And Noah deserved a home-cooked meal. "We'd love to join," I lied. "Can I bring anything?"

"No. You're not even settled yet. Just meet us on the patio in an hour."

"Sounds good." I watched them hobble back down the steps and across the yard, hoping this would be the beginning of a more stable environment for me and Noah. I could barely remember my own mother, but I knew she'd been a heroin addict. The state had removed me from her care at the age of six. My mother never made the slightest attempt to get me back, leaving me with a scar that would never heal. She'd died of her addiction more than a dozen years ago. I often feared her lack of maternal instincts was imprinted in my DNA. Every day since Noah was born, I tried not to be like her.

I inched further onto the landing, looking around at the suburban backyard with its sunny patio and tidy flower beds. This was my best shot at building a stable life with my son. I was amazed at my luck but unable to fully trust it. I'd lived a hundred lives, all abruptly cut short for one reason or another—childhood trauma, abandonment, my own bad choices. Self-doubt forced its way into my head whenever things were going too well. Once again, my destructive thoughts circled like vultures. And I couldn't help wondering how long it would take until my past caught up with me.

THREE

By 6:15, I'd showered and changed my clothes. Noah navigated the steps down to the yard, already more agile in dealing with the steep decline. The patio table was set with plates, napkins, and silverware. Just as we reached the bottom step, the glass slider opened, and Wendy rushed outside, oven mitts on her hands, carrying a steaming bowl.

"There you are! Perfect timing." She set the bowl on the table. "Take a seat."

George appeared, balancing four glasses of ice water in his hands. "I put some milk over there for the big guy."

Noah climbed into the chair near the milk, his chest barely reaching the tabletop. I took the seat next to him, noticing five places had been set at the table.

"I hope you don't mind. I called Cody and told him the good news. He's going to join us for dinner."

"Oh. That's great." I forced a smile, but nerves rattled through me. I had no idea what to say to him or what reaction to expect. Visions of awkward conversation left me dreading his arrival.

Wendy ran back inside and returned with a green salad and a plate of garlic bread, prattling around the table as she arranged everything. A tingling sensation moved across my back, causing me to turn. A white-haired woman peered over the fence from next door, her watery blue stare honing in on me.

I lifted my hand in a reluctant wave—anything to get her to stop looking at me like that. George followed my gaze, shifting his weight in his chair as he caught sight of the woman.

"Hi, Brenda. Nice night, isn't it?" George spoke loudly, annoyance pulling at his voice.

The older woman lifted her chin, a disapproving look in her eyes. "It was before all the ruckus. Please keep it down. I'm trying to enjoy my garden."

"We're allowed to eat dinner on our patio, Brenda. No one's stopping you from enjoying your garden." George shook his head, puffing air out of his mouth. He leaned closer to me as the woman turned away. "Remember Mrs. Harwood? She still lives next door. Lucky us."

"Oh, wow."

"Thankfully, a nice young couple bought the house over there." He pointed to the yard on the opposite side.

Wendy took a seat, banging the metal chair against the table. "Brenda is the worst kind of busybody. But she eventually goes away if you stand up to her."

Before I could respond, the gate clinked, and a lanky man in dark jeans and a form-fitting shirt strode toward us, dark stubble shadowing his face. He gave a curt nod to George and Wendy.

Wendy clasped her hands together. "There he is. Nice to see you, Cody."

George stood up. "What has it been? Almost three years?"

"Something like that."

I bit my lip. Three years? Wendy had talked about Cody as if they ate weekly Sunday dinners together, but clearly, that wasn't the case.

Cody turned to me, his brows lifting as he approached.

My fingers tightened around the edge of my chair as I awaited his reaction.

To my surprise, his arms stretched open. "Riley, what a surprise. We were all so worried about you."

My heart beat double-time as I stood to give him a quick hug and introduced him to Noah.

Cody waved to Noah, then returned his attention to me, staring for a moment too long. "Wow. You've really grown up."

"You too. I never would have recognized you." Cody had transformed from the shy, scrawny kid I remembered into a tall, confident man with an easy smile.

He glanced toward the garage. "And I hear you've moved into my old apartment?"

"Yes. I'm grateful to have a place to get back on my feet."

I was even more thankful when Wendy interrupted, ordering everyone to help themselves. We loaded up our plates and dug in as we talked about Cody's computer business and my desire to become a real estate agent.

When there was a pause in the conversation, Cody swirled the ice in his glass and tilted his head at me. "So, Riley, I hope you don't mind if I address the elephant in the room. Where have you been for the last fifteen years?"

A noodle lodged itself in my throat, but I swallowed it down. Wendy and George had stopped eating and were staring at me too. A gust of wind blew through a nearby tree, rustling the leaves.

"Well, it's a long story. I'm not sure if you want to hear about—"

"We've got lots of time, dear." Wendy glanced at George and Cody, who nodded.

Noah fidgeted beside me, and I told him he could run around the yard for a few minutes. Clearly, I couldn't put off telling my story any longer, so I set down my fork. "Okay. Yeah.

I guess it's the least I can do, considering how I left." I straight-ened myself up, clearing my throat. "Do you remember how I used to work part-time after school at Panda Express in the food court at the mall?"

Wendy nodded. "Yes. I remember that."

I told them how a guy named Max, who was in his early twenties, came by whenever I was working and chatted me up. He was good-looking and charming and took an unusual interest in me. I felt confined by the Eckharts' strict household and wanted freedom. This guy seemed to understand my emotions, boredom with school, and desire not to have to answer to anyone. On top of that, Max promised me money—lots of it. I'd been dirt-poor my entire life. He said he'd give me a free ride to Los Angeles. All I had to do was go out to dinner at fancy restaurants with rich, older men a few times a week. They would even pay for my meals. I'd live in a two-bedroom apart-ment with a shared swimming pool. There'd be three other girls with me, and we'd all be friends. But there was one catch. Max required me to keep our plan a secret and to cut off ties with everyone I knew. He said I had to ditch my phone so no one could track me. I agreed.

Wendy's face had gone white. "Oh my goodness. It's exactly as we feared."

"I always suspected someone older preyed on you." George wiped the back of his hand across his forehead, scowling.

I continued, telling them how things went fine for the first several days, how I thought I'd won, that I was smarter than everyone else. After a week or so, Max gave me drugs. Mari-juana at first, but it progressed from there. A few weeks later, he showed me how to shoot up heroin. I immediately became addicted. The weeks, months, and years that followed were a blur. Once in L.A., Max gave me a new identity, clothes, and look. I had no idea people were searching for me. I only did whatever it took to get more drugs. I paused, letting them fill in the blanks.

Wendy gasped, her hand covering her mouth. "Oh, you poor thing. I wish I had known."

George shook his head, eyes downcast.

Clearing my throat, I returned to the story. "Then, about five years ago, I got pregnant. I was devastated at first, but it turned out it was the best thing that could have happened. The pregnancy was a wake-up call. I realized I was repeating the pattern of my addict mother, and that was the last thing I wanted. A social worker had been approaching me on the street every once in a while, giving me a card with the address of a place that could help me. I escaped one night when Max was passed out and went to the address on the card, where I checked myself into a state-run rehab program. I got tons of counseling and took control of my life."

Cody's head tipped back. "Man. I'm sorry you went through all that. I had no idea that kind of trafficking went on here."

"You're a survivor," Wendy said.

"It must be difficult to stay clean." Cody leaned closer to me, a sheen of worry in his eyes. "Do you have support?"

"Yes. There are tough days, of course, but I go to NA meetings. I already located a chapter nearby. It really helps to connect with people who have gone through the same thing."

The others nodded.

Wendy lifted her chin. "You should be proud of yourself for realizing you were going down the wrong path and for deciding to make better choices. That takes a lot of courage."

"Despite everything, we're proud of you, Riley." George raised a glass, and I realized he was toasting me. "To Riley, home safe and sound."

"Hear, hear."

"Hear, hear."

Their glasses glinted in the dwindling daylight as they held them up, so I lifted mine, clicking it against the others. I felt unworthy of the toast but relieved they hadn't asked any additional questions.

We sat outside for another thirty minutes, chatting about people I used to know. My former best friend, Harper, and Jacob, the high school classmate I'd been dating when I disappeared. Apparently, they both still lived in town, and Jacob worked as an electrician. Harper was divorced and had a daughter who was about Noah's age. Wendy promised to throw a backyard barbecue and invite everyone so we could get reacquainted.

"Oh. You don't have to do that." The idea of facing so many people from the past caused the food I'd ingested to curdle in my stomach. "I'm not sure I'm ready to see everyone yet."

Wendy threw her head back in disbelief. "Don't be silly! I insist. Everyone will be so happy to see you again." She looked at George and Cody. "Don't you think we should throw a little party for Riley?"

"Yeah," Cody said, as George shrugged and said, "Sure."

Wendy's mind was set, so I rolled back my shoulders and nodded with a smile.

The sun sank behind the trees, and shadows grew longer across the backyard. I helped carry all the dishes inside, washing each plate and platter off in the sink as Wendy thanked me for my help. In the adjoining living room, George flipped on a news channel, where a newscaster reported on the weather nationwide. Cody found a hidden box of superhero figures and arranged them on the floor for Noah. When the last dish was put away, I joined them in the living room, noticing Noah's yawns and feeling my own exhaustion catching up with me.

As I was about to wrap things up and say good night, a face flashed across the TV, causing me to freeze. It was a close-up of

Drew Toven hobbling along a sidewalk, answering questions from a reporter who walked next to him. "I couldn't find a document I needed for a meeting the next morning, so I returned to the office that night to see if I'd left it there. When I walked in, I saw Sandra breaking into the safe. I was in shock for a second because that didn't fit with the woman I knew." His face perspired as he shook his head. "I went toward her, and she pulled out a knife and stabbed me in the gut. Thankfully, the blade was short, and she missed my organs."

The male reporter took over, the camera zooming in on his sculpted eyebrows. "Police are on the lookout for thirty-one-year-old Sandra Matthews, who could be living under a different name." The photo of me with wavy blonde hair at the company picnic popped onto the screen. I leaped toward the TV, standing in front of it to block the view.

George narrowed his eyes. "Everything okay?"

"Oh, yeah. Yes." My pulse thrummed in my ears. "I thought Noah was choking on that piece of plastic." I pointed to the action figures, anything to distract their attention from the TV.

"I'm not choking." Noah looked up at me, confused.

"I know. I thought you were, but you're not." I could still hear the reporter behind me talking about the supposed whereabouts of Sandra Matthews and her four-year-old son. "Thank you for such a nice evening, but Noah and I are exhausted. It's time for us to go to bed."

"No. I'm not tired." Noah's face crumpled, and he fell backward on the floor, crying.

Wendy gave me a knowing nod.

The news story had turned toward general statistics of theft by company employees. I scooped up my son and thanked everyone again, still in disbelief that the stabbing at Toven Brothers had made national news. Even with Noah writhing in my arms and the photo of me at the company picnic flashing in my head, I breathed easier once the night air hit my face. I climbed the steps to my new apartment, relieved Wendy, George, and Cody hadn't spotted the photo on TV and seen something familiar.

I hoped no one in this town would put two and two together.

FOUR

Noah hopped along the sidewalk next to me, stopping every so often to examine bugs. We'd taken it easy yesterday, getting our bearings, organizing our living space, and visiting a playground and an ice cream shop. Wendy had stopped by to tell me about a year-round preschool someone in her gardening group recommended, located in the basement of a Methodist church within walking distance of the apartment. I said I wouldn't mind checking it out, and she immediately pulled out her phone and arranged an appointment. My annoyance at Wendy's overstepping was quickly outweighed by how proud she seemed to have done something helpful. So I bit my tongue, and this morning, Noah and I met with Miss Beverly, a warm and bubbly woman who ran the preschool and spoke to me in an animated voice as if I were a child too. The space was clean and bright, the other kids looked happy, and the price was affordable. Despite being taken aback by Wendy's quick planning, I was sold, and I took home the form to enroll Noah. He could start as soon as Monday—just a few days from now.

The sun warmed my cheeks as we strolled back to the apartment, and I couldn't help feeling closer to the life I'd always envisioned. Once I had a few hours to myself, I could head to the Secretary of State with my lease and birth certificate and get a valid driver's license. They were the first steps to finding an honest job.

A car crept behind us, catching my attention because of the way it inched down the road. I stole a glance, breath catching at the sight of the vehicle—a police car out on patrol. The officer in the driver's seat stared at me through the window. I kept walking, the news story from the other night pulsing through my mind, along with the fear of being recognized as the fugitive Sandra Matthews. I pushed some black hair forward off my shoulder to cover half of my face and flashed a quick smile, then grabbed Noah's hand. *Act casual.* I asked Noah what he wanted for lunch so he'd look toward me instead of the officer. Although I hadn't seen it, Noah's photo could have been on the news too. At last, the patrol car passed us, pausing at the stop sign and turning onto a main boulevard.

I let go of Noah's hand, my head swiveling in every direction to ensure we weren't being followed. No one else was around except for a woman walking two mismatched dogs down the opposite side of the street. Hugging my purse to my side, I realized my paranoia had gotten the better of me again. There was no reason to worry. I'd changed my appearance. There were probably tens of thousands of single women with four-year-old sons named Noah. The chances of anyone making a connection between Sandra Matthews in Las Vegas and Riley Wakefield in Berkley were slim.

An hour later, we were back under the cover of our cozy apartment, stomachs full from the grilled cheese sandwiches I'd made for lunch. Noah and I lay on the couch, watching a wildlife show on PBS as the fan whirred in the window. Three hard knocks and Wendy's voice on the other side of the door jolted me to attention.

"Hello! Riley? It's me again."

When I opened the door, I found Wendy standing on the landing, her arms hugging a photo album and a high school yearbook.

"How did it go at the preschool?" she asked.

"It was perfect. Noah's going to start on Monday. Thank you for setting up the tour."

"Wonderful!" She edged forward, sliding past me into the apartment and looking around. She turned to face me, tapping the edge of the album. "I stumbled across these old photos and thought it might be fun to take a little trip down memory lane."

"Oh." I trailed her to the couch, mildly annoyed by the unexpected intrusion.

"I'm putting together a list of people to invite to the barbecue on Sunday. You haven't seen your old friends in so long. I thought it might be helpful to refresh your memory."

"I didn't realize you had photos from when I lived here."

"Of course! Not a ton, but you're in several of them."

Noah continued watching his show as Wendy plopped down on the couch. She patted the space next to her, and I sat as she hummed to herself, flipping through the thick pages. "Here we are! This was the day you moved in with us, remember? It was springtime."

I stared at the photo of a teenage girl I barely recognized, bony shoulders hunched forward, a duffle bag at her feet, and a sad smile pulling up one corner of her mouth. "Oh my gosh. I was so nervous. I look like a deer in headlights."

Wendy clucked, shaking her head. "You were thin as a rail. The food at that group home must have been just horrible."

"It was bad." I cringed, remembering one particularly horrific meal of colorless slop over mushy rice. The part-time cook at the group home had apparently never heard of spices, not to mention fresh fruits and vegetables. One especially vindictive worker would sometimes withhold our meals as punishment for talking out of turn or showing up late to therapy. And the group home bully, Marianne Clavey, often stole the best food from my plate, threatening to do something to me as I slept if I told on her. Memories of Marianne's cagey movements and catlike eyes were permanently seared into my brain. Phantom hunger pains stabbed through me just thinking about those years, but I smiled at Wendy. "I was grateful for your home-cooked meals, even if I didn't always show it."

"No matter how much you ate, you barely gained any weight."

"Well, that changed." I patted the extra padding on my stomach, which I hadn't been able to lose since Noah was born.

"It does for most of us." She let out an exasperated giggle. The plastic covering over the photos crinkled as she turned the page. A few pages later, she tapped her finger on another photo. "Here. That was you at school with your new friends."

I lowered my gaze, studying the image from a distant life.

"There's Harper." She touched the photo of a girl in a miniskirt with mischievous eyes and cornsilk hair posing for the camera with her hand on her hip. "She was always hot and cold, wasn't she? A real wild child. I wonder if that's what attracted you to her?"

"Maybe. I wasn't very confident."

"Those popular girls usually have strong personalities. But you seemed to enjoy her company."

I pulled the book closer. "I forgot how pretty she was. We looked so young."

She pointed to the boy with an intense gaze standing behind us. "And there's Jacob. He was bad news for teenage girls." She chuckled, but her tone was only half-joking.

"He was okay."

"I'll tell you one thing. He was heartbroken when you left."

"I didn't mean to hurt him."

We studied the faded photo again, neither of us speaking for a few seconds.

A sigh escaped Wendy's lips. "There were so many theories flying around after you vanished. I always thought that Harper and Jacob knew more about your disappearance than they let on, that one or the other was somehow involved."

"They weren't," I said, setting my jaw. "I left without telling anyone. That was the deal I made with Max."

"It's a relief to know I was wrong about them. For God's sake, I even accused Cody at one point. The gossip made everyone crazy."

"That's too bad," I said, willing her to change the subject.

Wendy's elbow jabbed me two times in the arm, an expectant grin on her face as her demeanor suddenly shifted. "I have some good news. I tracked down Harper's and Jacob's phone numbers while you were at the preschool. They can both make it to the barbecue on Sunday. They can't wait to see you again."

"Oh. That's amazing." Nausea turned in my stomach at the thought of facing them, but I put on a happy face for Wendy, who had clearly put a lot of effort into planning the get-together. "I wasn't sure how people would react to me returning out of the blue after being MIA for so long."

"They were both real quiet at first, like they didn't believe me." I could tell by the pucker of Wendy's lips and the distant look in her eyes that she was reliving the phone calls in her mind. "But you can't really blame them. It's shocking news. More than anything, they're relieved you're okay, just like George and Cody and me."

"I appreciate everything you've done."

Wendy waved her fingers at me. "Nonsense." She refocused on the photo album, flipping through more pages. Nostalgia shone in her eyes as she stopped at a particular photo. "Remember when you and Harper dressed like panda bears for

Halloween?" She lifted the book to show me. "I said you were too old for trick-or-treating, but you were so stubborn. I kept my mouth closed and let you do it. Figured you hadn't had much of a childhood."

I dipped my head, acknowledging there'd been no trick-or-treating in the group homes or money for real costumes. "Thank you for letting us do that. It was a fun night." Hot emotion rose in me as I ached for the girl in the photo, for the attempt at one normal Halloween before her childhood completely slipped away, for everything lost before and after.

She flipped another page. "And there's my sister, Leslie. You used to call her Aunt Leslie. She wasn't really your aunt, of course, but she was tickled that you felt comfortable giving her the title."

I stared at the photo of Wendy and her sister, who shared a similar smile and body type. They stood shoulder to shoulder in the backyard of the Eckharts' house during what looked like another summer barbecue.

"Aunt Leslie. She was always nice to me."

"Leslie will be here on Sunday too. She was so happy to hear of your safe return." Wendy winked.

Noah bounced up and down on the cushion on the other side of us. "Mom, can Aiden come over?"

"No, honey. We live far away from him now. But you'll make lots of friends at your new preschool." I caught Wendy's eye, shrugging. "Aiden was his friend in California."

Noah frowned. "Waaas Vegas, not California," he wailed, mispronouncing our previous location.

I shook my head at Wendy. "We were just watching a show about Las Vegas. He gets confused."

"No!" Noah stood in front of me now, hitting my knee. "You're wrong."

"Noah, please. Be quiet, or I'll send you to your room."

He stuck out his lower lip, and I willed him to put a plug in it. If there was one weakness in my plan to escape and shed my previous identity, it was Noah. He was only a child, but I should have given him a different name in Vegas or told my co-workers he was a girl. I hadn't done either for fear of confusing my story.

"I think someone's tired," Wendy said.

"Yeah. It's time to put him down for his nap."

Wendy handed me the yearbook she'd been balancing on her lap beneath the photo album. "And here's your old yearbook. The school delivered it to us after you disappeared, and I've been holding on to it all these years. I thought you might like to flip through it. Just for fun."

"Thanks, Wendy. I can't believe you saved it for me."

Noah stomped across the floor. "I want to see Aiden!"

"Oh, boy." Wendy eyed Noah over her shoulder. "I better be on my way. I was just so excited about the barbecue. I wanted to let you know."

"Can I bring anything?"

"Oh, no. There's no need."

"I insist. I make a pretty good potato salad."

"Fine. You're in charge of the potato salad." Wendy rose from the couch and headed toward the door. "And if you want to start your job search tomorrow, I can watch the little guy for a few hours. Just let me know."

"I might take you up on that." I watched her leave, not missing her not-so-subtle hint to look for a job as soon as possible. I'd hoped to take a week to get my feet on the ground and readjust to life in the Midwest, but Wendy didn't know about the thirteen thousand in cash I kept hidden in the freezer. And so, I had to act like someone desperately seeking employment. The money wasn't to be touched except for emergencies, although I'd had no choice but to burn through nearly two grand already on motels, food, gas, and new clothes since leaving Vegas. The money I'd stolen from Toven Brothers was meant to be savings, the down payment on a house or a condo where Noah and I would live and put down roots someday when we were no longer on the run. And I finally believed that day awaited me here on the not-too-distant horizon.

But dread replaced the excitement that should have been traveling through me because my plan wasn't foolproof. My face was all over the news, and someone could recognize me. In three days, I'd have to face Harper and Jacob, two people who had every right to harbor resentment against me. They'd been left in the cold back then. And if they suspected anything off about my story, they could ruin everything.

FIVE

On Friday afternoon, I left Noah with Wendy, telling her I was working on my job search. Instead, I drove to a nearby health center I'd found online where Narcotics Anonymous meetings were held. No meetings were happening now, but a stack of pamphlets with meeting days and times sat on a table just outside the door to a conference room. I peeked inside, envisioning myself sitting in one of the chairs. Then I pocketed a pamphlet and drove another twenty minutes south to Detroit, fueled by the fear that my identity and living arrangement weren't a sure thing. It was possible someone had seen me on the news and would recognize me as Sandra Matthews, and if that happened, I needed an escape plan.

I pulled into the parking lot of Lucky's Bar, swerving around a pile of broken glass, nailing a pothole instead. A rusty pickup truck sat a few spots down next to an SUV with a cracked windshield. The freeway roared beyond the narrow, two-lane road I'd followed for the last quarter mile to arrive at the address. The bar stood on a forgotten island of cement in the shadow of a dilapidated warehouse. Tires dotted a nearby area of overgrown weeds, and a stray dog nosed through a tipped-over garbage can. If there were ever a wrong corner of town, I'd found it.

I'd never been to Lucky's Bar, but I remembered the name from acquaintances at the group home, one who needed to fly under the radar to evade arrest and another who merely wanted a fake ID. A guy named Anthony kept his office here and helped them out for a price.

I entered the establishment, finding the bar's run-down exterior was only a sampling of what met me inside. My shoes stuck to the floor with each step into a dark and smoky room. At the counter, a man slumped forward, completely passed out at three in the afternoon. The irony of the name "Lucky's Bar" wasn't lost on me. No one experiencing good fortune would come to a place like this.

"Can I help you?" a woman behind the counter asked in a gruff voice.

I hadn't seen her standing in the shadows, and her voice made me jump. The stout woman leaned forward, eyeing me.

"Hi. I'm looking for Anthony."

"Ha." Her stubby fingers rubbed her forehead. "You're about six years too late for that."

"What?"

"Anthony is dead. Sorry, hon. Dropped dead of a heart attack." She grabbed a rag and wiped down the grimy counter.

My body seemed to sink into a hole as my only lead for a safety net disappeared. I edged closer to the woman. "Did someone take over for him?"

She stopped wiping the counter and fixed her eyes on me, a glint of recognition in them. "Not sure what you're talking about."

I leaned toward her, lowering my voice to a whisper because it was clear she knew exactly what I was referring to. "The fake IDs."

She stopped cleaning, fastening her stare on me once again. "What did you need?"

"A new identity, including a social security number and passport. One for my son too."

"You got cash?"

"Yeah." I patted my bag. "Right here."

The woman looked me up and down, tossed the rag aside, and waved me into a brightly lit back room. She pulled the door closed behind us and sat at a desk piled with papers while I took a seat in a folding chair opposite her.

"No passport. Too risky. But I can get you an enhanced ID that lets you cross into Canada without a passport. I'm Bea."

"I'm Riley."

"I'll need your phone number and a secure mailing address."

I'd opened a P.O. box this morning in anticipation of this meeting. I didn't want any of my mail getting mixed up with George and Wendy's. I gave Bea the information, along with my phone number, which she wrote down.

"I won't ask what you're running from." She glanced up from her paper. "Anthony taught me the business before he died. I can help you get a birth certificate, a matching driver's license, and a birth certificate for your son. Possibly social security numbers too. But it's gonna cost you. This ain't no run-of-the-mill fake ID you're asking for."

"How much?" I asked, scooting to the edge of my chair.

"Eight grand."

I nodded. I'd brought ten grand with me, removed from my freezer before I'd gone to bed and thawed overnight. The price was high but in the range I'd expected to pay for new identities that would withstand scrutiny. Still, it was a huge chunk of my savings.

Bea raised her chin. "And hopefully you're not in a hurry. There's a one- to three-month turnaround time."

The sinking feeling weighed me down again. Not having a backup plan for that long was dangerous. But I had no other options.

"Okay."

"Here's the deal. You never tell anyone where you got the documents if you get caught. Understand? Not even a whisper."

"I understand."

"If you do, there's going to be problems for you. Big problems."

"I understand," I said again, this time more forcefully.

She evaluated me for a second, apparently deciding to trust me. "Stand against that wall, and I'll take your photo. I'll get everything in motion once you pay."

"I can pay you now." I turned my back to her and counted the money, placing eight stacks of ten hundred-dollar bills on the desk.

Bea scooped up the money, stuffing it into a manila envelope, and I hoped she wouldn't take the money and run. "You're not messing around," she said under her breath. "How old are you?"

"Thirty-one," I said as I stood against a white panel affixed to the wall. Bea snapped three photos. "The documents will arrive at your P.O. box when they're ready. Don't come back here in the meantime. Don't call, and don't mention a hint of this to anyone. I need a visit from the police like I need a hole in my head."

I gave a nod. "Got it. Thank you." A puff of air released from my lungs as I made a beeline through the shadowy bar and back to my car. In one to three months, I'd have a safety net if needed. Until then, I'd keep my head down and live my life. I buckled my seatbelt and turned the ignition, hoping I'd just spent eight grand on something I'd never need to use.

SIX

A bowl of potato salad balanced in my arms as I navigated down the steps toward the long table where Wendy was setting up food and drinks. She and George had gone all out with pink and blue paper plates, cups, tablecloths, and balloons.

"It looks really nice, Wendy." I set down the heavy bowl, taking in the decorations and the sunny afternoon.

"I know pink and blue are your favorite colors. Or at least they used to be."

"They still are."

"Wonderful." Wendy folded her hands together, clearly pleased. "I hope you don't mind, but I invited a few friends from the garden club, and George has a couple of co-workers from the dealership stopping by too."

"I don't mind. I'm glad you invited some friends."

"And Harper's mom is coming with her." Wendy pursed her lips. "Not too surprising, I guess, considering how much time you girls spent together."

I offered a noncommittal shrug, but my nerves buzzed through me at the number of guests attending—many more than I'd expected. The gathering was set to begin in ten minutes.

George dumped a bag of ice into a cooler filled with drinks. Cody sat at the patio table, sipping a cold beer and playing Simon Says with Noah. I was thankful Noah had taken a good nap and was happily occupied. I smoothed down my hair, then tugged at my striped sundress, hoping I looked my best.

Wendy leaned close to my ear. "The guests should be arriving any minute. Remember to apologize to your old friends for the way you left."

My head tilted at Wendy's comment. Of course, I would apologize. She had a way of overstepping her bounds as if she were still in charge of me, which was becoming annoying. But I had to cut her some slack after all she'd done. Aside from the apartment, the preschool, and the party, she'd watched Noah while I was at the Secretary of State on Friday. I'd produced the original birth certificate I'd been protecting for years, my new lease, and the other necessary paperwork to obtain my Michigan driver's license. It was the first driver's license in years I hadn't purchased on the black market.

"Riley?" A beanpole of a woman with cropped hair strode through the gate, pulling a little girl about Noah's age by the hand and heading toward me. "It's me. Harper."

As she approached, I could see that it really was Harper. She'd grown taller, her face more gaunt now, and her hair blonder and shorter.

"Oh my gosh." I widened my stance as uncertainty jittered through me.

She stared for a second, absorbing the sight of me in much the same way I was doing with her. Tears filled her eyes as she dropped the girl's hand and wrapped her bony arms around me in a hug. She smelled wonderful, like vanilla and honeysuckles. "I can't believe it. I'm so glad you're okay."

Relief loosened my muscles as I hugged her back. Harper wasn't pissed. She was happy to reunite and didn't seem to hold a grudge. "I'm so sorry about the way I left."

Harper didn't respond but waved over a woman with a matching haircut who could have been her twin, except for the crow's feet around her eyes and the chunky gold hoops pulling down her earlobes. "Remember my mom?"

"Of course. Nice to see you again, Mrs. Parsons." I was too timid to lean in for a hug, unsure if the woman was as forgiving as her daughter.

She clasped my hands in hers, easing my nerves. "What a miracle. Welcome back, Riley! And please call me Lydia."

As soon as Lydia released me, Harper smacked my arm. "Why didn't you respond to my messages? Or reach out to me? I looked everywhere for you. I was so worried. I thought... I thought you were..."

My eyelids lowered as I looked at my sandals, anything to avoid making eye contact. "I couldn't take my phone. I mean, I thought I couldn't at the time. It's hard to explain, but I'm really sorry."

Harper pinched her lips together, shaking her head. "I'm not mad. We both did stupid things back then, didn't we?" She gave me a strange look, almost a challenge.

"You two always had your own ideas. Not always good ones," Lydia scoffed, shaking her head.

"Yeah." I picked at my cuticle, eager to bury the past and change the subject. I redirected my attention toward the girl at Harper's side, brightening my voice. "And who's this?"

She patted the girl's head. "This is my daughter, April. And Wendy told me you have a son?"

"Yes. He just turned four." Right on cue, Noah ran toward me, squealing.

"I see you've found each other." Wendy joined us, a wide grin across her face. Then she waved us closer together and took a few photos. Soon, Noah and April were hitting a balloon back and forth across the small yard.

Harper's mom wandered toward the food as Harper told me

about herself. She lived in a townhome on the other side of town and worked in marketing for a local e-commerce company. She'd graduated from Central Michigan after high school and gotten married young. She'd been divorced for two years now. She paused, her gaze skimming over me again. "Sorry. I just can't wrap my head around— Where have you been?"

"It's a long story, but basically, I was brainwashed by a slightly older guy. He promised me a better life in L.A., but he lied. He got me hooked on drugs by the time we got out there. I had to live under a new identity."

Harper chewed on her lip. "Was it the cute guy at the mall who you always talked about?"

"Yeah. That's the one."

"I mentioned him to the police but didn't know his name or what he looked like."

My fingers brushed her arm, letting her know nothing that happened was her fault. "It's okay. I didn't want to be found."

"I hope your running away didn't have anything to do with me."

"No. It absolutely didn't."

"I was so surprised you left like that, breaking the rules. You were always scared of getting in trouble."

"Those group homes put the fear of God in me." I spied Harper's mom walking toward us with a full plate. "I promise to catch you up more when we're alone."

Harper touched her chin, staring at my eyes, my nose, my body. "You look so good, like you've really grown up."

"I was thinking the same thing about you."

"I guess that's what fifteen years does."

More people streamed into the backyard as Wendy and George introduced me to a few friends and neighbors. I didn't recognize most of them, although several people claimed to have remembered when I lived with the Eckharts.

A woman with severely cut bangs and a pointy nose

approached me, frowning. "I'm Wendy's friend from the garden club."

"Oh. Hi."

Her scowl deepened. "You should be ashamed of yourself for wasting police resources like that. People thought you were dead."

My ankles wobbled in my wedge sandals, but I stood my ground. "I was young, and I made a bad decision."

She placed her hands on her hips. "What you did was nothing short of criminal. You should be punished for your lies."

I raised an eyebrow, looking around for backup, but Harper had wandered away, and Wendy, George, and Cody were deep in conversation with other guests. I squared my shoulders at the righteous woman. "Sorry. Do I even know you?"

"No. But everyone knows you. You were all anyone talked about for months!"

The disdain on the woman's face made me uncomfortable, and I bolstered my voice. "Ma'am, you don't have to be here. In fact, I think you should leave."

She mumbled something, but I'd already turned away from her. In the corner of my eye, I watched her stomp through the gate, crossing paths with another woman with a large bosom and a much happier demeanor. As the second woman entered the backyard, carrying a bunch of Mylar balloons that said, "Welcome Home!" I instantly recognized her.

"Hi, Aunt Leslie!" I raised my hand, calling out.

She trotted toward me, and we embraced.

"Oh, thank goodness! I was sick with worry when you ran away. You were always one of my favorites. I couldn't believe it when Wendy told me you were back. I had to come and see you for myself."

I thanked her, and she showered me with the same well-wishes I'd received from many others. We handed the balloons to the kids, who squealed with delight. The mood was light and celebratory again, and my nerves slowly dissipated.

After Aunt Leslie and I chatted for a minute, I joined a small crowd around the food table and helped myself to the spread, ending at the grill, where George dropped charred burgers onto our plates.

Wendy sidled up to me, giving me a nudge. "Everyone's raving about the potato salad. It's delicious. Cody and George have already had two helpings."

"It's a tried-and-true recipe." I winked. "I add apple cider vinegar to give it a little zing."

Wendy's head turned, and I followed her gaze toward the gate where Cody stood talking to another man of the same age, dressed casually in athletic shorts and a T-shirt. It took a second to realize he was a grown-up version of Jacob. My stomach somersaulted, and I fought the urge to run and hide behind the shrubs. A part of me had hoped he wouldn't show up. He stared directly at me, steely eyes pinning me in place. I forced my feet toward him, ignoring the way my heart thumped against my ribcage.

"Hi, Jacob." I offered a shaky smile as I neared him.

Cody took a few steps back, giving us space.

Jacob widened his stance, crossing his arms in front of himself. There would be no hug from him. Not even close. "Hi."

I shifted my weight. "This must seem weird."

"Um, yeah. How are you here?" His voice was cold. "I thought you ran off to Tahiti or something."

I grimaced at his comment, but I remembered what Wendy had said about Jacob being heartbroken when I left, and I supposed I deserved his reaction. "I came close a few times, but I made it. Thankfully." Jacob's stare was so fierce that I had to look away.

"And in fifteen years, you never thought to let anyone know

you were okay? You never bothered to contact me or say goodbye?"

"I didn't know..." My mouth was dry, and it was hard to form the words, but I tried again. "I wasn't thinking straight. And by the time I realized what I'd done, I assumed everyone here hated me. That's why I stayed away for so long. I was a coward." I edged closer, noticing the toll time had taken on Jacob's appearance—his receding hairline and deep creases around his mouth. But his expressive eyes and strong jawline were still as attractive as ever. And his teenage frame had filled out; his defined muscles showed off the time he must have spent at the gym.

He scowled and kicked at the grass. "You messed me up. You know that? I looked everywhere for you."

I gulped back a surge of guilt, but it swelled through me anyway. "I'm sorry."

The pain Jacob must have endured raged in his eyes, the downturn of his mouth. "It's not okay. You made us all think you were dead."

"You're right. I can't imagine what I put you through. It wasn't right, and you didn't deserve it."

Jacob tilted his head as if unsure about something. I followed his gaze to my shoulder, realizing he was studying the tattoo that peeked out from beneath the strap of my sundress. I stayed still, letting him examine it and hoping the image sparked a happy memory. When he tightened his crossed arms, I noticed that his left hand was free of a wedding band.

I snapped my attention back to his face when he caught me staring. "For what it's worth, it's nice to see you again."

His lips pulled back in something close to disdain. "I told Wendy I would come to your party, but I'm only here for her. I've got to get back to my girlfriend." He turned away abruptly, and I realized that was all I would get from him. The comment about his girlfriend was obviously meant as an extra twist of the knife, and I couldn't blame him.

My shell-shocked body remained motionless until Cody approached a few seconds later, speaking softly. "Don't take anything he said too personally. I'm not close with Jacob, but I heard he's had a rough time in general."

Harper moved closer, grabbing my hand. "He was heartbroken when you left. He told me once he'd wanted to marry you."

"Oh. I didn't realize." My feet anchored me in place as I felt another stab of guilt in my chest. I wondered if I'd made a huge mistake by returning here.

Harper made a face. "Jacob's girlfriend, McKenzie, is super jealous and possessive. I heard the most horrible stories from my friend who works with her. She and Jacob have broken up at least a half-dozen times." Harper gave me a sly smile. "Maybe the next time he and McKenzie break up, he'll have somewhere else to turn."

I steadied myself, my mind still reeling from Jacob's cold reaction. "He made it pretty clear he doesn't want anything to do with me. And I understand why he'd feel that way."

"It's more like he doesn't know what to do with his rush of emotions." Harper did a poor job of suppressing her grin. "He thought he'd lost the love of his life forever. And now you're back."

I sank into my sandals, trying not to let the situation overwhelm me. Wendy and George had put a lot of effort into making the party a success, and I needed to shake off Jacob's animosity and maintain the happy mood. It was important to show everyone I was grateful to be here.

I resolved to broaden my smile and make another round of chatting with the guests if only to double down on my story about how Noah and I had spent the last year living in a homeless shelter on the outskirts of L.A. I'd tell them how I'd worked various temp jobs trying to save enough money to buy a used car and get us out of there. It had taken so much longer than I'd thought. They didn't need to know the real reason I'd spent years on the run and the things I'd done to survive, including the recent disaster at Toven Brothers. But just as I stepped away from Harper, an unwelcome sight appeared on the other side of the fence, causing me to stop mid-stride, my arms dropping to my sides.

A woman with coiffed hair in a royal blue pantsuit approached the gate, waving to draw the attention of the guests. A cameraman and a woman carrying a boom microphone flanked her. The side of the camera said *Channel 4 Action News* in bright blue lettering.

The reporter projected her voice across the backyard, calling out to no one in particular. "Hi, I'm Melissa Miner from Channel 4 Action News. We got a tip that Riley Wakefield, the missing foster child, has returned. We'd love to break the story."

The conversation stopped, and all eyes turned toward me. The ground seemed to give way beneath my feet as panic erupted deep inside my body, rushing out to my extremities. Authorities were on the hunt for Sandra Matthews. Now Melissa Miner was here, and she was going to blow my cover.

SEVEN

"Riley's right there, in the striped sundress," Aunt Leslie yelled to the reporter, pointing at me and beaming as if she were announcing a lottery winner.

I felt Harper's palm on my back, urging me forward. "Go talk to her," she whispered. "This is so cool."

Dread seeped through my veins, thick and cold. I wished I could dig a hole in the ground and hide.

The guests mumbled among themselves, seemingly awestruck by the arrival of a local celebrity. They formed a half-circle around me as Melissa Miner made a beeline in my direction. She stuck out her hand, and I shook it as she introduced herself.

"I apologize for crashing your party. We got a tip at the station. This is the type of local, feel-good story we love to air on Channel 4."

"That's okay." Beads of sweat erupted over my skin as I pushed my hair forward, smoothing down my bangs to cover my eyebrows, anything to hide similarities between me and my previous identity. I motioned to Wendy and George. "Why don't you talk to my former foster parents, the Eckharts?"

"Of course, I'll talk to them too. But people will want to hear from you, especially."

With everyone staring at me expectantly, I agreed to a brief interview on the condition my son was kept off the air. Melissa reluctantly agreed to my demand, apparently caring more about being the first to break the story than whether she did the most thorough job. As I reapplied some lip gloss with my trembling hand, I wondered about the reach of the local news station. Hopefully, the broadcast was truly local, and no one in Las Vegas would ever see the coverage.

The cameraman counted down from three, then pointed at Melissa. She began the interview as everyone at the party watched.

"Hello, it's Melissa Miner reporting from Marigold Street in Berkley. We so often hear the heartbreaking stories of runaway teens, particularly those from difficult upbringings. Today, I'm happy to report a welcome twist to one of those stories. Fifteen years ago, Riley Wakefield, a sixteen-year-old foster child, disappeared from her foster home here in this quiet neighborhood. Riley's foster parents, George and Wendy Eckhart, her friends, and her neighbors feared the worst. Authorities concluded she'd escaped to the streets, her location and fate unknown. And after years of no trace of Riley Wakefield, most of those who'd known her presumed she'd met a tragic fate.

"But a few days ago, Riley showed up on the doorstep of the foster home where she used to live, healthy and unharmed. I'm here at a welcome home party with Riley and her former foster parents."

My intestines twisted as the camera guy appeared to zoom in on me.

"Nice to see you, Riley. We're all glad you're safe and sound." She held the microphone inches from my face.

"Thank you." I focused on Melissa's thick eyelashes to avoid looking at the camera.

"Did you know so many people had been searching for you for so many years?"

"No. I thought maybe a few people were initially, but I didn't think about the effect my running away would have. It was a terrible decision I made back then, and I regret the hurt and worry I caused everyone."

"It looks like everyone here has forgiven you." Melissa smiled as she motioned toward the backyard partygoers, many bobbing their heads up and down. "Have you been living on the streets all this time?"

"More or less, yes." I proceeded to tell a trimmed-down story about meeting the man at the mall and how he convinced me to go to L.A., got me addicted to drugs, and used me in his sex-trafficking ring.

Melissa gasped, placing her free hand over her heart. "How terrible. I'm sorry to hear that happened to you. Has the man been arrested?"

"He died a few years ago. I eventually got clean and moved into a homeless shelter that provided counseling, rehab, and job training. I worked temporary jobs until I'd saved enough money to buy a used car and return to Michigan."

"And no one from your life here in Berkley knew where you were?"

"No. I was scared. I wish I'd handled things differently, but I didn't know how people would react."

Melissa offered some words of sympathy, admiration, and encouragement, then turned her attention toward the Eckharts.

"And Wendy and George, how did it feel to open the door and see Riley standing there?"

Wendy folded her hands together as her mouth stretched wide. "It felt a little like I was seeing a ghost. I just couldn't believe it." She glanced toward George. "We were both so happy and relieved."

The reporter's face turned serious. "I looked back at the

police report you filed after Riley disappeared. She'd stolen quite a bit of money from you the night she left, didn't she? A thousand dollars."

Wendy waved away the question. "That was the least of our concerns. We only wanted her to be safe."

Melissa faced me. "Riley, do you have plans to pay the money back?"

"Yes." I swallowed as I considered using the money I'd taken from Toven Brothers to reimburse the Eckharts immediately and lessen my guilt. But as far as they knew, I was destitute to the point of being homeless. I couldn't act like I was sitting on a secret pile of cash. "I'm still getting on my feet right now, but as soon as I'm able, I will pay them back. That has always been my intention."

Melissa nodded her approval, then turned back to Wendy and George. "And is it true that you were no longer allowed to host foster kids after Riley disappeared?"

"That's true, yes," George said, tucking in his chin.

Wendy inched forward, clearly eager to expand on George's answer. "No one knew what had happened to Riley. The police were questioning everyone close to her, as they should have. The social workers at the agency were being extra cautious in not letting us take in more kids. But we understood the decision they made, and we moved on."

"Does Riley's safe return feel a little bit of a vindication against those who thought you'd done something wrong back then?"

Wendy shrugged. "I suppose so. It proves that we've always told the truth. And so did the others who were questioned about her disappearance."

The reporter's eyes found me again. "Enough about the past. What's next for Riley Wakefield?"

"I'll be looking for a waitressing job while I study to get my real estate license. That's all I know right now."

"That sounds like a promising plan, and I wish you the best of luck." Melissa prattled on for another minute about how Channel 4 strives to regularly report stories with heartwarming outcomes and how she was glad she brought everyone this breaking news first.

At last, the interview was over. Melissa told us we did a great job, and I took it as a win that I would only be on air for less than five minutes and that she hadn't mentioned Noah. As her colleagues packed their gear, she leaned closer to me as if to share a secret. "Riley, I contacted the police about your return while we were preparing for the interview and was surprised you hadn't stopped by to talk to them yet."

A sour taste filled my mouth as I stared at her berry-stained lips. "I guess I should have done that first thing. I wasn't thinking."

"They may be following up with you in the next day or two so they can officially close the case."

"Okay. Thanks," I said, turning away. I'd prepared myself to have to talk to the police at some point, but the imminence of a police interview sent a new ripple of dread through me. I reminded myself to keep my emotions in check. I was Riley Wakefield, the runaway foster child who'd spent years as a homeless woman in the L.A. area. The authorities had no reason to suspect I was also Sandra Matthews, the woman from San Antonio who'd stabbed a man in Vegas, or any of the other identities I'd lived under. So, I watched the Channel 4 Action News team leave, forced a happy expression onto my face, and returned to the party.

EIGHT

Clanging metal and squeaking brakes awoke me before daybreak. My mind was foggy, and it took a second to get my bearings in the darkened room, to remember I was safe inside the little apartment with Noah sleeping on his air mattress in the corner. I sat up, realizing the noise was a garbage truck beeping through the alley behind us. Noah sighed and turned over. He was a heavy sleeper, and the commotion outside didn't disturb him. Yesterday's events had worn us out, with the last guests not leaving the barbecue until after 10 p.m.

I lay in bed for a few minutes, closing my eyes and trying to go back to sleep, but my mind flipped back to the TV interview I'd done yesterday. Maybe I shouldn't have agreed to it. But that would have seemed suspicious to everyone. I reassured myself that I had made the best decision, given the unexpected arrival of the news crew. The smartest move had been to get the interview out of the way and simply hope that not many people outside a fifty-mile radius watched the Sunday night local news on Channel 4. I would turn down any future interview requests. The last thing I needed was for someone from my past to recognize me.

I slipped out of bed and tiptoed out of the bedroom, heading to the kitchen to brew a pot of coffee. As I turned on the light and poured the water into the reservoir, my vision caught on something out of place. Next to the front entrance, the door to the narrow coat closet hung slightly ajar. I would have noticed the open closet when I'd checked the lock on the front door before I'd gone to bed. I disliked open closet doors—lingering fears of the boogeyman from my childhood—and I never left them open, especially at night. The closet door had been closed. I was sure of it.

A chill skittered across my skin as I turned in every direction, inspecting the rest of the apartment. I froze as I noticed something else: the little rug I'd bought at Target and placed in front of the door sat slightly askew. I didn't remember it being like that last night. I stumbled backward, placing my palms on the counter to support my weight. Had someone been inside my apartment while Noah and I slept in the next room?

I pulled in a breath and grabbed a butcher knife from the drawer. Then I crept toward the closet, facing the span of black filling the opening. My heart thumped wildly as I flung the door open, preparing to defend myself against the intruder. Only three lightweight coats hung from the rack, a few pairs of shoes lining the bottom, and some odds and ends on the top shelf. No one was there.

Whoever had been here was gone. I studied the front door again, noticing it was still locked. Did the intruder have a key? Or could someone have gotten in through a window? The window in the living room had a box fan wedged into the opening and a screen on the other side. Someone might have entered that way, although putting the screen and fan back in place from outside would have taken some work. There was a fan in the bedroom window too. But surely we would have heard someone busting their way into our room, even if we were sound asleep?

My frantic thoughts veered to who would have broken into the apartment during the night. The obvious answer was that Drew Toven had followed me here. What if he'd seen the news report? But it seemed unlikely that someone in Las Vegas would arrive so quickly unless they were already in the area. Maybe a guest at the barbecue was angry that I'd returned so suddenly without any communication for many years. The belligerent woman forced her way into my thoughts, followed by Jacob's stony glare, but I couldn't imagine what either of them would have accomplished by breaking into my apartment in the middle of the night. I turned more options over but was no closer to an answer.

The cash I kept hidden in the freezer propelled me into action. I yanked open the freezer door, scanning over the frozen dinners and chicken nuggets until I found the ziplock bag marked "frozen spinach." Wrapped in a paper towel inside was the pile of $100 bills I'd stolen from Toven Brothers—$5,000 remained after my travel expenses and the payment to Bea. *Thank God it was still there.* I ran into the bedroom and reached underneath the mattress, finger grasping the manila envelope stuffed with my important documents and the only family heirloom I owned—a silver chain necklace with a heart pendant. The necklace was of average quality and virtually worthless from a monetary standpoint but priceless in emotional value. It had been sealed in a plastic bag and stuffed into the file I'd received when I'd left the group home. A note taped to the bag merely stated *This belonged to your grandmother.* Noah breathed heavily as I sifted through my most precious belongings, accounting for each one. They hadn't been touched.

I flopped on the bed, clutching my head. *Was I going crazy?* Maybe no one had entered the apartment during the night. Everything of value was still here. Perhaps Noah had gotten up to go to the bathroom and wandered around, opening the closet for some reason and messing up the rug. Of course. That was a more likely explanation.

An hour after dropping Noah at his first day of preschool, I found myself inhaling stale air in a cramped room at the local police station with the Eckharts next to me. I'd stumbled across Wendy and George in the garage this morning, measuring the oil levels of their matching silver sedans, and told them about my plans to stop by the station. They insisted on accompanying me for moral support. Now, Officer Mason, a potbellied man with a crew cut sat across from us, flipping through papers.

The officer addressed me with a tight-lipped smile. "I understand you're here with an important update."

"Yes," Wendy said before I could respond. "Our former foster daughter, Riley Wakefield, ran away fifteen years ago and was considered a missing person. But now she has returned." Wendy patted my arm. "Here she is. You probably saw her on the news yesterday. Channel 4."

The officer's eyes darted from me to Wendy and back again. "No, but I talked to the reporter and reviewed the file. Thank you for coming in. You saved me a trip."

I gave a half wave. "Hi. I'm Riley. I'm no longer missing." I placed my ID and birth certificate on the counter. "I ran away from my foster home when I was sixteen and got mixed up with some bad people. It wasn't anyone's fault but my own."

He took a minute to inspect the documents. "These look authentic."

"They are." I touched my chest. "It's me. Everyone recognizes me. You can ask anyone who was at the party yesterday."

"She has a tattoo." Wendy tapped my shoulder. "It's the same strange black bird she got when she lived with us. I was so angry after she got it. I told her she'd regret it later." She chortled. "But now I guess it was a good thing."

"It's a dove, but it's black." I stretched my collar over my shoulder to reveal the inked image.

The officer leaned forward to get a better look, then flipped through the slim file, landing on some notes. He studied a series of old photos, glancing at my face every few seconds. "It certainly appears to be you, Riley. It's an amazing turn of events. I'm glad you're safe and sound."

"Thanks. I'm really sorry for wasting the police department's resources." I shifted in my chair, remembering the angry woman at the barbecue.

He twirled a pen between his fingers as he tilted his head. "Would you like to tell me more about this man at the mall who lured you out to California? We can coordinate with the authorities out there."

"His name was Max. He said his last name was Smith, but I think that was a lie." I paused, shaking my head.

"That last name does seem a little too generic."

"And there's nothing to be done at this point because he's dead."

The officer frowned, centering himself on his chair. "Oh..."

"Yeah. I heard from a mutual acquaintance that he was shot by a gang member. It happened about three years ago. It wasn't a big surprise, considering the kind of life he was leading."

"I see. Well, I guess that simplifies things in some respects." Officer Mason lifted a paper, his jowls sagging.

George cleared his throat. "We'd like to take back that claim we made about the stolen money. Just erase it from the record if you can."

"That's right," Wendy said.

Officer Mason waved them off. "The statute of limitations expired years ago, so it's a nonissue either way."

I sat up straighter. "I'm going to pay them back."

"It's fine, dear," Wendy said, patting my arm.

"You were a minor then anyway, so none of this affects your

adult record." Officer Mason shut the folder. "I'm going to make some copies of your documents and officially close your missing person case. It's nice to have a happy ending to these types of cases once in a while."

"Thank you." I sat up taller, aware of the tension leaving my body. "I appreciate all your work trying to find me, and I'm sorry again."

Officer Mason shrugged, glancing toward the rows of filing cabinets. "In the grand scheme of things, you didn't do anything too bad. Sometimes I have to deal with murderers and rapists and child abusers. I'll take a teenage runaway any day." He grabbed my birth certificate and ID to copy and left the room.

I lowered my eyelids, thinking of my prior illegal acts and hoping they weren't written across my face—the lies I'd told, the money I'd stolen, the people I'd injured, and worse. I released the gulp of air I'd been holding in my lungs, thankful that Officer Mason hadn't felt it necessary to take my DNA or fingerprints. I'd always been careful, but I wasn't completely certain I hadn't left traces behind at Toven Brothers or other locations. As far as the local police knew, I was nothing more than a runaway who'd returned home after many years. I was a file they could stamp with a happy face and add to their list of closed cases so they could move on to more pressing matters.

And that was exactly how I wanted it.

NINE

Noah squealed as I pushed him on the swing, thankful for the afternoon breeze. Dark sunglasses shielded my eyes from the bright sunlight and deflected the obvious stares I'd been receiving from people all over town.

Harper stood next to me, pushing April on the neighboring swing. I'd shown up ten minutes late for our Wednesday afternoon playdate and was surprised by how offended she'd been, from giving me the cold shoulder after we arrived to answering my questions with clipped, one-word answers. I wasn't completely up to speed with playdate etiquette, but her reaction felt over-the-top for such a minor infraction.

"I'm sorry again about being late," I said for the third time. "I left my phone and had to go back for it."

"It's fine." Harper's voice was flat, and it was clear my late arrival wasn't fine.

I was anxious enough about spending time with her, and her overreaction only amplified my nerves. "Should Noah and I leave?" I asked.

"No. Why would you do that?" Harper shrugged as if our

tardiness had been no big deal after all, her voice suddenly buoyant. "I'm glad this worked out."

"Me too," I said, hoping she'd finally gotten over it.

The swings creaked as we pushed the children. The early August heat was sweltering, and sweat gathered in my armpits.

Harper gave a big push to April and then turned toward me. "It's so crazy how our lives turned out so alike. I mean, we have kids practically the same age, we're single, and now we both live in Berkley."

"Yeah." I bit my lip, aware the twisting path I'd taken to arrive back at this spot would be unrecognizable to her. "I guess there was a reason we were friends."

"Higher, higher!" April yelled.

"Higher!" Noah joined in.

We pushed them higher, their giggles drifting through the humid air.

Harper stepped back. "Do you remember the night I stole that beer from the 7-Eleven and we ran to this park and drank it?" She pointed to a nearby maple tree. "Right under that tree. You were so nervous and freaked out about the whole thing like the police were going to track us down and arrest us."

I looked toward where she pointed, finding a young woman sitting on a blanket and playing patty-cake with a two-year-old. "You were fearless. And I was nervous about being sent back to the group home. I hated it there."

The sparkle in Harper's eyes vanished, replaced by something darker. She stopped the swing and helped April to the ground before returning to me. "I wish that was the worst thing we did."

I lowered my head, focusing on the tufts of grass below. I wasn't sure which teenage escapade Harper was talking about, but I was positive I'd done much worse things alone.

I kept my face still as I turned toward her. "We were really stupid."

"I shouldn't have..." Harper's lip twitched as she stopped mid-sentence.

"What?"

"Never mind. Nothing." She set her jaw, clearly changing her mind about whatever she'd been about to say. "Did you know I was the first person in my family to get a college degree?"

"That's great, Harper."

"It was really important to Mom."

"She must have been proud."

"She was. She still is. That's why I did some of the things I did. I couldn't let Mom down." Harper stared at the horizon for several seconds. "When my grades tanked our junior year, I was devastated because I thought that was the end of my college dream. And then it was so hard to focus after you left, but I turned things around and made college happen. Mom was over-joyed. She visited me at Central almost every weekend."

"She did?" I knew that Harper and her mom had been close. Someone had even mentioned at the barbecue that they were more like sisters than a mother and daughter. But driving several hours every weekend to visit her daughter while at college seemed overkill.

"Yeah. Mom was always there for me. I missed you so much after you disappeared. I blamed myself for what happened to you."

"It wasn't your fault."

Harper continued talking as if I hadn't spoken. "I remember how annoyed you were with George and Wendy's rules. I didn't realize they bothered you so much that you would run away with a strange man."

"It was a bad decision."

"All this time, I wanted you to be alive. I prayed for you every night." Her voice was quiet, and I wondered if she was talking to me or herself.

"I'm sorry. I should have figured out a way to text you from someone else's phone."

Harper picked at her nails. "It's okay. That was a long time ago."

I registered the hurt on her face and knew it wasn't okay. Still, the past was the past, and there wasn't much else I could do to make it up to her other than try to be a good friend going forward. As Harper helped her daughter back onto a swing, she told me she'd met her ex-husband a few years after college and left him a year after April was born because he loved beer more than them.

"That must have been difficult," I said.

"It was, but I'm happier without him." The distant look in her eyes conveyed something else: that the life she'd envisioned for herself hadn't turned out exactly as planned.

I wanted to ask if she was dating anyone new, but she spoke first.

"I can't believe Creepy Cody was at the barbecue."

I tilted my head at the juvenile nickname. It was mean, and I didn't like it, especially aimed at someone like me who'd grown up without parents. "He seems a lot more normal now. He's good with Noah."

Harper stared into space. "You've been through so much." She lowered her face toward mine. Her voice had changed to something softer and more serious. "You must have dealt with some really terrible people."

"Yeah."

"I bet really bad things happened to you out there." She looked around the playground at the handful of adults and kids absorbed in their fun afternoon. "It's just us. I won't tell anyone."

My back pressed into the bench slats as terrifying memories tore through me—the hunger pangs clawing through my insides, the time I was locked alone in a dark room, not knowing when I'd be let out, the nights I woke up with a calloused hand over my mouth to stop me from screaming, or the times I hid beneath my bed hoping my tormenter wouldn't find me. I had, indeed, been through some horrific things. I squeezed my eyes shut, willing away the rest. "Bad things happen everywhere, Harper."

"Yes, but not like that. It sounds like you were sold into a life of prostitution. You were just a kid."

I watched a crow fly over our heads, unwilling to trust Harper with my secrets. "It's behind me now, and I don't want to talk about it."

"But don't you want those men to be held accountable?"

"Of course I do. But Max is dead. That's the best karma I could have hoped for. I don't know the names of the others." I glanced toward Noah, who piled sand into a mound. "I went through counseling at the shelter. Even got my G.E.D. Now I want to move on."

Harper shifted on the bench, uncrossing her legs. "Okay. I understand. But I'm here if you ever feel like talking."

"Thanks."

"Not everyone is smart enough to get themselves out of a situation like that. But you did. You're a strong person, and I'm proud of you."

I took in Harper's words, noticing the sheen in her eyes.

"I did what I had to do."

She pulled me into a one-armed hug, and I relaxed on the bench, comforted by her proximity. We chatted about high school memories and watched our kids build lopsided sandcastles as clouds gathered across the blue sky.

An hour later, Noah and April had had enough of the park.

I brushed the sand from Noah's palms when a dark figure

moved in the corner of my vision, sending a bristle up the back of my neck and drawing my eyes toward a grove of pine trees on the far side of the playground. I peered between the gaps in the distant branches, catching a glimpse of someone behind the foliage wearing a pop of royal blue. The person strode in the opposite direction and vanished among the trees.

TEN

A kid screamed from another corner of the playground.

"What's wrong?" Harper was looking at me, concern pulling down the corners of her mouth.

"Nothing. I thought I saw someone hiding over there." I nodded toward the trees.

She craned her neck in the same direction. "I don't see anything."

The movement had stopped, and the trees stood quietly, only a few birds flitting from branch to branch. "Yeah. I guess I was wrong."

"We need to get going." Harper checked her phone. "I have most Wednesday and Friday afternoons off. Let's do it again soon."

"Definitely."

I opened my bag and packed the water bottle, snacks, and sunscreen. A few minutes later, Noah was buckled in his car seat, and I pulled out of our parking space adjacent to the playground. A black SUV pulled up behind us, leaving a larger-than-normal gap. I did a double take in my rearview mirror at the BMW with tinted windows. I couldn't identify the driver through the windshield, only the silhouette of a person wearing a hat and dark sunglasses. The driver followed us through several turns, and my hackles went up. Without using my signal, I turned right down a random residential street, and the BMW turned too. The light shifted across the windshield, and I gasped as I glimpsed a royal blue baseball cap on the driver's head. I exited the neighborhood, and at the next light, I put on my turn signal but gunned it straight through the light just as it turned red, then slammed on the brakes to avoid hitting the car in front of me.

"Ow!" Noah said, clutching his seatbelt.

"Sorry. I didn't see that car." My foot stayed squarely on the accelerator as I drove in the opposite direction of home, my heart racing along with our car and only returning to normal once I was sure the SUV was no longer visible in my rearview mirror.

I wondered who could have been tailing me, but only one name lingered in my thoughts. What if Drew Toven had somehow seen Melissa Miner's news report and followed me here? Between denying my former boss's advances, stabbing him, and stealing his money, I'd done more than enough to ensure he'd want retribution. Still, it was too soon to freak out, and I was well aware of my tendency to imagine the worst. But even as I told myself it could have been a coincidence, I couldn't ignore the sickening feeling writhing in my gut.

I held Noah's hand as we cut across the Eckharts' front yard and through the gate. The afternoon had turned gray, the threat of rain thick in the air. As we entered the backyard, I tossed one last glance over my shoulder, confirming that the suspicious car hadn't followed us.

"I guess I have a celebrity living next door."

The scratchy voice made me jump, and I looked toward the

source. Mrs. Harwood stood on the other side of the fence, wearing a white bathrobe that matched her tufts of hair. As she stared at me, a clump of hair fell into her eyes, and she made no effort to move it.

"Hi. Mrs. Harwood, right?"

"You can call me Brenda." She pulled the robe tighter around her bony frame as she nodded toward George and Wendy's house. "That was a big party they threw for you. Of course, I wasn't invited."

"Oh. I'm sorry."

She swatted away my apology like a pesky fly. "I saw you on the news the other day. And I remember when you used to live here."

"You do?"

Brenda glanced toward the second-story bedroom window, then back to me. "You had a mind of your own, didn't you?"

"I guess so." I heard the note of disapproval in her voice, and my gaze dropped to my feet.

"But you were more polite than some of them."

Noah moved toward a soccer ball lying at the edge of the yard. My impulse was to go with him, away from the awkward conversation with the old lady. Instead, I forced myself to stay and act as the polite person she remembered.

"I don't blame you for running away. Not one bit." She eyed the Eckharts' back door and made a face like she'd gulped sour milk. "I wouldn't want to live with those two either."

A guffaw spilled from my mouth at her unfiltered honesty. From what I'd witnessed, there was no love lost between Brenda and the Eckharts, and I could see how Brenda would be a difficult person to have as a close neighbor. "They did their best. I wasn't the easiest teenager."

Brenda scowled. "They're horrible neighbors. They chopped down the big maple tree that shaded my yard. Then they had all those wild kids running around for years on end, always yelling to do this or stop doing that. I thank you for putting an end to it."

I hugged my arms around myself, her comment placing me in an awkward position. "To be fair, I didn't realize my running away would prevent them from fostering other kids."

She flipped her hand in the air, waving away my statement. "Regardless, you did a good thing."

"Okay."

"And, as long as I have you here, can you please keep that light off?" She pointed toward a floodlight above the door to my apartment. "It shines directly into my bedroom window and interferes with my sleep."

"Sure. Sorry. I didn't realize it was on." I stepped away, hoping the conversation was over. But she spoke again.

"And let's put an end to the late-night visitors. It makes me feel unsafe to have strange people prowling around in the dark."

I stepped back, confused by her statement. I scanned the yard, looking over the fence to see what I could of the alley. "What late-night visitors?"

"I saw someone wandering around your apartment very late the other night. Your light was off then, so I couldn't see who it was. The person went right in the front door. I assume you let them in."

The ground seemed to give way beneath me as I remembered the open closet door and the off-kilter rug. I hadn't let anyone into my apartment late at night, but what if someone had let themselves inside? "Sorry. That's not..." I shook my head. "I don't know who that was."

She peered down her nose at me, her eyes sinking further into the hollow sockets as if she didn't believe a word I said. "Very well."

"Was it a man or a woman?"

"I can't say. It was dark, like I said. And my vision is poor without my glasses."

A raindrop landed on my forehead. Another hit my arm, and I looked up at the angry sky. "We should get out of the rain."

Brenda nodded and shuffled away. I waved Noah up the stairs, letting us into the apartment as the rain grew heavier. It should have been a relief to take shelter from the downpour. But when I locked the door behind us, I no longer felt safe inside.

ELEVEN

I wedged a chair underneath the door handle as a torrent of rain fell outside the open window. I considered closing and locking the window too, but that would turn the second-story apartment into a sauna. Besides, the intruder hadn't entered that way. Brenda said she'd seen the visitor go in through the door. She thought I'd let someone inside.

"Why are you doing that, Mommy?" Noah pointed to the chair propped underneath the door handle.

"So Mommy can hear if we have any visitors."

"Oh." He returned to his matchbox cars, accepting my explanation at face value. I wondered again what kind of horrible mother I was for making my child think it was normal to wedge a chair beneath a door handle to ensure our safety. I hoped he was young enough that he wouldn't remember this when he was older.

I checked the bedroom and the bathroom for anything out of place, but everything was exactly as I'd left it. The manila envelope was under the mattress. To make things more difficult for a thief, I removed my valuable documents and the plastic bag containing my grandmother's necklace, folded them into an empty box of tampons, and placed the box behind the toilet paper in the cupboard beneath the bathroom sink. Back in the kitchen, the ziplock bag marked "frozen spinach" was still in the freezer with the money inside.

The edge of the counter dug into my hip as I watched Noah play, satisfied that no one had entered the apartment while we'd been gone. An image of the car with the tinted windows prowled through my mind. If Drew Toven was the driver, he could have been the same person who'd entered my apartment the other night. Then again, it was just as likely that someone local had discovered the truth about my sordid history. Neither option was good.

I turned toward the small kitchen window, watching the alley deluged with rain. As far as I could see, the narrow road sat empty. Things felt dire, but I'd been in tight spots before and always figured a way out. My ability to sniff out the bad guys was a by-product of navigating the volatile personalities I'd encountered while living in group homes. The girls were cliquey by nature, and I'd quickly learned who to ignore, stand up to, or sweet-talk to avoid a punch in the teeth or worse. Without any parents to guide me, I'd had to be resourceful to survive.

Hiding behind my schoolwork had been my preferred strategy for surviving the group homes. Burying myself in a book, a math problem, or a scientific theory was my invisible armor, an easy way to escape reality and keep the other kids at a distance. The approach worked with almost everyone except for Marianne Clavey, who had it out for me no matter what I did. Still, the praise I received from my teachers outweighed Marianne's torment most of the time. My college dream never came true. A life on the run didn't lend itself to a four-year degree, but my street smarts gave me an advantage now. I would keep a close watch on my surroundings and figure out who was tailing me. And then I'd find a way to make them stop.

.   .   .

Over the next few days, my senses were on high alert, but I masked my watchfulness with a good-natured smile and plenty of small talk whenever I was outside the apartment. At night, I turned off the floodlight outside the front door for the sake of Brenda Harwood's sleep, but I left the living room and bathroom lights on. I wedged the chair beneath the door handle and locked the windows in the main living space, aware I was leaving only the bedroom window for an intruder to enter. But it was too stifling to sleep without the fan.

Despite my constant surveillance, I spied no strangers following me. I found no items out of place in the apartment. I couldn't help wondering if the person at the playground had merely been another parent, if the black BMW tailing me had only been a person heading the same direction, and if the shadowy figure Brenda had seen entering the apartment was merely Wendy or George dropping off toys or photo albums. Things were looking up, and I hated to view my life through a filter of paranoia. Noah was enjoying his new preschool, I'd started the online real estate class, and a local breakfast and lunch spot called Songbird Café had hired me as a part-time waitress, agreeing to a flexible schedule.

On Monday at 11 a.m., I breathed in the scent of maple syrup, coffee, and a generic cleaning product. A black polo shirt with "Songbird Café" stitched in one corner felt scratchy against my skin. I wiped down a recently vacated table as my manager, a feisty woman named Suzie, had instructed. I'd noticed Suzie observing me from afar, nodding her approval as I made small talk with the customers in a corner booth, distracting them from the fact that I'd initially served their food to the wrong table, then winning them over with some good, old-fashioned charm. They'd left me a thirty percent tip, which made me hopeful I could make enough money at the café to pay for next month's rent without dipping into my cash savings.

"I got tables six and eight confused, but I fixed it," I said to Suzie, out of earshot from the diners.

She puckered her lips and gave me an encouraging nod. "You'll learn the table numbers. You have a nice way of relating to the customers. That's something I can't teach. Keep up the good work."

I bit my lip and turned away. I'd spent years honing my people skills as adapting was necessary for survival. I wouldn't share that information with Suzie. Still, I was thankful she'd overlooked my lack of references after I'd shared a sad story about the fictional place where I used to work in California, which I'd told her had gone out of business after a grease fire.

The door chimed behind me as I dropped the dirty rag in the bin in the kitchen and washed my hands.

"A new group just arrived for you." Tabitha nodded toward the dining room. She was the only other waitress on duty and a pretty, twenty-something, part-time college student. "Table four."

"I got it. Thanks." I lifted my chin and strode toward the bright dining room, enjoying the flood of natural light after spending so much time in my dark apartment. But my feet stopped moving when I caught sight of the couple sitting at table four. It was Jacob and a petite woman with bright red lipstick, who I presumed was his girlfriend, McKenzie.

Jacob's eyes widened at the sight of me, and it seemed he hadn't planned this encounter on purpose. I wanted to run back into the kitchen, but Suzie was perched at the register, watching me.

"Hi." I forced out the word as I slapped down two menus, heat creeping up my neck. "Can I start you with some coffee?"

"I'll have a Diet Coke," the woman ordered without looking at me, touching her large forehead with a manicured finger.

Jacob gave me a sheepish look. "Sorry. I didn't know—"

"Didn't know what?" McKenzie's gaze traveled from his face to mine. She read my name tag, a realization solidifying as she leaned back and stared at me. "Oh. Riley. Riley Wakefield. The long-lost foster child from the news."

"Yep." I shifted my weight, hoping Jacob would spit out his order so I could retreat to the kitchen as quickly as possible.

She raised her eyebrows at Jacob. "Your ex-girlfriend is serving us. How awkward." Her laugh sounded dangerous, like a smattering of bullets.

"McKenzie, stop." Jacob huffed out a breath.

Her cackling stopped abruptly, and she motioned toward me. "What am I supposed to do? Ignore the fact you brought me to the restaurant where your ex-girlfriend works? She made you think she was dead!"

Jacob glanced up at me, ignoring McKenzie's rant. "Coffee would be great. Thanks." He seemed to have softened toward me since the last time I'd seen him, and I couldn't help noticing the depth of his eyes. As I turned my back and hurried toward the kitchen, I heard him say, "Grow up, will you? I didn't know she worked here."

I puffed out a breath when the door to the kitchen swung closed behind me, thankful I didn't have to listen to McKenzie's response.

"You okay?" Tabitha cocked her head at me, tapping a small notepad with the tip of a pen.

"Yeah. I just..." I clenched my teeth. "My ex-boyfriend is out there with his girlfriend. What are the odds?"

"Stuff like that happens all the time. Literally, everyone in town eats here for some reason. I mean, the food is average, at best." She made a face toward a row of eggs sizzling on the stove and then peered over my shoulder through the tiny window in the swinging door. "Is it table four?"

"Yeah."

"I'll cover it for you. You can have table ten. They're just about ready to order."

"Thanks."

Tabitha pushed past me, straight toward Jacob and McKenzie. I collected myself, and when I was ready, I exited the kitchen, making a beeline toward table ten. McKenzie made a smart comment about how I'd switched tables, and I could almost feel the sear of her eyes against my back. I focused on the man and woman in front of me, on their orders of whole-wheat toast, veggie hash, and sunny-side up eggs. Then I checked in on my other table, forcing a smile at the two elderly men who requested a fourth coffee refill. At the edge of my vision, Jacob and McKenzie sat across from each other, not speaking. At the barbecue the other night, Harper had mentioned Jacob's tumultuous relationship with his girlfriend, and my presence had clearly caused another argument between them. A swell of sadness for Jacob expanded in my chest. For his sake, I hoped McKenzie had a kinder, softer side.

As I had the thought, my gaze flicked toward her. I immediately wished it hadn't. She locked eyes with me, refusing to look away. It was the kind of stare that had something to prove, an icy glare that chilled my bones. I stumbled backward and turned toward the kitchen, barging through the swinging doors. Something about McKenzie made me uneasy, and I couldn't get away from her fast enough.

TWELVE

We found Wendy standing at the edge of the patio with a shovel and yellow work gloves covering her hands. Noah jumped and hopped as he walked toward her, excited about the two leftover cinnamon rolls I'd snagged for him from the café. But my feet dragged, my body tired from working long shifts two days in a row.

"Welcome home!" Wendy said with a broad smile. "How was school?"

"Good." Noah held up a watercolor painting and waved it in the air. "We painted."

"Wonderful." She turned her attention toward me. "And the new job is still going well?"

"So far, so good." I didn't want Wendy to worry about my ability to come up with rent, so I hadn't told her about any of the negative parts of my job or yesterday's run-in with McKenzie and Jacob.

"That's great." She examined the ground. "I'm just figuring out the best place to plant some native grasses. It's a little late in the season, but they can establish their roots for next year."

"That looks like a good spot." I nodded toward the far side of the patio bordering the McKneelys' house.

Wendy grunted in disagreement. "I'm going to plant two little trees over there to get more shade in the late afternoon. It's a bigger project than I can do on my own, so I might have to ask someone from the garden club to help me." She eyed the house next door. "The McKneelys are leaving on vacation tomorrow for a month, so at least they won't be home to mind the commotion."

"That's good. I don't know much about gardening, but I'm sure it will look nice when you're done."

Wendy refocused on her native grasses as Noah and I continued across the yard and up the stairs. I would have loved to have a quiet afternoon lounging alone in the yard while Noah played with his soccer ball. However, between George and Wendy, one of them always seemed to be puttering about in the yard, tending to the garden, or sitting on the patio talking on the phone or flipping through a magazine. It was a constant reminder that the space was not mine, that we were living on someone else's property. It made me yearn even more for a home of my own. A private residence was a luxury I'd never been afforded since the state had removed me from my mother. Still, I reminded myself that the Eckharts' constant presence, coupled with Brenda Harwood's watching eyes, created an extra layer of security against anyone who might have been following me.

That evening, I sat at our little kitchen table with my laptop while Noah built a wooden train track across the floor. On my screen, a woman taught the second session of my real estate class as I made notes in my workbook, feeling extra motivated to succeed in my new career. There was no limit to the number of commissions I could earn, and my people skills would help me connect with clients. More than that, I'd always envied home-owners, envisioning the happy families inside the walls and the roots firmly attached to a place. For most of my life, I'd only had dusty shoes, a duffle bag, and a bunk room. A home with equity and a mortgage payment felt like a commitment to a better life, one that was safe and stable. It would be fulfilling to help others achieve their dreams, even if I was still a few years away from getting Noah and me there.

The teacher was lecturing about the ownership differences between a single-family home, condominium, and co-op when something banged from outside. It sounded as if a person had tripped and tumbled against the wall. I sat up straighter and listened, hearing faint footsteps beyond the door. Anxiety prickled over my skin. Wendy and George knew about my real estate class and wouldn't want to interrupt. Who else would be out there? I scraped back my chair, waving Noah toward the bedroom.

"Stay in here for a minute, okay? Don't come out until I come back."

Noah pouted. "Can I take my train?"

"Yes." I handed him his train and a few pieces of track. I closed the bedroom door and approached the front entrance, jumping at the sound of three knocks. "Who is it?" I yelled through the door.

"It's Jacob."

I recognized his deep voice but couldn't imagine why he was here. Gripping the handle, I cracked the door wide enough to peek through.

Jacob lowered his face, his eyes bleary. "Sorry. Is this a bad time?"

"Kind of. I'm taking my real estate class right now."

"Oh." He stepped sideways, sliding his hands down the sides of his athletic shorts as if he didn't know what to do with them. "I won't keep you. I was just wondering if..." He looked toward the horizon, clenching his jaw. A second later, he took a breath and turned his focus back to me. "I was wondering if I could take you out for dinner on Friday night. You know, for old times' sake. I wanted to apologize for the way I acted at the barbecue."

I swallowed, surprised by his invitation. But McKenzie's death stare pierced through my mind like a warning. "Um. I don't think your girlfriend will be cool with that."

"No. She wouldn't be. But I broke up with her yesterday. For good this time."

"Oh." I looked at my feet to hide my shock as the teacher droned on through my laptop. I hadn't been on a romantic date in five years. Not since I'd dated Noah's dad for a few months. He'd left me the moment I'd told him I was pregnant. I didn't want to cause Jacob more pain. He had grown into a good-looking guy, objectively speaking, but there was no spark from my end. Still, a dinner out wasn't a big commitment. We could smooth things over and go our separate ways. "Okay. I'll have to arrange a sitter for Noah, but it shouldn't be a problem."

"Great. How about I pick you up at six forty-five? There's a nice Italian place about five minutes from here."

"Sounds good."

"Can I get your number?" He dug into his pocket and pulled out his phone, and I told him my phone number. A smile twitched at his lips. "I'll let you get back to your class. See you Friday."

I closed the door, noticing how my pulse was racing and my palms had turned clammy. Was I making a mistake? I squeezed my eyes shut as I admonished myself for overthinking everything. The past was the past. It was only a dinner; it didn't need to turn into anything else if I didn't want it to. I let Noah out of the bedroom with a smile, offering him a pudding cup for being so good. Then, I returned to my laptop, finding it almost impossible to focus.

.   .   .

The next morning, I dropped Noah at preschool and returned to the house on Marigold Street. Despite the humidity, I felt lighter as I stepped along the walkway and through the gate to the backyard. It was a relief to have a day off from the café after two days of learning the rules, balancing heavy trays, and wiping down tables. And I was looking forward to a nice dinner out with another adult, even though a friendship with Jacob could be tricky to navigate.

As I crossed the patio, I spotted Wendy sitting in in her living room in front of the TV but looking at her phone. I knocked on the glass, and she waved me inside, where a blast of cool air and the jingle of a commercial greeted me.

"Good morning." She grinned, scooting to the edge of the couch.

"Hi. Don't get up." I held up my hand.

Wendy smiled as she pointed to her phone. "George and I just received an invitation to a luncheon from a local charity that supports foster kids. Isn't that wonderful? They said they saw us on the news."

"That sounds great, Wendy." She told me all the details about the event before I spoke again. "I was just stopping by to ask a favor."

"Oh?"

"I ran into Jacob at the café on Monday. He and his girl-friend were there but not really speaking to each other. Anyway, I guess he broke up with her. He asked me out to dinner on Friday night."

Wendy clutched her hands to her heart, gasping. "I knew he'd come around. I just knew it."

I bit my lip but couldn't help smiling at her dramatic reaction. "It's only dinner. And it's just to catch up on old times. But

I was wondering if you could watch Noah for a couple of hours."

"Of course. We'd love to have the little guy stay here for a while. I bought some Play-Doh at the drugstore yesterday. I saw it in the aisle with all the odds and ends, and I thought, 'I bet Noah would like that.'"

"That's nice of you. Thank you."

Wendy patted the empty couch cushion next to her. "Sit for a minute."

I'd been hoping to change into my workout clothes and get in a morning jog before the heat became unbearable, but Wendy had just offered to watch Noah for me, and I didn't want to be rude. I lowered myself next to her on the couch as a reporter on the cable news channel she and George watched incessantly droned on about falling stock prices.

"I bet it's strange to see Jacob again after so long." Wendy's voice was softer now. "Do you think you still have feelings for him?"

The boldness of her question caused me to lean away from her. "I'm not sure. People change a lot over fifteen years. It's just a dinner between two friends for now."

"Hopefully, that old spark will still be there. You two made such a cute couple."

"Maybe we did back then, but I'm guessing we've grown in different directions. I don't really see it going anywhere."

Wendy fiddled with her ring, turning it around her finger. "Well, if there's really nothing there, you should be upfront with him and tell him you're not interested before a second date. Let him down easy." She stopped fidgeting and frowned. "It wouldn't be right to break his heart twice."

"Yeah. Of course." I dropped my gaze to my lap. Maybe Wendy hadn't been overstepping as much as I'd thought. She was concerned for Jacob's well-being, and I couldn't blame her.

Wendy's face changed, her eyes holding a sheen of nostalgia. "I remember when Jacob took you to the spring dance right before you ran away. What was it called? The junior prom?"

"Yes. That's right."

"It was held at the Hilton, and the school decorated the ballroom with lights and flowers and such. There's a photo of it in the yearbook I gave you. Anyway, you wore a pink dress with a giant ruffle across the top." She stifled a giggle. "I told you that you looked like a pink princess. I meant it as a compliment, but it made you mad for some reason, and you wouldn't even let me take your picture. Remember?"

"Ha. Yeah. Thankfully, my fashion taste has evolved since then."

"Jacob picked you up in that beat-up white pickup truck he always drove around in. And then you and Jacob never came home that night. I was worried sick. Then you showed up at four in the morning, all disheveled." She drew in her chin and raised her eyebrows. "You claimed to have been out with Harper, but I knew what you and Jacob were up to."

I leaned forward, my face radiating heat. The conversation had taken an extremely awkward turn, and I felt an urgent need to get away from her. "Hey, Wendy, I was hoping to fit in a run before it gets too hot. And I have my NA meeting at one." I began to stand, but Wendy put out her hand, indicating that I should stay put.

"I only brought it up because when you ran away, I thought you might have been hanging out somewhere with Jacob again. Or Harper. That's why it took me a day to report you missing."

"That makes sense. But I wasn't with him."

"Yes." She placed her warm hand on top of mine, giving a pat. "I know that now."

We both sat motionless, turning our attention to the TV, which, to my horror, switched to a story of national interest in Las Vegas, reported by an eagle-faced woman with flowing locks. "Authorities are still searching for a woman who stole funds from a Las Vegas area construction company and stabbed the co-owner of the company. The woman known as Sandra Matthews was employed as an administrative assistant under a stolen identity."

A poor-quality image of my face filled a quarter of the screen, with the reporter on the other side. It felt as if someone had their hands around my throat. It was the photo from my company ID taken on the first day at Toven Brothers. My hair was different—bleached blonde, long and wavy, and without the bangs I now had. My makeup was more garish. But my face was right there on the screen.

"Authorities have been unable to locate Matthews since the day of the stabbing when she attacked Drew Toven, who walked in on her stealing money from the company safe. The victim's injuries were relatively minor, and he is at home recovering well. Authorities believe Matthews may have ties to San Antonio, Texas, where she told people she was from and where police have located another woman named Sandra Matthews whose name and social security number were used by the perpetrator without her knowledge."

"How horrible." Wendy clucked and looked at me, apparently not making the connection between me and the pixilated photo.

I stood, throat constricting further. "I've got to get going."

The TV wouldn't stop. "Sandra was so nice." Benji, a guy who operated large machinery like backhoes and bulldozers, popped on the screen, confusion swimming in his eyes. My former co-worker continued talking. "I would never have guessed she was capable of stabbing someone or living under a fake identity. But now that I think about it, I never really knew anything about her, except that she had a little boy who was about three or four, and she made one heck of a potato salad at the company picnic. It was really good."

My body froze, held in place by fear. Surely Wendy would

notice the similarities between me and the woman they were discussing on the news. I'd made the same potato salad for the barbecue on Sunday, the one people had been raving about just like they had at the Toven Brothers company picnic. It was a stupid thing to do, a mistake. There should never have been threads connecting me to my past, not even a potato salad recipe.

Wendy chuckled. "Well, he should have tasted *your* potato salad. There's no beating that one."

I'd been poised to sprint to my car for a fast getaway. But Wendy's statement hit me first, nearly knocking me over with relief. She didn't see me in Sandra Matthews, even with a different version of my face right there on the screen. Like most people, she only saw what she wanted to see. My fingers tightened around the handle of the glass slider as I found my voice. "Thanks, Wendy. I've got to go now." Before she could respond, I slipped out the door, eager to close myself inside my apartment as quickly as possible.

THIRTEEN

After escaping the uncomfortable moments in Wendy's living room, I changed into my running clothes and was out the door, the brim of a baseball cap pulled low on my forehead. I traveled along the suburban streets, one foot stretching in front of the other in an urgent cadence. Jagged breaths heaved from my mouth, and I clutched the cramp forming in my side. Despite being out of shape, I was desperate for exercise and wouldn't let a little discomfort stop me. My muscles began to loosen as the sun peeked out from behind a cloud and warmed my skin. I passed more rows of tidy houses on quarter-acre lots, thick-trunked trees, and patchy lawns.

The news report replayed in my head, and I was dumb-founded by both my misfortune and my luck, relieved I'd looked so different in the photo from my Toven Brothers ID. Wendy hadn't recognized me from the grainy photo, so I hoped no one else would either. My stride lengthened at thoughts of the police focusing their search in the wrong direction. Drew must have told the police about my mismatched ID. Authorities had figured out that I'd swiped the social security number and name of Sandra Matthews in San Antonio, assuming I'd lived there at

some point. But I'd never been to San Antonio. I'd purchased
the identity information on the dark web for $600 when I'd
lived in Santa Fe under the name Kayla Macon in another
failed attempt to start over. I hadn't known that another living
person named Sandra Matthews with the same social security
number actually existed. Even if I hadn't stabbed Drew, my jig
would have been up as soon as I filed taxes. Either the IRS or
the real Sandra Matthews would have noticed the inconsis-
tency. Living under fake identities for so many years was difficult, but I'd learned things with each failure and had gotten
better at it. I should have known that a few hundred dollars had
been too cheap.

The quiet streets spit me out at a busy intersection, where I
jogged in place, waiting for the light to turn, relieved that I'd
only inflicted a minor injury on my former boss. My lifetime of
emotional baggage was heavy, and the guilt of having done
serious harm to him—possibly resulting in his death—might
have debilitated me, even if I had been acting in self-defense. I
hoped the less serious injury meant the police would move on to
more pressing matters. Regardless of the level of the police's
interest in the case, I worried Drew Toven wouldn't let my
betrayal slide, especially if he had the strength to travel. He was
a man with a big ego who would win at any cost. My actions
must have humiliated him. I'd overheard enough conversations
through his office door to know that not all the deals he made
were on the right side of the law, which made me worry about
his next move. My head was dizzy as I pictured the person with
the blue hat behind the trees at the playground and the SUV
with the tinted windows following us, driven by someone with
the same colored hat.

The light changed, and I continued across the four-lane
road, jogging ahead for another third of a mile, then turning into
a quaint pocket of commercial storefronts and restaurants. A
retail space with nondescript siding and a sign that read *Inter-*

Tech in red lettering sat among a bank, coffee shop, bookstore, and clothing boutique. I slowed to a walk, realizing it was the office where Cody worked. I leaned toward the glass to spy through the reflection and catch a glimpse of the interior.

"Riley?" A deep voice caused me to spin around. I was surprised to see Cody standing behind me, a cardboard cup in his hand.

I adjusted the brim of my hat, feeling a little like I'd been caught. "Oh, hi." I pointed toward the sign. "I just realized you work here."

"Yeah. I needed some coffee." He glanced at the coffee shop, then back at me. "I didn't know you were a runner."

I couldn't help laughing. "I'm not really. Sometimes, I just need to let off some steam."

"I get it." He took a sip. "And how's the apartment working out?" He crossed his arms, his moon-shaped eyes reflecting in the sunlight.

"Fine." A bristle of attraction rushed through me, and I fought to ignore it even though I'd felt a similar reaction to him a few days ago in the Eckharts' backyard. Cody had been so good with Noah; he was gentle and fun in explaining his made-up games instead of acting in the fake manner that adults often do with children.

He stared somewhere over my shoulder, eyes glazing over for a second as if lost in a thought. "George and Wendy said they made the place nicer since I lived there. It was a dump."

"It's nothing fancy. Lots of odds and ends."

"I moved out after you ran away." He stepped closer, his arm brushing against mine in a way I didn't mind. "It felt like total freedom living on my own, away from them."

I bit my lip, mildly surprised by his comment. "I always thought you had it so good in the garage apartment."

He shrugged. "Compared to what I came from—what we both came from—yeah. But it wasn't perfect by any means." A half smile formed on his mouth as he shook his head. "But you know that already. You wouldn't have run away otherwise."

"Right. So many rules."

He stared at me for a beat too long. "I was stunned when you came back."

"I didn't have anywhere else to go. Up until Max died, I was afraid to live under my real name. He was the type who would have tracked me down."

"That sounds like such a scary and stressful way to live. I'm sorry."

I got lost in Cody's eyes for a second and forgot to speak. "Where did you go after you left the apartment?" I managed to say, turning the conversation away from myself.

"I turned eighteen a few weeks after you disappeared. I moved into a crappy rental with my buddy from the group home and got a job with the Geek Squad at Best Buy, which wasn't the greatest but forced me to get my shit together and apply for college."

"I'm glad you've done so well for yourself. You should be proud."

He looked toward the red-lettered sign, then shrugged again. "I've always liked messing with computers, writing code and all that. It's a steady paycheck."

A person hurried past us, entering the store, and I realized I was probably holding Cody up. "I'll let you get back to work."

He raised his cup. "See you soon."

As Cody disappeared behind the door, I picked up my pace, my pulse racing but not from the exercise. I was impressed with Cody's determination and easy manner. There was something different about him beyond his ability to roll with the punches. He and I had much in common, and I wanted to ask him a hundred more questions about his time in foster care, his relationship with George and Wendy, and his life in the intervening years. But it wasn't the right time, and I needed to take things slowly. Although he felt like an old friend, I reminded myself that I didn't really know him at all.

I continued along my path, deciding to run another half-mile, then turn around and head home. As I struggled to keep a steady pace, my thoughts circled back to the apartment. Brenda Harwood's raspy voice scratched through my head, admonishing me for letting in a late-night visitor. Cody had lived there once, many years ago. Would he still have a key? I imagined the Eckharts would have changed the locks at some point, but they liked to save money wherever possible, so maybe not. As much as I was drawn to Cody, I wondered if there was any chance he could have been the one who entered my apartment while Noah and I were sleeping.

FOURTEEN

At 6:47 on Friday night, four solid knocks sounded at my door. I smoothed down the skirt I'd purchased from the local thrift shop and stole one last glance in the mirror to make sure no excess lipstick stained my front teeth. Then I headed toward the door and opened it, finding Jacob standing there with a nervous smile. A hint of his cologne reached me, smelling like leather and oak barrels. He'd traded his athletic shorts for stone-colored pants and a navy polo shirt.

"Hi." His smile widened. "You look nice."

"Thanks. You do too." I closed the door and locked it behind me, hoping that agreeing to this dinner wouldn't send him the wrong impression. He led the way down the steps, commenting on the clear night and the break in the humidity. Then we walked shoulder to shoulder past the Eckharts' house, where I'd dropped Noah with Wendy and George about twenty minutes earlier, Noah wearing his dinosaur pajamas.

"Have you been to Francesco's?" Jacob asked as we arrived at his truck, doors unlocking with a beep.

"No." The anxiety coursing through me had all but extinguished my appetite. "I haven't eaten out at all since I've been back."

He made a sad face that made me giggle as he opened the passenger door for me.

I touched the frame of the vehicle. "You still drive a white pickup truck, huh?"

"This one's a lot nicer than the one I used to have."

"Yeah. I remember." I climbed up, and he closed me inside.

The dim lighting and tealights burning between us created a romantic atmosphere. A sense of unease pooled in my stomach as I wondered how Jacob viewed me. Sitting across from him in a cozy booth, I studied the strong line of his jaw as he talked about his day, and I realized again that he'd grown into an attractive man. But for now, I was satisfied that Jacob no longer seemed angry with me over the past.

We ordered drinks, and he asked me how I liked working at Songbird Café.

"It's not so bad. Unless you have to serve rude customers." I winked. "Then it kind of sucks."

He laughed. "I guess it took me too long to realize I was in kind of a toxic situation. I couldn't see it until you came back." He looked down, folding and refolding his napkin, before raising his eyes. "Did you ever think about us over all those years? About how we used to be?" His stare intensified.

"Of course I did." My mind flipped through the past as I searched for the right words, unsure what to say.

"This might sound dumb, but I always thought we'd get married."

The conversation had gone from zero to a hundred, and I wasn't quite ready for it. "I'm sorry. It's not dumb. I didn't mean to hurt you like that." I squirmed in my seat, itching to change the subject to something less weighty. I remembered the photos

Wendy had shown me the day before. "Hey, remember when we went to the junior prom? My dress was so hideous with that big ruffle."

Jacob shrugged. "I didn't think so."

I sipped my white wine, setting a breadstick on my small plate and unsure what to say next. "That was such a fun night."

He stopped drinking mid-sip, peering at me from the corner of his eye. "Was it a fun night?"

"I thought so." My foot tapped beneath the table.

"We had a pretty big fight, though, didn't we? You were acting so secretive. Then you thought I was cheating on you or something." He grunted, shaking his head. "I wasn't, but you ran off with Harper instead. I had no idea that would be the last time I'd see you."

I nibbled some bread, chewing slowly as I nodded along. "I forgot about the drama. My memory is so hazy sometimes. It seems like a long time ago, doesn't it?"

"In some ways. Not in others."

The waitress interrupted to take our orders. When she left, I mentioned one of Jacob's high school baseball games when he'd hit the winning home run. His face shone at the memory, and he immediately recounted all the details of that game, taking in my expressions as he spoke. When the story was over, his eyes grazed over me again, traveling from my eyebrows to my nose, to my cheeks and mouth.

"Why do you keep looking at me like that?" I felt like a specimen under a microscope and I shifted in my seat.

"Like what?"

"Like you're memorizing my features." I raised my eyebrows at him. "It's a little creepy, to be honest."

He held my gaze. "I'm staring at you because you're pretty. Even more beautiful than I remembered." His hand reached across the table, grasping mine. "I hope we can spend a lot more time together."

I looked away, fumbling about how to respond, my feelings toward him still lukewarm. "Thank you." I blinked a few times, remembering Wendy's warning. "I just..." I cleared my throat. "I have to be honest with you."

"Okay."

"I'm glad we're reconnecting, but I need to start as friends. Nothing more. You're fresh out of a relationship, and I have a son now. I can't rush into things."

He tipped his head back and released a long breath, failing to camouflage his disappointment. "That's fine."

"And I..." My throat constricted.

"What?"

"And I don't want to hurt you again."

"Right." Jacob crossed his arms. I waited for him to speak, but he kept his mouth closed.

Our food arrived, breaking up the uncomfortable silence. We ate quietly for a minute, and I sensed he remembered how it had felt to be seventeen and have his girlfriend leave him cold, to ditch him with no explanation and never see her again. I twirled some pasta on my fork. At last, Jacob spoke, telling me that he'd seen me on the news the night of the barbecue and that he was sorry for what happened to me. "It must have been rough out there."

"Yes."

"You can talk about it if you want."

"I'd prefer not to right now if that's okay."

His fork hit his plate, clanking loudly. "Sure. Another time."

As I ate, I caught him looking at me again.

He must have realized he was staring because he tapped the table, a new smile pulling at his lips. "Hey. Do you remember when we drove to Detroit and walked along the riverfront? We ended up at that Irish bar where they never checked IDs, and we drank beer. You told Wendy we were at the library."

"Oh, yeah. We were so bad."

Something changed on Jacob's face, the brightness dimming like he'd thought of something horrible.

"What's wrong?" I dabbed my mouth with my napkin as a sinking feeling glued me to my seat. I must have slipped and said the wrong thing.

"Nothing." He flashed a smile, quickly masking whatever had bothered him. He asked me about Noah, and I rambled on about him for a few minutes. We took the last few bites of our food, and when the waitress walked past, Jacob asked for the dessert menu. "I'm glad we could do this."

"Me too. I'll pass on dessert, though."

He rapped his knuckles on the table. "C'mon. We have to look."

"Sure. We can look."

I checked my phone. We'd been at the restaurant for less than an hour, but something about Jacob's sudden shifts in demeanor made me grateful it would be an early night.

FIFTEEN

"Back so soon?" Wendy's body filled the doorway as she waved me inside.

"Yeah. It was just dinner." I kept my voice light, but guilt tugged at me for the way I'd abruptly ended our date. When the waitress returned to take our dessert order, Jacob insisted we share one. I turned him down, making up an excuse that I was trying to cut back on sugar. He swiped the bill from the table and paid it with a smile and a wink. As we left the restaurant, he reached for my hand, suggesting we go for a long walk and rehash old times. The hopeful look in his eyes told me he hadn't given up on us and still believed he could win me over if only he put in enough effort. Not wanting to lead him on, I yawned and said I was tired and needed to pick up Noah. During the short drive home, we chatted about his work as an electrician before he pulled up front and said good night, staring straight ahead as he waited for me to get out of the truck.

I followed Wendy into the living room, where Candyland was set up on the coffee table and the aroma of buttered popcorn filled my mouth.

"Mommy!" Noah jumped up from the floor.

"Hey, buddy. Did you have fun?" I kissed him on the head.

"Yeah. I won." He pointed to the colorful game pieces.

George nodded from the couch. "He's the Candyland champion."

"Cool." I dug out a few bills I'd earned from tips at the café and forced them toward Wendy, who waved the money away.

"There's no need this time. You're still getting on your feet."

"Thanks for watching him," I said, touched by the gesture. I gathered Noah's things, and we said good night, then traipsed across the backyard under a pinkish summer sky. It was just after 8 p.m., and still light outside. I let us into the apartment, kicking off my shoes and beginning Noah's bedtime routine. After I tucked him in and read him two books we'd checked out from the library, I returned to the living room, preparing to veg out on the couch and watch TV.

But as I crossed to the kitchen to retrieve a glass of water, my vision snagged on something amiss. Not the closet or the rug this time, but the skinny drawer under the desk where I kept my laptop. It sat slightly ajar. My mind raced backward, retracing my memory for the last time I'd removed the laptop from the drawer. Yesterday evening, I'd done a Google search on Drew and Toven Brothers to see if there had been any updates to the police search, but I'd found no new information. The drawer had been closed when I'd left for dinner, hadn't it? Or was my paranoia taking over again? Maybe I'd left it slightly open and hadn't noticed. I strode toward the desk and pulled open the drawer, removing the laptop and flipping it open. It fired up immediately, asking for my password, a four-digit code. I released a breath as I typed it in, finding everything as it should be.

I peered around the walls. The windows were locked from the inside. I'd opened the bedroom window when I put Noah to bed, but it had definitely been locked while we'd been out. I leaned into the couch cushion, flipping on the TV and settling on a reality show about plastic surgeries gone wrong.

Even with the distraction, my thoughts circled like ravens. I reminded myself not to self-sabotage. It was more likely that no one had violated my space, and I was freaking out. Not many things had gone my way over my lifetime, but this latest attempt to establish a new life had gone better than expected. A free five weeks in an apartment, preschool for Noah, a warm welcome from former foster parents and friends, a waitressing job, and the beginnings of a real estate career. I wasn't used to things working out. I imagined people doing shady things because that's what the past had taught me. It was the world I'd lived in for so many years. But my future could be different. I sprawled my body across the couch, muscles loosening as the reality show gave me a glimpse into someone else's life and let me forget about my problems.

A text buzzed on my phone.

How did your date with Jacob go?

I inhaled a deep breath before responding.

It was fun. No spark there, but good to catch up!

Harper gave it a thumbs-up, and I returned to watching the reality show. Just as my worries faded, someone banged on the door. I bolted upright, heart pounding. Two more knocks. I pictured Drew Toven, angry and looking for revenge.

"Riley, it's me. Jacob."

Seriously? Jacob was here again? I exhaled, standing and moving slowly toward the door. I thought I'd made myself clear that I wasn't interested in him, and annoyance needled through me at his refusal to respect my feelings. Then again, maybe I'd merely forgotten something in his car.

"Hi." He stood there as I opened the door, wearing the same clothes he'd had on earlier, his hands shoved into his pockets.

"Hi."

"Sorry. I know nothing's happening between us, but I forgot to tell you something. Can I come in for a minute?"

I peered over his shoulder, alarmed to see Brenda Harwood standing ghostlike in her backyard, with her white housecoat billowing in the wind. Her glare iced over me, and I gave her a little wave, imagining what she must think about a gentleman caller showing up at my door. Eager to escape her prying eyes, I stepped out of the way, allowing Jacob to move past me. After we were shut inside, I held a finger to my mouth, nodding toward the bedroom. "Noah is sleeping."

"Okay." He crossed his arms in front of his chest, eyes darting around. I couldn't tell if he was nervous or angry.

"It's getting late, Jacob," I said, keeping my voice down. "Why are you here?"

He motioned toward my midsection, eyes narrowing. "Can I see your scar?"

"Huh?"

"The big scar on the side of your abdomen?" The set of his jaw let me know that it was more of a demand than a question. "The one you got from that knife when you were three or four? It was the reason they took you away from your mom." His eyes bore into me, a challenge.

I felt dizzy, the floor seeming to tilt beneath me. "No. I don't feel comfortable."

"C'mon. Just flip up your shirt for a second. I'm not going to make a move on you or anything."

I wrapped my arms tightly around myself, taking a step backward. "I don't have that scar anymore. I had a laser treatment."

He barked out an incredulous laugh that made me jump.

"So you lived on the streets and then in a homeless shelter, but somehow you had enough money for a laser treatment?"

I couldn't look at him. I couldn't breathe, much less form another word. There was no good answer.

"You may have fooled a lot of people in this town with your sad story and your tattoo. You tricked the Eckharts and everyone at the party. You pulled one over on the press and the police because you sure as hell look like a grown-up version of Riley Wakefield. But I was close to her. Really close. I knew her. You aren't fooling me." He scowled, talking through his teeth.

My heart thumped as I looked toward Noah's bedroom door and then back to Jacob, thinking fast. "My appearance may have changed over the years, but yours has too." I touched my chest. "I'm Riley."

He kicked the floor. "Bullshit! We had a horrible time at the junior prom. We never went to Detroit, walked along the riverfront, or drank beer at an Irish bar. I made that story up." He stepped toward me, blocking my path. "I was testing you, and you failed."

A desperate cry formed in the back of my throat, but I swallowed it down, preparing for the worst. My fresh start was shattering into a thousand pieces, and now it would be impossible to put it back together.

Jacob sneered. "I don't know who you are or what you're doing, but I know one thing for sure." He pushed his face against mine, his hot breath whispering in my ear. "You're. Not. Her."

Each word hit me like a punch to the stomach. I couldn't speak. I couldn't move. I'd been so close to getting away with it. But this man was standing inches from me, seething with anger because he knew my secret. He was correct. I wasn't Riley Wakefield. My real name was Gina Holland.

And now I was in a great deal of danger.

SIXTEEN

Jacob tore his death glare from me and headed toward the door. "I'm going to the police."

"Wait! No! Please."

He flinched when I grabbed his arm, his eyes blazing with hatred.

"Jacob, wait! Please just hear me out before you go to the police or tell anyone else. I can explain." I motioned toward the couch, desperate to convince him to keep his mouth shut. "Will you sit? Give me five minutes. That's all I ask."

His hands rested on his hips, a vein bulging down the center of his forehead.

"Please! You can turn me in if you don't like what I have to say." I nodded toward the couch.

Jacob threw his head back, letting out an exasperated sigh. "Fine. Five minutes." He sat down, placing his hands on his knees and refusing to look at me.

I lowered myself next to him, knowing my only chance at getting out of this mess was to tell him the truth. "My name is Gina Holland. I'm Riley's sister."

He tilted his head but said nothing.

"I'm three years older than her."

Jacob shook his head, frown lines etching the contours of his mouth. "Riley didn't have a sister."

"She didn't know I existed until a couple of weeks before she disappeared. Our mom was a drug addict. We were separated at a young age. Riley was only three when she cut herself with that butcher knife, the one that left that horrible scar on her stomach. She was placed with a foster family. I went into a group home at the same time. I was six."

Jacob raised his head to look at me, a flicker of compassion showing in his eyes.

"I remember asking about Riley a lot those first few months after we were separated but was told she was living with a family who was giving her a good, happy home, and I had to be strong on my own. After a year in the group home, I was placed with a foster family, where I stayed for three years. Whenever I asked my foster mom about my sister, she insisted that I didn't have any siblings. She said they only had one spot and requested an only child. She convinced me the little girl I remembered must have been a cousin or a neighbor."

Jacob's eyes were trained on me as I continued.

"I was shuffled around a few more times after that. My memories of having a sister grew more vague with each passing year. By the time I was fifteen, I gave up hope of ever reuniting with my mother. Through my court-appointed representative, I learned that she'd never taken advantage of any of the resources offered to her by the agency, had never once requested a visitation, and had failed to show up to the court hearings related to my custody. I was so angry at her, and my pain was obvious to my social worker. When I told her I didn't want even one thing connecting me to the woman who had abandoned me, not even her last name, she wrote a letter to my representative requesting approval of the name change for the sake of my mental health. It only required some paperwork signed by a judge to change my name from Gina Wakefield to Gina Holland. Holland was the last name of a favorite teacher I'd had in school a couple of years earlier."

I glanced at Jacob, whose face held a strange expression as if he wasn't sure I was telling the truth.

"I landed in my last group home in Roseville when I was fifteen, about six months after my name change. It was the worst place I'd ever lived. Horrible things happened there." I averted my eyes, aware of my parched throat as visions of Marianne Clavey invaded my thoughts. I had never forgotten her smattering of freckles and her light-green eyes rimmed with yellow, always calculating how to torment me, or the years living in fear of what she'd do to me next. I hated her. The image of her face always lurked just below the surface of my psyche, her cruel acts often slithering their way into my nightmares. I unclenched my fists and continued. "I worked a part-time job, saved my money, and moved out of the group home the moment I turned eighteen. A charity had donated a beat-up car to me, and I found a full-time job cleaning houses, renting the cheapest studio apartment I could find to save money for college. From the file I received when I left, I learned that my mother was still alive at the time and had moved to some small town outside Grand Rapids. There was no mention of a sister in my file, and I realized I must have been confused or imagined the whole thing."

Jacob shifted his weight, tossing me a suspicious glance. "Are you really Riley's sister?"

"Yes. One day, I was scrolling through the local news on my phone and came across a feel-good article about a group of high school students who had volunteered at a soup kitchen in Detroit. My eyes stopped on the name Riley Wakefield. The name rang a bell, like when you vaguely remember a flash of a dream you had the night before but can't quite put your finger on it. I found her face among the students in the photo and couldn't believe it. She looked exactly like me. I realized that my memory of a sister hadn't been false. She was real, a student at Berkley High School, just a fifteen-minute drive from where I lived. Someone had left Riley off my records many years earlier."

"Why would someone do that?" Jacob asked, incredulous.

"I'm not sure, but everyone knows it's easier to place a single child than a pair of siblings. Maybe whoever did it thought they were helping us in some warped way so that we could be placed with families more quickly. Or it could have been an innocent mishap, a wrong keystroke on the computer by someone who was likely overworked and underpaid."

Jacob's posture remained rigid. "That sucks. For both of you. But it doesn't excuse what you're doing."

I ignored his comment, willing him to listen to the entire story. "I followed her home from school one day. I could see by the way she walked, talked, and laughed that we were definitely related. She was living here with the Eckharts."

"Did you visit her here?"

"It took a few days of watching from a distance to work up my courage. But the third day, when she went inside, I knocked on the door. George and Wendy weren't home, but Riley answered. It was almost like looking into a mirror. I was a couple of inches taller, and she was skinnier, but our features were so similar. I told Riley who I was, and she was shocked. She had no memory of me, but she knew by our resemblance that I was telling the truth. I was her sister."

The wheels turned behind Jacob's eyes as he registered everything I told him. "Do you know where Riley is?" he asked, a note of hope in his voice.

"No. I wish I did."

His face fell, and I hated myself for putting him through this, for dashing his hopes once again.

"I've looked for her many times, but there's never a trace. At least, not recently." A wave of emotion hit me, and I took a second to find my voice. "Back then, we became close very quickly. It was so strange to meet someone who shared my mannerisms, my voice, and even my laugh. I'd never had a family before, much less anyone who looked and acted like me. Discovering a long-lost sister was surreal for both of us. We planned to move to California together. She hated school and thought the Eckharts were too strict, so she wanted to run away immediately. But I told her she was lucky to be placed with them. She needed to graduate from high school. I told her it was good to have people like George and Wendy, who cared enough about her that they set boundaries. But she was persistent. She craved independence. We'd both been moved around like furniture our entire lives."

Jacob leaned forward, pressing his palms into his thighs as if I'd knocked the wind out of him. But I could see by the look on his face that he recognized a nugget of truth in my description of Riley.

"She mentioned you a lot, Jacob. She'd grown tired of Harper. Said she was pushy and selfish. You were the only person who might have kept her here."

He gave a slight nod, but his mouth was downturned, his feelings hurt.

"Anyway, I stayed over that night. Wendy and George didn't allow Riley to have overnight guests, so I hid out in her room. She snuck me food from dinner, and I used the bathroom after they went to bed. The Eckharts never knew I was here. I remember looking out of Riley's bedroom window toward this very apartment. Cody lived here then, and I watched as he came and went as he pleased. I was jealous. I'd never been given my own space like that at any foster home."

"What teenager wouldn't want to live in their own apartment?"

"Right." I looked at Jacob, happy at least that he was listening. "Anyway, that night, Riley and I talked about everything. She showed me photos of you and Harper and bragged about your home run at that baseball game. She showed me her scars and her tattoo. She was annoyed about how upset Wendy had been over the tattoo, but I convinced her, again, that it was nice to have someone who cared enough to be upset. She told me about her job at Panda Express and the guy named Max Smith, who'd been hanging around whenever she was there. He was recruiting girls to go to Los Angeles, all expenses paid. He even promised them free room and board just for going out to dinner with rich guys. I warned her to stay far away from Max; his offer was too good to be true."

Jacob ran his fingers through his hair, the color draining from his face. "I can't believe she never mentioned him to me."

"I was worried she would leave with this shady guy at the mall instead of waiting for me and finishing high school, so I told her I'd go to California with her whenever she wanted to leave. I planned to find a college out there and encourage her to finish school. We had both craved a real family for so long, and we decided we could have our own little family. It was a better option than her going with Max, so we set a date two weeks from the night I slept over. She wanted to go to the junior prom with you before she left. I was supposed to meet her in my car at the end of the block at one in the morning the night after the dance. She said the Eckharts kept a thousand dollars in cash in some secret drawer in Wendy's desk, and she would steal the money to help us pay for our first month's rent once we got to California. She gave me an envelope filled with important papers to take with me so she'd have less to pack and less to forget. Her birth certificate was in there. I've saved it all these years."

"Did you run away together?"

I massaged my temples, memories surfacing from the dark corners of my mind as I prepared to confess the terrible sequence of events that followed.

SEVENTEEN

I'd never spoken to anyone about what I'd done, and I felt my throat tightening as I faced Jacob and forced the words out. "Two days before Riley and I were supposed to leave, I did something stupid. Something horrible." I paced the floor, taking a few deep breaths. "There was a girl at the last group home where I lived." I swallowed the name Marianne Clavey, not willing to give Jacob more information than necessary. "She was mean to everyone, dangerous. She got the most pleasure from tormenting me, in particular—spitting in my hair as I did my homework, stealing my clothes while I showered, dumping milk on the special piece of cake I got once a year on my birthday, tripping me in the hallway, getting the other girls to gang up on me, and even lighting her bed on fire as I slept only feet away. Our supervisor only punished her for the fire. I was overjoyed when I turned eighteen and escaped the group home to an apartment several miles away. I thought I'd never have to see her again." I pinched the bridge of my nose, organizing my troubling thoughts.

"What happened?" Jacob's question nudged me back to the story.

"She showed up at my apartment a few days before I was supposed to go to California with Riley, all smiles like we were old friends. She gave me a soft punch on the arm and said, 'Hey, Holland. Look at us, both out in the real world.' I couldn't believe it. She always called me by my last name, Holland, when she ridiculed me at the group home, but now she was saying it in a friendly way. She said my bunkmate from the group home had given her my address. She needed a place to crash until she could find her brother. It would only be a day or two. Otherwise, she'd have to live on the streets. I didn't want to let her in because she'd been so cruel to me. She was mentally unstable, and I was scared of her. But a bad thunderstorm was expected that night, and a part of me feared she'd do something for payback if I turned her away. I figured I was leaving for California in a few days anyway, so I let her sleep on the couch."

Jacob sat perfectly still, his chest rising and falling, and I could tell he was hanging on every word.

"She was still sleeping when I went to work the next morning, and I was grateful she hadn't burned the place down. By the time I returned from a day of cleaning houses, I was exhausted and ready for a shower. But when I walked through the door of my apartment, I caught her digging through my personal things. She stood up quickly and shoved something in her pocket, but not before I caught a glimpse. It was my necklace, the only valuable thing I owned, a family heirloom from my grandmother, and the only object tying me to my roots. I'd planned to give it to Riley once we got out west."

"Jeez." Jacob's mouth opened slightly, but his eyes remained trained on me.

I paused, my throat dry, before continuing. "I asked her what she was doing. She said, 'Nothing,' and tried to walk past me. I grabbed her arm, telling her to give me back the necklace. She punched me in the stomach, and I doubled over. It took a second to catch my breath. I was in a rage, not only at her but at myself for being stupid enough to let her in. I charged at her from behind, hitting her hard. She probably wasn't expecting it because I'd never fought back before. She flew forward, hitting her head on the corner of the table—a glass top with metal legs. She didn't get up, and I left her there on the floor while I took back my necklace. An hour passed before I realized she wasn't merely unconscious. She was dead. She must have been in frail health or had some kind of medical condition. I didn't realize pushing someone could kill them."

"What?" Jacob's face had taken on a horrified expression.

"I panicked. I was scared to call the police because I had caused her death. I should have called 911 when she didn't get up, but I didn't. I should have let her leave with the necklace, but I didn't. Everyone at the group home knew how much I hated her. I'd even mentioned getting back at her someday to a couple of them. No one would believe what happened to her in my apartment was an accident." I squeezed my eyelids closed, remembering how frantic and terrified I'd been at that moment, my entire future disappearing into the abyss. "I texted my sister a message that said, *I love you.* Then I grabbed my things and immediately skipped town, throwing my phone in the river and stealing a plate for my car along the way. I didn't want to bring Riley into my mess or get her in trouble, so I didn't tell her what I'd done or that I was leaving. I figured I'd try to contact her a few months later. That was the first time I learned how to disappear. But Riley must have been hurt when I didn't show up that night. I can't even imagine how betrayed and abandoned she must have felt, especially after what our mom did to us." My voice cracked, and I rubbed my eyes, wiping away the tears. I'd never forgiven myself for leaving my sister cold. "I knew she had it good with the Eckharts, and I hoped more than anything that she'd stay with them and finish high school. She must have made a different decision, though. She must have stolen that thousand dollars from George and

Wendy and left with Max instead. I haven't seen or heard from her since."

"And you didn't go after her?" Jacob's voice was tight with judgment.

"Once I got settled in a new city under a new name, I texted her. And called her many times from my new phone. But her phone was out of service. I'd seen the news stories about how she'd gone missing. I knew Max was responsible and that he'd probably taken away her phone, gotten her hooked on drugs, so he could control her."

"Man. Poor Riley. That's even worse than I imagined." Jacob sucked in a long breath. "So you aren't a recovering addict?"

"No. I've never done drugs, but I'm sure Riley did once she ran away. Guys like Max use drugs to keep women working for them. Addiction leads to desperation."

Jacob closed his eyes but didn't speak.

I continued. "About a month later, I went to L.A., looking for her. After a week of searching and staying in a youth hostel, I found a woman on a dirty street corner who recognized Riley from the photo I'd brought. Her name was Stacy, and when I told her that Riley might be with a guy named Max, she nodded like she knew exactly what I was talking about. She remembered seeing Riley with him a few days earlier but said Riley was using a different name. Stacy couldn't remember what it was but promised to keep an eye out for my sister and pass along any messages or money. I gave Stacy all the cash I had, about two hundred dollars, to give Riley. Stacy and I exchanged numbers, and I left town.

"When I didn't hear from Riley after a week, I called Stacy. She told me she'd seen Riley again a day or two after I'd left and had given her the money but didn't know where she was staying. I decided I needed to try harder. I moved to Bakersfield, about two hours from L.A., where I lived under a fake identity

THE FOSTER DAUGHTER   111

and worked cleaning homes during the day and as a waitress at night. I took the shuttle to L.A. every week or two for over a year and searched for Riley. Sometimes, I'd find Stacy instead, who usually told me she'd seen Riley again but still couldn't tell me where she was staying. I looked everywhere, sometimes in drug-infested neighborhoods, combing the streets late at night. But I never caught a glimpse of her. I often gave Stacy envelopes to pass on to Riley. They always contained my phone number, a note, and what little extra money I had."

"And you never heard from her?"

"No. Things got bad for me in Bakersfield when my employer realized my social security number wasn't real. I had to leave town and change my name, still on the run for what I'd done to the bully from the group home. But I continued calling and texting Stacy in the months and years that followed. She rarely picked up, and when she did, she was confused. She could never provide any details. During one of our last calls, she told me Max was dead. He'd been shot by a gang member."

Jacob sat up for a second. "Riley's alive."

"That was three years ago, but yes. According to Stacy, she was alive then." I shook my head, not wanting him to get his hopes up. "But there hasn't been any other trace of Riley since then. I've been back several more times..." My words trailed off before I found my voice again. "My gut tells me something bad happened to her out there. A part of me thought that by coming back here, I might be able to find another piece to the puzzle. Maybe try to meet someone who knows what happened to her in L.A. I know it probably sounds stupid."

"It's not stupid." Jacob snapped out of his trance-like state, his momentary hope swinging in the opposite direction and hardening back to anger. "But even if all that is true, you can't show up here after fifteen years pretending to be Riley. You can't just dye your hair, get a tattoo, and tell everyone you're her."

I followed his pained stare to my shoulder, remembering
how I'd stopped at a tattoo shop in Salida at the beginning of my
long drive from Vegas, showing the toothless guy who worked
there a sketch I'd made of Riley's tattoo. The design was simple
and small but required Noah and me to hole up in a motel room
in Indiana for over a week to wait for it to heal.

"It's not right." Jacob's spittle flew toward me as he spoke.
"It's not fair to everyone who knew her. I loved her."

I leaned closer to Jacob, forcing him to look at me. "I loved
her too. I didn't want to do it like this. My son and I are in
danger. My former boss is looking for us. He's not a good guy. I
stole some money from him, and I'm out of options. I didn't
want to assume my sister's identity, but I can't use my real name
ever again. It only takes one person to recognize the name Gina
Holland and call the police. The girl I killed has an older
brother who is probably still seeking revenge against me."

I thought back to three days after Marianne Clavey died at
my hands. I searched my crime online, hoping it had been over-
shadowed by more important events. After all, a poor, parent-
less eighteen-year-old from the wrong side of the tracks wasn't
the type of victim who typically garnered public outrage and a
demand for answers. While the coverage of Marianne's death
was fleeting—and it appeared that the investigation had been
too—I'd been horrified to find an article in *The Detroit News*
describing how I'd allegedly killed Marianne in a fight,
bolstered by a statement from a girl who'd lived with us at the
group home, confirming Marianne and I were sworn enemies.
But it was the two sentences quoted from Marianne's older
brother, Lee Clavey, that had been repeating through my head
for fifteen years: "I vow to hunt down the person who killed my
sister, no matter how long it takes. I will never stop searching
until I find Gina Holland."

Lee Clavey's threat still kept me awake at night. It only gave
me minor comfort that my searches for him in the following

years revealed that he lived in Indiana and had had numerous run-ins with the law, including two years in prison for felony grand theft auto. Not the type of guy authorities would bend over backward to help dig for answers or even communicate with. I assumed he had never learned my last name by birth was Wakefield. My name change occurred when I was a minor, and the records were sealed. I'd never seen any evidence that the authorities had dug deep enough to uncover that information either. But they likely still had their antennas up for anyone named Gina Holland. I'd found no online trace of Lee Clavey for over ten years and I didn't know where he currently lived or if he was even alive. His complete lack of presence on the internet seemed almost as suspicious as mine.

I leaned toward Jacob, continuing my effort to sway him to my side. "They'll put my son in foster care. Please. Don't do this to Noah. He's a sweet and curious boy. The system will destroy him." Hot tears streamed down my cheeks, and I didn't bother to brush them away.

Jacob sighed again, hunching over as if he couldn't bear to look at me. "This is a lot to take in."

"I know. Please give me a few weeks to take my son somewhere else. Find a different name. I'll make this right."

"Ha. It's a little late for that. You could have come forward and helped us find Riley fifteen years ago." He stood abruptly and paced away from me. "For all these years, I thought it was my fault that Riley left the way she did. I thought I wasn't a good enough boyfriend. But it was never because of me. It was because of you. You bailed on her."

I closed my eyes, his words spearing through my heart.

Jacob moved toward the door, each foot landing with an angry thud. He looked over his shoulder, sneering as he jabbed his finger toward me. "You better take your son and get the hell out of town. You have twenty-four hours to leave and change your name, or I'm telling everyone the truth. That's all you're getting from me. Twenty-four hours. And that's only because I feel bad for Noah." He let himself out, slamming the door behind him.

My hands covered my face, my body unable to move, like an animal caught in a trap. I'd only just gotten settled here. My backup identity, the one I'd purchased at Lucky's Bar, was meant as a last resort I hoped never to use. The documents could take several more weeks, or even months, to come through. It was possible Marianne Clavey's death had finally caught up with me, that my true identity would be revealed. I would lose my son. I doubled over at the realization as if Marianne Clavey herself had punched me in the gut once again. I needed to think fast, or I was screwed.

EIGHTEEN

Not long after Jacob gave me the twenty-four-hour ultimatum and stormed out of my apartment, I devised a desperate plan. I called Harper and told her I was on my way to the emergency room because I nearly cut my finger off slicing an apple and was sure I needed stitches. Could I drop Noah at her place on my way? Harper was alarmed and agreed without question. She even offered to drive me, but I told her I was capable.

Wrapping a bandage around an uninjured finger on my left hand, I tucked a roll of medical tape in my pocket to apply later. I'd have to keep up the act for a few weeks, at least when Harper was around. I removed my remaining money from the freezer and zipped it into an oversized purse. Then I scooped Noah out of his bed and loaded him in the car, dropping him at Harper's house five minutes later as I pretended to clutch my hand in agony.

My body ran on pure adrenaline as I drove past the hospital without slowing and continued south on I-75 toward Detroit. By the time I arrived at Lucky's Bar, it was after midnight, and the parking lot held a half dozen cars and one greasy-haired woman leaning against a pickup truck. I hoped Bea was working tonight. I'd tried calling the bar before my finger injury act, but not surprisingly, no one answered.

A couple of men playing darts stared at me as I entered, the cigarette smoke in the air even thicker than last time. I stifled my cough and continued toward the counter. An older couple at the bar watched me suspiciously, a sign that they were regulars and I wasn't.

Bea stepped out of the back room, her features hardening as I approached. "Can I get you a beer?" Her voice was detached; apparently, she was pretending we'd never met.

"No." I leaned closer, lowering my voice to a loud whisper. "I need to talk to you. It's an emergency."

"This isn't the time. We're busy right now."

"Please. I won't leave until you talk to me."

"The stuff isn't ready yet," she said through clenched teeth.

"Hey, Bea. Another round over here!" a man yelled from the other end of the counter. Bea left me standing there and served her customer.

The older couple exited the bar, leaving a five-dollar bill next to their empty glasses. I took one of the seats. Bea passed me, pausing to say, "You're gonna have to wait."

I dipped my head in agreement, although waiting even one minute longer felt like torture. Jacob was holding a ticking time bomb over me. He had information that could blow up my life. He knew I wasn't Riley Wakefield, and unless I moved quickly, soon everyone else would know too. I had to get this done now. There was no option to return at a less busy time.

Lifting my phone, I wrote another lie to Harper.

It looks like I still have a long wait here. I'll text you when I'm leaving.

She wrote back immediately.

Don't worry. Just go home when you're done. You can pick up Noah in the morning. Mom's coming over first thing to help.

My eyes closed in relief. I would wait here all night if I had to.

Thank you!

I settled onto the barstool, where I sat for another hour until most of the people in the bar had stumbled out the door.

"You got a lot of nerve coming here, you know that?" Bea said to me at last, untying a stained apron from her waist.

I looked toward the closed office door. "Can we talk in the back?"

She huffed, peering around the empty bar before waving me off my chair. "Come on."

My eyes blinked against the bright lights as I followed Bea into the small room, shutting the door behind us. "Did you order the documents the day I paid you?" I asked.

"Yes. But I go through a guy who buys information from another guy. It's complicated. It takes time to do it the right way so you don't get caught in the end. I told you not to come back here."

"I know. I'm sorry, but my situation has changed." I balled my hands, feeling my clammy palms. "I need a new identity for me and my son by five o'clock tomorrow."

Bea laughed but stopped when she saw the look on my face. "That's impossible."

"Nothing is impossible for the right price."

"What kind of trouble did you get yourself into?" Bea held her palm toward me and made a face like she'd sucked on a lemon. "Don't answer that."

"I'm going to lose my son if I don't get a new identity tomorrow." My voice cracked as I spoke. "He's four."

She looked up at the ceiling. "Oh, lord. You're a tough one, ain't you? My guy could have a package ready to go quicker, but it will take at least twenty-four hours. I did it once for someone. But the price for that is high."

"How much?"

"Ten thousand. Maybe fifteen."

Dread tunneled through me at the price tag. I only had five thousand left of the money I'd swiped from Toven Brothers, but there were other ways to cover the shortage—valuables inside the Eckharts' house. Or maybe the out-of-town next-door neighbors were less obvious targets. There were opportunities to swipe wallets from the diners at Songbird Café. I didn't want to target innocent people, but the alternatives were even worse. A murder conviction. Jail time. Losing Noah. Stealing the money would let me avoid those outcomes. "I'll pay ten. I don't have enough with me now, but I'll bring you the money tomorrow."

"Okay, hon. But I don't want to tell you what will happen if you don't." Bea released an elongated sigh. "I'll be here a few minutes before noon, and I'll see what I can do."

I nodded and left the bar, but not before I heard her say, "Take care of yourself."

When I returned to the apartment, I opened my laptop and considered my next destination. Mexico wasn't a possibility because I'd need a passport for that. Canada made more sense. Toronto was a five- or six-hour drive away, and I had no ties there. Noah and I could cross the bridge from Detroit to Canada with only birth certificates and an enhanced driver's license for me. I located a few affordable motels on the outskirts of town. One would have to do until I could save some money and figure out where to go.

.   .   .

After a short and restless sleep, I awoke early, showered, and bandaged my finger with the medical tape. I needed to pick up Noah as soon as possible. My descent down the exterior stairs offered a clear view through the Eckharts' back windows. Through the glass, George and Wendy puttered around their living room. They stopped when they saw me and stared out. I gave a half wave, and Wendy waved back as I continued toward my car, feeling guilty for the possibility of bringing more trouble to their door. I worried that Jacob hadn't kept his word and had gone to the police sooner than promised. But as I buckled my seatbelt, I reined in my fears. The police would have arrived at my apartment to question me already if Jacob had reported me. I still had time to steal five thousand dollars from either the out-of-town neighbors or the café, pick up Noah, deliver the money to Bea, claim my new identity, and get out of town before anyone learned the truth.

My frantic thoughts had settled down by the time I approached Harper's front step, silently rehearsing the story about how I'd sliced my finger and had needed two stitches. No one answered when I pressed the doorbell. After a minute, I rang it again. Harper should have been expecting me because I'd texted her before I'd left. I checked for approaching police cars. No one else was around except for a woman watering her flowers across the street. A black minivan was parked in front of my car, and I wondered if it belonged to Harper's mom. They were probably playing with the kids down in the basement and couldn't hear me. I waited a few more seconds, then knocked several times.

At last, the door creaked open, and Harper stepped back, slumping in the shadows.

"Harper?" I asked.

She looked up, the morning light hitting her bloodshot eyes and the tears streaming down her cheeks. Cold dread trickled through me as my mind filled in the blanks. *She knew. Shit. Shit.*

Jacob must have told her I'd been lying about who I was. I only hoped she'd hand Noah over without any physical altercation. I needed to have him with me, to wrap my arms around him and tell him I loved him more than anything in the world, that I was sorry I was such a horrible mother.

Harper squeezed her eyes closed. "I can't believe this. It's really too much."

I kept my face still, deciding to play dumb. Maybe I could still talk my way out of it, deny everything, and convince her Jacob had lied.

"Have you heard?" she asked with a sniffle.

Acid churned in my stomach as I steadied my feet. "I'm not sure what you're talking about."

Harper moved into the doorway and took my hand. "Jacob got hit by a car this morning. I'm so sorry, Riley... He's dead."

NINETEEN

My brain could barely register Harper's words. I'd been expecting a slap in the face. Instead, I'd gotten plowed over by a freight train.

"Jacob is dead?" My feet felt unsteady beneath me. "What happened?"

Harper's arm looped around my shoulders as she pulled me inside and closed the door. "A hit-and-run. A friend of mine who works at the hospital just called me. She said Jacob was jogging when he got hit. It sounds like he might have crossed somewhere he shouldn't have."

"Who hit him?"

"I don't know. Nobody does yet." She spoke in hushed tones. "I guess no one else was around, and the car took off."

I pressed my fingers to my temples, feeling the medical tape on my left hand. "I can't wrap my head around it. I just went out for dinner with him last night. We had a nice time." My mind spun as I stared out the window. I'd never tell her the next part when Jacob confronted me for impersonating Riley and threatened to expose me if I wasn't gone in twenty-four hours.

"I know. I can't believe it." Harper wiped her tears away. "Mom's upstairs, resting."

I hadn't wanted Jacob to die. Of course not. But I couldn't deny the relief rippling through me at the news. With Jacob's death, the threat to my well-being was gone. Maybe I didn't have to change my identity again and flee to Canada. Maybe Jacob had kept his promise to wait until tonight before reporting me to the police, and my secret had died with him. I closed my eyes, allowing the new reality to settle over me and debating whether I was a horrible person for feeling equal parts shock and relief at the news of his death.

Beyond Harper's shoulder, Noah and April perched on the couch, watching cartoons. I moved toward Noah, kissing him on the head and smelling the scent of his hair. Tears filled my eyes. I wasn't going to lose him.

Harper ushered me toward the adjoining kitchen. "I'll make some tea."

I nodded, leaving the kids to their show and balancing against the counter as my thoughts went haywire. The timing of Jacob's death was odd, and I couldn't help wondering if someone was protecting me. But I couldn't imagine who would do that. Nothing made sense.

Harper's hand shook as she handed me a steaming mug. "How bad is your finger?"

"Not terrible. Only two stitches. It seems like nothing now, but thank you for helping me out."

"Of course. That's what friends are for." Harper slurped a sip of tea, then set down the mug. "Do you think..." She stopped, making a face and shaking her head.

"Do I think what?"

"Never mind. It's crazy."

"This whole situation is crazy. Just tell me."

Harper looked at her hands, then sighed. "I was going to say, do you think McKenzie could have hit Jacob with her car?"

Harper's words rushed over me like a bucket of cold water. "I can't see her doing that."

She leaned closer, speaking in an urgent whisper. "But look at the timing. Jacob broke up with her. Then he took you out for a romantic dinner last night. She could have followed him. I'm sure she was insanely jealous. And angry."

I remembered how McKenzie had acted at the diner. She was immature and impulsive. The possibility of a jilted lover getting revenge hadn't occurred to me, and the theory seemed only mildly feasible now that Harper had mentioned it. "I guess it's possible. Would she be that stupid, though?"

"Who knows?" Harper lifted her mug, then lowered it. "It could have been a freak accident, I guess. I remember when that biker got hit a year or two ago."

"I'm sure the police will do an investigation."

I stayed at Harper's for another few minutes as we continued talking through our emotions and disbelief. Then, I drove Noah back to the apartment, thinking about returning to Lucky's Bar as soon as possible and explaining to Bea that I needed to cancel my astronomically expensive request for the urgent identities. Unless I learned otherwise, I had to believe Jacob hadn't told anyone else my secret.

We cut across the backyard, Noah hopping beside me toward the garage.

"Oh, there you are!" Wendy's voice startled me. I turned to find her rising from a chair on the patio. She headed toward me, her skin blotchy and her eyes bleary. "Oh, dear. I can see by your face that you've heard the awful news."

I nodded and released a sob. Wendy's arms wrapped around me, and I leaned into her, thankful for her warm body. I imagined this was the type of emotional support moms were supposed to offer, the kind I'd never had.

She stepped away from me after a minute. "Cody called me

this morning just before I saw you leaving. I didn't have the heart to tell you about Jacob."

"Harper told me. I still can't believe it."

"What a tragedy." She rubbed my back as concern clouded her eyes. "You need to be nice to yourself today. Take Noah to the park or watch a movie. I'll make some soup and bring you a couple of servings before dinner."

"Thanks, Wendy," I said, although I had no appetite and couldn't imagine eating.

A movement caught the corner of my eye, and I turned to see Brenda Harwood standing by the fence, staring at me. I nodded in her direction, causing Wendy to turn.

Brenda frowned, shaking her head. "There's always some commotion going on over at your apartment, Riley. I saw that man on your doorstep late last night. Lots of coming and going. This used to be a peaceful place to live."

Wendy growled, tipping her head toward the sky. "This isn't a good time, Brenda. We're having a private conversation." Then she made a face at me, clearly exasperated by her meddling neighbor.

A chill slid down my spine, reaching into the depths of my body. Brenda had seen Jacob return to my apartment late last night, hours after our date ended. I hoped she wouldn't realize that the person she'd seen was the same man who had died this morning. She would surely report the information to the police.

Wendy turned her back to the neighbor and whispered in my ear, "Just ignore her." She squeezed my arm again and hobbled into her house. Following Wendy's advice, I averted my eyes from Brenda and led Noah up the stairs, retreating into the apartment. My reality had been completely altered since I'd stood on Harper's front step an hour earlier. My body lowered into the couch as myriad thoughts swarmed my head. The timing of Jacob's death was convenient to the point of being suspicious. It could have been a coincidental freak accident, I supposed. Or McKenzie could have taken out her rage on Jacob as Harper had suggested. But there was another option: Drew Toven. Could it have been him at the park, hiding behind the trees? Everything he did was self-serving, and I wouldn't put a hit-and-run past him. But what would he gain from eliminating Jacob, whom he had likely never met? I wondered if he had mistaken Jacob for my new love interest.

My gaze skimmed over the apartment walls, pausing on the light fixture attached to the ceiling. Someone had been inside these walls the other night. I was sure of it. Was Drew capable of wiring my apartment? Maybe he'd heard Jacob's threat and stopped him from exposing me, although I couldn't imagine why.

Anxiety pressed in on me, and I couldn't stop myself from dragging a chair to the middle of the room, standing on it, and unscrewing the glass covering over the ceiling light. There were no electronic devices hidden inside. After replacing the glass dome, I checked all the lamps, finding nothing. One of the outlets appeared to stick out from the wall more than it should have, so I found a screwdriver in the kitchen drawer and unscrewed the outlet cover. There was nothing other than standard wiring behind it.

"What are you doing, Mom?" Noah faced me with wide eyes, a bin of Legos weighing down his little arms.

"I'm making sure everything fits together the way it should." I gave him a wink to let him know not to worry.

"Like my Legos?"

"Yes. Exactly like that." I looked at Noah, desperate to preserve his innocence. "Hey. Can you build me a car?"

"Yeah!" Noah plopped down on the rug and began sorting through pieces. With Noah distracted, I continued around the apartment, unscrewing everything that came apart and inspecting nooks and crannies for anything suspicious. After nearly thirty minutes of searching, I came up empty. No one had bugged my apartment.

Feeling slightly ridiculous and only marginally more secure, I made a peanut butter and jelly sandwich for Noah. Perhaps my hunch had been wrong. Maybe Drew hadn't followed me. I was determined to keep my mask firmly in place and continue as my sister, Riley Wakefield. It was my only chance to set down roots for Noah and get insight into the life my sister had lived before she ran away.

I glanced at my watch, finding it already after eleven in the morning. I returned the pile of cash in my purse to the freezer, realizing I needed to contact Bea before she got too deep into the request I'd set in motion last night. Dialing the number for Lucky's Bar led to several rings, and I almost gave up.

"Yup?"

I was shocked when she picked up, and it took a second to spit out her name. "Bea?"

"The one and only."

"It's Riley."

A disapproving puff of air.

"You know what we talked about last night?"

Deep breathing reached my ears. "Yep."

"I need to cancel that request. I'm sorry. Tell them I don't have the money."

"I already made a call."

"Please, cancel it. My situation has changed." I swallowed, aware I was pushing my luck. "Don't cancel the first one, though, the one I already paid for. I still need that as a backup."

A pained sigh heaved through the phone. "Are you kidding me? I couldn't stop the first one, even if I wanted to. Don't ask me for any more favors. And don't call this number again." The phone slammed down on the other end of the line, and the call went dead.

Bea was pissed, and rightly so, but I'd handled it. I'd done as much damage control as possible, could keep my savings, and wouldn't have to resort to stealing from the people around me. Still, questions about Jacob's hit-and-run stained my thoughts. I hadn't done anything intentionally to harm him. But I couldn't shake the feeling I was somehow responsible for his death.

TWENTY

A few hours later, after Noah and I had returned from the park, I was getting ready to shower when someone knocked on the front door. I pulled my clothes back on and smoothed down my hair, expecting to find Wendy in the entryway with a Tupperware container of soup. Instead, when I cracked the door, Cody wavered in the opening, his hair damp and his face clean-shaven.

"Hi." I struggled to hide my surprise as I opened the door wider.

"Sorry to stop by unannounced like this." He shoved his hands in his pockets and shifted his weight from foot to foot. "I heard about Jacob. I'm sorry for your loss. I remember how close you two used to be."

I looked at my feet, hoping to disguise that I'd never really known Jacob until very recently. "Thanks. It still doesn't seem real."

Cody cleared his throat, hesitating for a moment. "Do you need anything? I can watch Noah for you or bring you some food."

I studied him briefly, noticing the warm way he spoke and

his thoughtful eyes. He was handsome in a boy-next-door kind of way that I found disarming. "That's so nice of you to offer. I'm fine. Really."

He peered over my shoulder. "Is the apartment still working out?"

"It's fine for now. Noah and I don't need much."

"Are George and Wendy driving you crazy yet?"

"That's up for debate." I chuckled, and Cody smiled too. The Eckharts probably checked in on me too frequently and sometimes didn't fully respect my boundaries as an adult woman, but their concern for my well-being seemed genuine, and I suspected they were a bit lonely. "They mean well and they've done a lot to help me."

He nodded, looking toward the Eckharts' house and then back to me. "I was wondering if I could treat you to lunch some-time? Whenever you're feeling up to it."

I rolled onto the balls of my feet, happiness bursting through me for the first time in days. It seemed Cody felt the connection between us too. "Sure. Does Wednesday work? I don't have any shifts at the café that day, and Noah will be at preschool until three."

"Wednesday it is. There's a pretty good lunch spot near my office if you don't mind meeting me there."

We exchanged phone numbers, and he gave me the name of the restaurant where we planned to meet at noon on Wednesday.

Noah joined us in the doorway, jumping up and down at the sight of Cody. "Want to play with me?"

"Sure, big guy."

I placed my hand on Noah's head to keep him in place. "I'm sure Cody is busy. And I have to get myself cleaned up."

"Aw. But I want to," Noah whined, sticking out his lower lip.

"I'm not busy." Cody leaned down to Noah's eye level. "I

have an idea. How about we play hide-and-seek in the backyard and give your mom a break?"

"Okay!" Noah was already halfway down the stairs.

"Are you sure?" I asked Cody.

"Positive. I've been looking for someone to play hide-and-seek with all day." He gave me a sly smile and followed Noah down the stairs. "You hide first," Cody yelled as he stood by the fence, covering his eyes and counting loudly. I was grateful to have met a man who was so kind to me and my son. But I was just as thankful to have a few minutes to myself to take a hot shower and wash the stress of the last several hours away. I stood watching them for a minute, filled with disbelief at how drastically my luck had changed over the course of a single day.

I rinsed the last suds from the container Wendy had dropped off before dinner. My appetite hadn't returned yet, but I thanked her profusely and ate the soup anyway, remembering everyone's advice to keep my strength up. My phone buzzed from the counter, so I dried my hands and picked it up, seeing a local number I didn't recognize.

"Hello?"

"Is this Riley Wakefield?" It was a man's voice, deep and stern.

"Yes."

"This is Detective Brinmore from the Berkley Police Department. Do you have a minute?"

Oh, crap. My stomach dropped, and the fear of Jacob having spilled my secret before he died tore through me, but I did my best to steady my voice. "Yes. Of course."

"I'm calling about a hit-and-run that happened this morning, resulting in the death of Jacob Fletcher."

"Okay."

"I understand you were with Jacob last night."

"Yes. We went out for dinner. I still can't believe he's gone."

"I'm very sorry for your loss."

"Thank you."

"Can you tell me more about the dinner?"

"Sure. We went to Francesco's. Jacob was my boyfriend back in high school, but we hadn't seen each other in about fifteen years. Not since I ran away."

"Yeah. I'm familiar with your story and glad it had a happy ending." He paused, not sounding happy at all. "What time was the dinner?"

"He picked me up at six forty-five and dropped me off about an hour later."

"So around seven forty-five p.m.?"

"Yes. You can verify the timing with George and Wendy Eckhart. They were babysitting my son at their house while I was out with Jacob."

"And did you see Jacob after that? Last night or this morning?"

"No." I spit the word out without hesitation, hoping to cover the lie.

"Did he say anything unusual during dinner? Maybe he was having problems with someone?"

"Wait. Do you think his death wasn't an accident?" I asked, tightening my voice.

"Not necessarily. I'm investigating all angles."

"The only person I ever heard Jacob complain about was his ex-girlfriend, McKenzie. He broke up with her a few days ago."

"Right." A strange noise caught in the back of the detective's throat before he spoke again. "And did he break up with her because he wanted to be with you?"

"I don't think so. I told him over dinner that I thought we worked better as friends. He agreed." I closed my eyes, hoping again that he couldn't detect my lies.

"Did McKenzie know that?"

"I'm not sure. You'd have to ask her."

The detective grunted. I tried to imagine how his conversation with McKenzie must have gone.

"Was Jacob heading anywhere else after he dropped you off?"

"Not that I know of. I assumed he was going home."

"Are you still living at 1189 Marigold Street?" he asked.

"Yes. In the garage apartment."

"What color and model of car do you drive?"

"A blue Honda Accord." I paused. "What color was the car that hit him?"

"We're not releasing that information just yet."

I could hear fingers clicking against a keyboard before the detective thanked me for my time and asked me to call him if I remembered anything else that might be important. I agreed, heaving out a sigh as I ended the call. I hoped I'd cast enough suspicion toward McKenzie to avert the spotlight from me. She was the easiest target. It would have been reckless to mention the black SUV I suspected had been following me. I couldn't reveal anything that would lead them back to Sandra Matthews. But just like Detective Brinmore, I wondered where else Jacob had gone after leaving my apartment.

And who would have gone to drastic lengths to keep him quiet?

TWENTY-ONE

My feet ached from working another six-hour shift at Songbird Café. I removed my shoes, listening to Noah sing a song he'd learned at preschool about the days of the week. I nodded along as my mind wandered back over the last two days. When I arrived at the café yesterday morning, my co-worker, Tabitha, had given my shoulder a sympathetic touch. "Hey, Riley. I heard about Jacob. Are you okay? Everyone would understand if you needed to take a few days off."

"Thanks. I'm okay," I'd said with a sad smile. "I think it's better if I keep myself occupied." My body had moved slowly as I took orders and served food. Although I'd only known Jacob briefly, the loss of the man who had loved my sister burrowed through me at unexpected moments.

There'd been some chatter at the café about Jacob's death. Bits and pieces of conversation reached my ears as I walked past tables, people talking in somber voices about the tragic accident. I'd overhead McKenzie's name more than once but wasn't sure in what context. Still, I guessed most of the diners had never met Jacob or McKenzie.

A sudden silence pulled me from my thoughts. Noah had

stopped singing, looking at me expectantly. I snapped back to the present and clapped for him. "You did a great job singing that song! I'm going to clean up for a minute. Then maybe we can play a game or something."

"Okay!" Noah pulled a box of crayons and a coloring sheet from his superhero backpack and positioned himself at the table.

Enclosing myself in the bathroom, I washed my hands and inspected my appearance in the mirror, letting visions of tomorrow's date with Cody wander through my imagination. But the harsh lighting made my face look gaunt and my eyes haggard. I hoped I could improve my appearance with a little makeup. I leaned toward my reflection and flicked back my hair, cursing at the line of light brown growing from my scalp. The roots were a completely different shade than the rest of my shiny black tresses. Riley's hair had been much darker than mine—the color of ink—giving her a dramatic and mysterious look. Thankfully, black was an easy color to duplicate with hair dye, but the solution was temporary and required constant upkeep. I needed to cover my roots before anyone noticed this wasn't my natural color. In the cabinet below the sink, I found one of the extra boxes of hair dye I'd purchased at the drugstore.

I skimmed the familiar instructions, draped an old towel over my shoulders, and got to work, squeezing the cool solution onto my scalp and combing through it. The solution had to sit for fifteen minutes, and I could use the time to play a game of Uno or Candyland with Noah. With my hair plastered to my head, I grabbed the box with the instructions, set a timer on my phone, and joined Noah in the living room, where he did a double take and started laughing.

"What's so funny?"

He pointed at my head. "What did you do?"

"I'm making my hair look pretty. I have to keep this cream on it for fifteen minutes."

"You look like a seal."

I couldn't help giggling at that. I told Noah he looked like a puppy dog, which made him laugh harder. We decided on Uno, and I shuffled the cards, dealing out our hands. A few minutes passed as we played our cards. It was fun, and I realized these were the times I treasured most, the little moments of laughter spent with my son, the same moments my own mother had missed out on with me and Riley.

Three loud raps on the door interrupted our game.

I lowered my cards. We hadn't been expecting any visitors.

"Riley! Noah! It's Wendy," Wendy's voice projected from outside.

I looked around, panic overtaking me. Her unannounced drop-ins were becoming a liability. My hand flew to my head, touching the cold cream by accident. I couldn't let her see the hair dye. Before I had time to think or speak, Noah ran to the door and opened it. "We're playing Uno!" he said, jumping up and down, oblivious to what he'd just done.

I stood, deciding to make a run for the bathroom.

"Oh! Look at you." Wendy was inside now, and she'd already seen me.

My feet stopped, and I turned, finding her broad smile flattening to a straight line.

"Hi, Wendy. I was just covering some grays."

"Grays? At your age?"

"Yeah. I guess it's hereditary."

She stepped further into the kitchen, picking up the Narcotics Anonymous flier I'd left conspicuously on the counter and giving an approving nod. Her gaze gravitated toward the box of black hair dye. "I never would have known. Your hair always looks so perfect."

I exhaled with relief.

"Mommy used to have yellow hair." Noah looked at Wendy with a solemn face.

Wendy's eyes popped. "Oh?"

"Oh, no." I waved my hand to dismiss the idea. "He's remembering when I dyed my hair bleached blonde for a while. It was way too much upkeep and only lasted a few weeks."

Noah stuck out his lower lip. "No. It was long and yellow when we lived in Was Vegas."

My molars clenched together. I fought the urge to tell Noah to keep his mouth shut, but I couldn't do so with Wendy standing there. The poor kid had no idea he was doing anything wrong. I shrugged toward Wendy. "He's confused. We drove through Las Vegas on our way here, and it really made an impact."

"Noooooo! I'm right!" Noah's words came out like a howl.

Noah was only telling the truth, and I should have rewarded him with a hug. Instead, I placed a hand on his shoulder and gave Wendy an exasperated look that said, *Kids. What can you do?*

She returned a knowing nod in my direction. "In any case, I only came by to see how you were doing. I heard from Betsy Parker, who lives down the street, that Jacob's parents returned to town yesterday. They live in Florida now but are having the funeral in Berkley. It's at the Lutheran church on Friday morning. But you probably know all of that already."

I gave a slight nod. Harper had texted me the details of Jacob's funeral this morning while I'd been at work. I hadn't responded because I couldn't shake the feeling that Jacob would still be alive if I hadn't returned to town pretending to be my sister and if he hadn't called me out on my lie. A few days had passed since his sudden death, but I still couldn't make sense of the strange coincidence.

"I'm assuming you're going," Wendy said. "I know Jacob was a big part of your life. He cared for you so much."

An image of McKenzie's angry face pulsed in my mind. I didn't want to go, but Wendy was correct. Jacob had been a big part of Riley's life, and I'd been among the last to see him alive. I had to go. "I'll take the morning off work and pick up an extra shift another day." My phone made a loud beeping noise, and I turned off the timer. "I've got to wash this stuff out of my hair."

Wendy raised a hand. "I'll be on my way. Just let me know if you need anything." As suddenly as she'd arrived, she was out the door.

Noah stomped toward the couch, pouting. "I'm right."

I looked at my watch, aware I needed to wash out the dye but knowing this was far more important. "Hey, buddy. Let's talk." I kneeled to meet him at eye level. "There are some things we need to keep private. I don't want anyone here to know we used to live in Las Vegas, okay? It's a secret between you and me. We can't tell anyone else."

"Why?"

"Because a bad man is looking for me, and I don't want him to find me."

Noah's eyes widened, and I immediately regretted telling him the truth.

"It's nothing to worry about." I tugged at the hem of my shirt, backtracking. "But we're going to tell people that Mommy's hair has always been this color—black. And that we moved here from California. As far as anyone knows, we never lived in Las Vegas. Okay?"

Noah chewed his lip as he nodded.

I worried that my propensity for lying would scar my son for life, the same way my mom had scarred me and Riley by abandoning us. But he jumped up and skipped over to the little table. "Can we play Uno again?"

My chest heaved as I reminded myself I wasn't like my mother. I'd made plenty of parenting mistakes, but my son knew I loved him. I was already doing better than she'd done. "Sure, buddy. Let me wash my hair first."

.   .   .

Ten minutes later, I returned to the living room wearing comfy pants and a T-shirt. My damp hair was combed straight and colored as black as the night sky from root to tip. Noah sat in front of the TV, flipping through the channels, most distorted with static.

"I can't find my shows." He tossed the remote on the couch, leaving the TV on a station playing the local news as he headed toward the table.

I was about to turn it off when I saw Melissa Miner, the local newscaster who'd crashed my backyard barbecue a few weeks earlier. She stood on a corner in front of a commercial building and a sign that said *Market Street*, with an alley running past her in the other direction.

"Jacob Fletcher lost his life on Saturday morning while jogging past the intersection of Market Street and this unnamed alley. He was the victim of a hit-and-run. Unfortunately, the police are no closer to knowing who the driver of that vehicle was. The only clue is a chip of black auto paint left at the scene. The authorities say the paint is a common shade of black used on multiple makes and models of cars. We ask that you call the tipline if you have any information relating to this tragic death." Melissa Miner gave herself another not-so-subtle pat on the back as she reminded viewers that she'd brought them the story first.

I sucked in a sharp breath. The investigators had found black paint. Black like the SUV I'd seen following me around town, the one I worried was driven by Drew Toven.

I'd gone past the crash site on my way home from work yesterday, but the remnants of the accident had already been cleaned up. I hadn't noticed anything out of the ordinary. The intersection was just a few blocks from where Jacob told me he lived. I knew from our conversation at dinner that he jogged regularly, and he most likely followed a certain route. Anyone familiar with his routine would know where to find him and where would be the best place to strike without being seen. Surely, a hidden alley would make the top of that list.

Detective Brinmore's questions cycled through me. *Did Jacob mention a problem with anyone?* I'd given McKenzie's name in response, but Jacob also had a big problem with someone else. Me. *Where did Jacob go after he dropped you off?* I never told the detective that Jacob had returned to my apartment a second time to threaten me just hours before he died. Brinmore hadn't contacted me again, and I took that as a sign that he still didn't know that Jacob had returned to confront me after our dinner date. It didn't sound like McKenzie had been arrested. I wondered what color car she drove and if the detective had uncovered any solid answers. Because I certainly hadn't.

TWENTY-TWO

Cody strode through the door of the InterTech office and into the sunlight as I exited my car.

"I saw you pull up," he said with a sheepish expression.

"Sorry, I'm a couple of minutes late."

"No worries."

In truth, I was late for our lunch date because I'd changed my clothes three times, searching for an outfit that was both casual and alluring. Something that hinted at being sexy without being obvious about it. I'd decided on a sleeveless sundress and wedge sandals. I wasn't sure if Cody's lunch invitation had been intended as a real date or simply a catch-up session between two former foster kids who'd been taken in by the same couple. But unlike my encounters with Jacob, I couldn't deny my attraction to Cody. While Jacob had been a good catch for someone, things could never have gone anywhere between us. Pursuing a romantic relationship with my sister's former boyfriend felt weird and wrong. Cody, on the other hand, didn't have any strings attached.

"The restaurant is only a block this way." He pointed past me, and we walked in that direction, reaching the casual bar and grill a minute later. A host seated us at a small table next to the front window. I liked how the sunlight shone across Cody's face, reflecting off his neatly combed hair and turning his eyes a lighter shade of brown. We chatted briefly about his career in tech and my hope of becoming a realtor and quitting my wait-ressing job.

After a waitress served us the iced teas we'd ordered, a somber expression clouded Cody's face. "I'm sorry again about Jacob. That must have been a real shock for you."

"It was."

"Talk about being in the wrong place at the wrong time."

"I know. What are the odds?" I sipped my tea and cleared my throat, ensuring our waitress wasn't approaching. "Do you think someone could have targeted him?"

Cody's brow furrowed. "Hit him on purpose?"

"Yeah."

"Hm. Not likely. There are so many really terrible drivers out there. Besides, who would want to kill him?"

"Maybe McKenzie was pissed off that Jacob broke up with her and immediately went out to dinner with me." I sat back, testing out Harper's theory on him.

Cody touched his chin, considering. "It's possible, I guess. But running over Jacob still seems like a big leap. And don't most people who get dumped hold out hope of getting back together with their ex, at least for a week or two?"

"That's true," I said, although I couldn't relate from any personal experience. I'd never let myself grow too attached to anyone. Even when Noah's father ditched me, I took it as a sign that he couldn't be trusted. The idea of trying to win him back had never occurred to me. "Do you know what color car McKenzie drives?" I asked.

"No idea. Why?"

"They think someone driving a black car hit him."

"Ha. That doesn't really narrow it down. Half the people in

this town drive black cars, including me. George told me once that black and silver cars are the most popular colors at the dealership."

"Yeah. It's not exactly a smoking gun."

Our food came, and we shifted the conversation to Noah—his preschool, what he liked to eat, his favorite games, and even his favorite color. I told Cody he was good with Noah and would make a good dad someday.

He waved away the praise. "You should be proud of yourself. You didn't have a role model for a mother, but you're still a great mom, one either of us would have been lucky to have."

"Thanks." I fiddled with my napkin as heat crept up my neck at the best compliment he could have given me. I noticed him staring and automatically turned my head away, hoping he didn't notice any differences between me and his memory of Riley. It seemed he and Riley had never been particularly close, but I wasn't sure. I lifted my gaze. "At least we had the Eckharts for a while."

"Yeah. It could have been worse. I couldn't have survived much longer at the group home."

A knowing look passed between us. Kids over the age of fifteen were the least likely to be taken in by foster families and even less likely to be adopted. I'd heard of it happening, but it was rare. Cody and Riley had lucked out, going to live with the Eckharts in their teens.

Memories of the group home in Roseville churned through my thoughts, painful flashbacks I would have loved nothing more than to forget. Even before Marianne Clavey arrived, it was much worse than the other places I'd lived. I described the place to Cody, pretending it was where I'd lived before landing with the Eckharts and assuming Riley's experiences at her group homes had been somewhat similar. I told him how the woman who oversaw the place acted like a dictator, enforcing tight security at all hours, especially nights and weekends. She assigned solitary confinement for anyone who acted out or spoke out of turn, once locking me in a room alone for a full day with no food. There were ten girls with tragic childhoods and difficult personalities living together, stealing each other's belongings, and ganging up on the most vulnerable. Without using Marianne Clavey's name, I told him about the brutal bully who was usually the source of trouble, the ways she'd tormented me, and how the social worker had dismissed my complaints about her, labeling me as overly sensitive.

"That's scary. You didn't deserve any of that." A flash of sadness crossed Cody's face before he spoke again. "My last group home was pretty bad too. I remember watching a kid die."

"What?"

"Yeah. He was choking. The guy overseeing us was new and decided to call his supervisor to ask what to do instead of calling 911. By the time he got an answer, it was too late."

"That's horrible. I'm sorry."

The glazed look in Cody's eyes disappeared. "So when I got placed with the Eckharts a year or so later, I was relieved. And the apartment was more freedom than I'd ever had."

"You deserved it. We both did."

"Because of your return, I've seen George and Wendy more these past few weeks than in the last fifteen years. I guess I kept my distance after I moved out."

I nodded, understanding why he'd want some space from them now that he was an adult. I'd experienced a little of the Eckharts' overbearing nature and imagined they would have been even more involved with their foster kids. Riley had complained about how strict the Eckharts were with her, not letting her out past ten o'clock most nights and prohibiting her from having people over to the house after dinnertime. She said Wendy had flipped out when she'd gotten the tattoo on her shoulder, making her spend an entire Saturday helping to clean the house. Now that I was a mother, I recognized that the

Eckharts' reaction to Riley's behavior seemed more like sensible parenting than a horrible punishment.

I caught Cody staring at me again but realized he wasn't looking at me in the intense way Jacob had been inspecting every inch of my face; it was more like a moment of admiration. I smiled, and he smiled back, lowering his eyelids. There was definitely something more than friendship between us.

He spoke again. "It's too bad we didn't know each other better back then. Maybe I could have kept you from running away."

I averted my gaze. "My mind was made up. I don't think anyone could have stopped me."

"You *were* a little hard-headed. No offense." He snickered. "You've mellowed out since then."

I gave a guilty shrug. "Having a kid changes you."

"And you quit doing drugs cold turkey? That's amazing."

I looked at the napkin in my lap, realizing I had to stick with the narrative I'd spun about Riley. "I go to NA meetings when I need to," I said, wondering if I should be alarmed at how easily the lies rolled off my tongue. "I never want to go back to that life."

"You're doing an amazing job." Cody reached across the table and interlaced his fingers with mine, sending a shimmer of warmth through my body.

The waitress returned, and Cody grabbed the bill. We continued talking as we left the restaurant and walked along the sidewalk.

"Are you going to Jacob's funeral on Friday?" I asked.

"I don't think so. I didn't really know him."

"Oh."

Cody must have sensed my disappointment because he added, "But if you want me to go with you for moral support, I can."

"That's okay. Harper is driving me."

He took a few more steps. "Are you spending much time with Harper?"

"Here and there. She's been a big help with Noah."

Cody's feet stopped moving. He stared toward the street as if debating whether to tell me something.

"What's wrong?"

He turned to face me, his expression darker. "You've changed over the last fifteen years. You've grown as a person and bettered yourself." He paused. "Harper is still making bad decisions."

"She is?"

"I worked with her ex-husband, Danny, to link the computers at his office. The stories he tells about her are kind of scary. She's impulsive and vengeful. She has threatened his life more than once and turned their daughter against him."

"Really?"

"Yeah. And that's not all. When Danny started dating someone else, Harper just happened to run into them whenever they went on a date. She'd always be there, watching, like a stalker. It was super off."

"That doesn't sound like her."

Cody raised an eyebrow. "It should. From what I remember, she was a pretty bad influence on you back then. Or maybe it was the other way around." He grinned to let me know he was only poking fun.

"Right. We both made some bad decisions." I nodded my agreement, although I felt like I'd been thrown into unfamiliar waters. It wasn't clear exactly what kind of bad influence Harper had had on Riley, but I recalled how bitter Harper had been when I'd shown up ten minutes late to our playdate. Something about her extreme reaction to such a minor infraction didn't sit right.

Cody kept talking, clearly eager to finish his story. "And, one day, someone broke into Danny's girlfriend's apartment and went through her things. They couldn't prove it was Harper, but they just knew. The girlfriend broke up with him because she was too scared about what else might happen."

"Are you sure? Doesn't Danny have a drinking problem? I mean, he probably tells some tall tales."

"Danny? No. Not that I ever saw. He might have a beer once in a while, but nothing beyond that. Harper is the one who lies all the time."

"Oh." It was difficult to reconcile the Harper I'd gotten to know, the woman who'd graciously taken in Noah during my middle-of-the-night emergency, with the person Cody was describing. I pushed back. "There are two sides to every story. And divorce brings out the worst in people."

"That's true." He shifted his weight. "Look, I'm not telling you to ditch her. Just don't piss her off. I'm sure you remember how she was back then. Such a drama queen at school. Always desperate for attention. After you disappeared, Wendy and George were convinced she'd done something to you."

"Really? Why?"

"You would know better than me. People said you left the dance to find her after you and Jacob argued. You told Wendy the next afternoon that you were going to meet Harper. Then you were gone. Harper said she had never made plans with you."

"Well, she was telling the truth." I angled my face away from him, hoping to sound convincing.

Cody gave me a friendly smack on the arm. "Hey. I had a really nice time, and I don't want to end on a bad note."

"Me too. The lunch was great, and I appreciate you telling me about Harper."

"Next time you need help with Noah, maybe call me first. I'm more fun than Harper. And George and Wendy, for that matter." Cody winked. "And Noah is pretty fun to hang out with."

"I appreciate that. Noah loves all the games you play with him."

"Do you want to do this again? Maybe dinner next time? Noah can come too."

I nodded, stopping myself from squealing. "I would love to. I'll even host you in the old apartment if you're up for it."

"Sounds great. See you soon, Riley." He gave me a quick hug and then turned and went through his office door.

My insides fluttered as I got into my car, but my euphoria was fleeting. I wished I could come clean with Cody, confide in him that I wasn't Riley but Riley's sister, Gina. A relationship based on a lie would be difficult to maintain. Then again, I'd spent my entire adult life honing the craft of deception. Living as someone else felt like second nature. Cody was the first man I'd been genuinely attracted to in a long time. I had to give it a try.

TWENTY-THREE

My spine pressed into the wooden pew as I averted my eyes from the closed casket surrounded by flowers at the front of the church. Enormous stained-glass windows rose toward a peaked ceiling on either side of me as somber organ music droned through the space.

Harper leaned into me as she stretched to see who was still funneling into the chapel. She settled back into her seat and patted me on the arm. "How are you holding up?"

"I'm hanging in there."

"I brought tissues if you need one."

"Thank you. I'm so glad you're here with me."

The conversation with Cody from a couple of days earlier circled through me. Cody was smart and kind, but maybe he was wrong about Harper. She wasn't scary and evil. His only knowledge of Harper had come from her ex-husband, so his view of her was negatively skewed. Harper had been open with me about her messy divorce. She and her ex had probably both made exaggerations about the other's behavior.

The Eckharts sat on either side of me, studying the program. I kept my head low, trying not to look at the older couple quietly crying in the front row, who Harper had identified as Jacob's parents. I wondered if Riley had known them. McKenzie sat in the row behind them, dressed all in black. Apparently, she was acting as the grieving girlfriend despite Jacob having broken up with her. An older woman, who I presumed to be McKenzie's mom, sat beside her and rubbed her back.

Harper elbowed me, nodding toward a bald man in a black suit diagonally across the aisle. "That's Detective Brinmore," she whispered. "He called me the other day. I heard him introduce himself to someone a few minutes ago."

My insides turned as I took in the detective I'd spoken to on the phone about my date with Jacob. I wondered if he'd learned anything else about me and if he was attending the funeral in a personal or professional capacity. The second option seemed more likely. Maybe the person who'd hit Jacob was inclined to be here, but I wasn't sure. Despite the mistakes I'd made, my knowledge of criminal behavior didn't extend much past run-of-the-mill identity fraud.

The service began, and the minister's calm voice soothed my thoughts. He spoke about God working in mysterious ways and everlasting life. Jacob's older brother took to the podium and shared his favorite memories of Jacob growing up. Then his cousin spoke, sharing an anecdote and momentarily breaking down. Everyone rose after a couple of hymns were sung and some Bible verses read. The immediate family was to follow the casket to the cemetery where Jacob would be buried.

Wendy looked at me and Harper, her eyes bloodshot. "That was a nice way to remember him, wasn't it?"

"Yes." Harper's cheeks were wet with tears.

I nodded along as a bit of hot emotion rose to my face. Harper handed me a tissue, and I blew my nose.

McKenzie walked past with the family, leaning into her mother as if her legs were too weak to stand. Her head jerked back when she saw me, her eyes tightening on me like screws. I nodded as if to say, *I'm sorry,* but the gesture had no effect. She glared at me like a rabid animal who wanted to rip the flesh from my bones. McKenzie's mom, who had missed the entire exchange, tugged her daughter forward, and she reluctantly followed.

I exhaled as the mother and daughter exited through the back door. McKenzie's emotion felt raw and real. She seemed devastated by Jacob's death. Or was she devastated by what she'd done? I couldn't be sure. The only clear thing was that she carried plenty of resentment against me.

Wendy and George headed out for lunch, and Harper drove me home, dropping me out front. She had to return to work, and I needed to catch up on my real estate coursework. I remembered how nervous I'd been about applying for the class. It turned out it was easy enough to forge Riley's G.E.D. certificate. No one had asked any questions. I cut across the yard and up the stairs, lost in thought as I opened the door. But something wasn't right as I stepped inside. A light shone from the kitchen, one I hadn't left on. Fear bristled over my scalp, but before I could turn and run, an arm reached out from behind the front door and wrapped around me. A man's hand covered my mouth, the odor of spearmint gum filling my nose. I twisted my neck to the side to find Drew Toven gripping my body.

"Hi, Sandra. Or should I call you Riley?" The combination of his hot breath and sweat-covered face gave me the sensation of bugs crawling over my skin.

I blinked, afraid to scream or move. Drew had found me, and he knew too much. The closed hand on my mouth made it difficult to breathe.

"I'll release you, but you have to stay quiet." He never

stopped chomping his gum. "Scream, and I'll get you locked up for years. But I prefer not to get the authorities involved."

"Okay," I said through his fingers. He loosened his grip, removing his hand from my mouth. My lungs filled with oxygen. I stepped away from him, still gulping for breath and terrified he had come to get what I'd denied him, that he'd pin me down and overpower me.

He sniffed through his nose. "You stole my money. I want it back."

I widened my stance, relieved the money was foremost on his mind. He could turn me in for stabbing him. Still, I was sure he didn't want me talking to the police about how he'd sexually harassed me or about his company's ongoing shady dealings with developers and politicians any more than I wanted my previous identity exposed.

"Give me the fifteen grand, and I'll walk away and never look back."

"I don't have all of it, but I can give you five thousand."

He tilted his head, smiling. "Tell you what? We can spend a few minutes in the bedroom right now, and I'll forgive the rest."

"No!" The disgusting man's proximity made me want to vomit, and I was desperate to get him away from me. My body stiffened at his suggestion, and my resolve hardened too. "My son is getting dropped off here any minute," I said, lying. "They'll see you. I'll pay you back what I have. I'll send the rest later."

Drew sighed and touched his shirt in the same spot where I'd stabbed him. I presumed there was a bandage underneath, covering a wound that was still healing. Maybe he realized he couldn't overpower me. "Get the money."

Thoughts of Noah going through life without a mom sent a flash of terror through me. I opened the freezer door, locating the ziplock bag of cash.

"Clever," he said, raising his eyebrows. "I saw you on the

news. Recognized you right away, although I preferred you with blonde hair and those big eyelashes. You have all these people so convinced you're that teen runaway. I almost believed you myself." He motioned toward the bag. "Hand it over."

I gave it to him. "That's all the money I have."

"Not my problem."

"I don't have any other money," I said, repeating the truth.

"You're ten thousand dollars short. That's not the deal we made."

I squeezed my eyes closed, feeling the walls closing in on me. I had no other money, but I'd never sleep with him. "I'll get you the rest. I promise. Just give me a week or two."

Drew blew out a long, low whistle. "That's too long. I need to get back to the office. I'll give you two days. Meet me in the alley out back at four p.m. on Sunday. Once you pay in full, we'll go our separate ways." He cracked his gum. "Or there's always option two."

My feet were glued in place as he leered at me. I had no other money. "What if I can't get that much money by then?"

"Then things will get worse for you. I'll tell the nice couple who think you're their long-lost foster daughter who you really are. You'll be charged with robbery, attempted murder, and identity theft." He looked at me like I was something he'd scraped off the bottom of his shoe. "Man, I thought I was low."

"You don't know anything about me."

"I'm pretty sure I know more about you than anyone else. And don't try running again. I'll find you." He jabbed a finger toward me. "Four o'clock on Sunday."

"Wait." I stepped forward as he turned to leave. A thousand questions swarmed my mind, but one bothered me more than the others. "There's something I don't understand."

Drew turned back, annoyed.

"Why did you kill Jacob?"

"Huh?"

"You didn't have to do that."

His eyes narrowed into slits. "Who the hell is Jacob?"

"Jacob Fletcher. He was killed in a hit-and-run last week, hit by a black car just like yours. He was about to expose me. You would have lost your leverage. Or maybe you thought we were dating."

"Ha." Drew rubbed his jaw. "I saw that on the news, but it wasn't me. I'm not in the business of killing people. Never have been." He fixed his stony eyes on me, and I felt myself withering beneath his glare. "Focus on getting the money."

Drew stomped out the door, and I stumbled over my feet as I rushed to lock it behind him. I paced around the apartment, fighting the urge to punch the wall. An open window in the bedroom was missing the screen. The fan lay face-down on the floor. That was how he'd gotten in, from the platform outside. He hadn't left any obvious signs of entry the other times, but maybe he hadn't bothered tidying up today because he knew he was confronting me.

I replaced the screen and locked the window as sweat erupted over my body. Ten thousand dollars was an impossible sum to come up with in two days. I raced to the bathroom and opened the tampon box, relieved at the sight of the necklace, Riley's original birth certificate, and other documents related to my previous identities still folded inside. The identity I'd ordered through Bea hadn't arrived yet and probably wouldn't for several weeks, if it arrived at all. At least I still had these.

I turned over several money-making schemes in my mind, but they were all criminal, and most would take too long. I scoured my brain, recalling what Riley had done when she'd needed money. She'd stolen it from the Eckharts' secret drawer. There'd been a thousand dollars in it back then. As much as I didn't want to betray the Eckharts, the people who had helped me the most, I couldn't help wondering how much they kept there now. I paced into the living room, stopping when I reached the small window next to my front door and peering toward the back of their house. They were out for lunch at Beau's Tavern, a nice restaurant that would take at least an hour to complete their meal. I probably had at least twenty or thirty minutes to get myself in and out. I silently vowed to repay anything I took within six months.

Trying to ignore the guilt pulsing through me, I tiptoed out of the apartment, locking the door behind me. No one was outside in either of the neighboring backyards, but I felt exposed. In case Brenda was spying out the corner of a window, I walked casually down the steps and across the backyard as if I were merely stopping by to ask for a cup of sugar. I'd overheard Wendy telling Aunt Leslie that they kept a spare key in a fake rock in the corner of the patio. Before I opened the fake rock, I checked the slider, which was rarely locked when they were home. I had a hunch they also forgot to lock it on occasion when they left the house.

Sure enough, the glass door slid open as soon as I gripped the handle, allowing me to walk directly into their living room. This was almost too easy. My pulse raced as I closed myself inside and scurried through the deserted rooms and up the stairs until I reached Riley's old bedroom, which was now Wendy's office. They'd moved the desk with the secret drawer into this room. I opened the bottom drawer. The false panel installed above was exactly as Riley had described. I dislodged the panel, hoping to find a windfall, so much cash that they wouldn't even notice if a few thousand was missing for a matter of months. Instead, the secret compartment stared back at me. It was empty.

Shit! I slumped forward as any remaining hope drained out of me. My hands shook as I replaced the false panel and closed the drawer. I knelt there for a second, cradling my head. A part of me was relieved there was no money stashed away here because I didn't want to steal from Wendy and George, who had been nothing but kind to me and who had provided my sister a home so many years earlier. Hot shame coursed through me at what I'd been prepared to do and how I'd led a slimeball like Drew Toven onto their property. I stood up and exited the house as quickly as possible, relieved at least that Wendy and George hadn't returned home while I'd been inside.

"What a shame."

An unexpected voice made me jump. I turned toward it, finding Brenda Harwood lurking behind the fence. She'd caught me breaking into the Eckharts' house. I had to think fast to come up with an excuse.

She peered down her nose at me. "I saw another man at your apartment today."

My body froze as I took in her words, realizing her disapproving comment was about something else entirely. I straightened my shoulders and smiled. "Yep. Just a friend."

"I'd prefer if you didn't have so many people over. This is supposed to be a quiet neighborhood."

Her complete lack of understanding about my situation raked through me as I suddenly gained a greater appreciation for George and Wendy's annoyance with their meddling neighbor. How could a person have so little going on in her life that she had to create problems? I stepped toward her, brightening my voice. "Hey, Brenda. I have an idea."

She perked up.

"Why don't you mind your own business? Seriously. Back the hell off." My words whipped toward her like a sling blade, surprising us both.

Brenda threw up her arms in disgust, backing away from the fence. "You young people have no respect these days."

I watched Brenda scurry toward her back door, slightly ashamed of my outburst. But I continued toward the stairs, hoping she'd be so taken aback by my verbal attack that she'd forget she'd seen me exiting the Eckharts' house while they weren't home.

Once inside my living room, I fell onto the couch, defeated. There was no choice but to reevaluate how to proceed. This wasn't how I wanted to live: always under threat, always on the run, betraying my friends and loved ones, and afraid to get too close to anyone. I'd done criminal things in the past, but I wanted to be a better person going forward for Noah. And for myself. I would figure out another way to pay off Drew. My former boss had appeared to be telling the truth when he'd said he wasn't responsible for Jacob's death. But that didn't mean he wouldn't do something horrible to me.

TWENTY-FOUR

I invited Cody over for pizza and a movie on Saturday night. He immediately accepted and insisted on bringing the food. The outdated TV in our apartment came with an old DVD player, so Noah and I went to the library and checked out a DVD of *Finding Nemo*. At 6 p.m., Cody arrived with a large pizza and a bottle of sparkling water. I gave him a three-second tour of the apartment, and he confirmed that it looked pretty much the same as when he'd lived here, except for two new mismatched cabinets above the sink. We sat at the tiny table, eating our food and giggling at Noah's antics. I told Cody about Jacob's funeral and the people I'd seen, including McKenzie and Detective Brinmore, but leaving out the part about my former boss showing up in my apartment, propositioning me again, and taking back some of the money I'd stolen. Although I did my best to act light-heartedly, terrible thoughts poked at my consciousness. Was this my last night of freedom if I couldn't come up with the remaining ten thousand dollars? Would it be my last night spent as Riley Wakefield? Would Cody still like me after I asked him for money?

After eating most of the pizza, we put in the movie and squeezed together on the couch.

"Good choice, guys. I love this one." Cody rubbed his hands together and winked at me. His presence was a balm for my ragged nerves.

I decided to enjoy the moment and settled into him. Every once in a while, Cody's arm lingered near my body, sending a pulse of attraction through me. At one point, his calloused hand rested on top of mine, and he gave a little squeeze. We smiled at each other. Our connection was real, and Cody was a good man. I didn't want to screw it up. But Drew Toven's leathery face hung over me like a bad dream. He would expose my true identity if I didn't come up with the money by tomorrow at 4 p.m. My house of cards would collapse. I would go to jail and lose Noah and surely Cody too.

When the movie credits rolled, I encouraged Noah to build something with his Legos in the bedroom to give me and Cody a few minutes alone. As Noah scampered into the other room and closed the door, I prepared myself for a difficult conversation. Before I could speak, Cody looped his arm around me and leaned in for a kiss. I closed my eyes and kissed him back. For a moment, the world disappeared, and I only felt the heat of his body, his lips on mine. His arms were sturdy around me, and I felt safe for the first time since I could remember. I didn't want the moment to end, but he eventually pulled away.

He brushed his fingertips across my cheek and gave me a crooked smile. "I've been wanting to do that for a while."

"Me too."

He ran his fingertips along my hair, a mystified look in his eyes. "I can't believe I never noticed you back then. I was such an idiot."

I shrugged. "We were kids."

"Yeah. Dumb kids."

We laughed in agreement and leaned back on the couch. I

rested on his shoulder, not wanting to ruin the mood, while I listened to him tell me about what he'd been up to the last few days.

When there was a lull in the conversation, I decided I couldn't put it off any longer. I straightened up and faced him. "Cody, I need to tell you something."

"Okay."

I stared at my hands for several seconds before beginning. "I did some illegal things when I was living out west. I was desperate, and I wanted to do right by Noah to give him a better life."

Cody gave a little nod as if encouraging me to continue.

"Anyway, long story short..." The words were difficult to say, and I coughed a mouthful of air from my lungs. "I stole money from a bad man before coming here. He tracked me down. Yesterday, when I got home from the funeral, the guy was waiting for me here. I gave him all my money but still owe him another ten thousand."

"Oh, wow..." Cody's eyes practically popped out of his head. "Are you serious?"

"Yes."

"Are you okay?"

"Yeah."

"Did you call the police?"

"No. And I won't. I can't. I'll go to jail and lose Noah, so that's not an option. I have until four tomorrow afternoon to come up with the rest."

He looked around the apartment. "This sounds dangerous. What should we do?"

Heat flushed through me, surging into my face. I leaned forward, resting my palms on the tops of my thighs. "I was wondering... and I know this is crazy because you don't even know me, really... but I was wondering if I could borrow the money from you? I'll pay you back as soon as I earn my first real estate commission. I promise I'm good for it." I sat motionless, waiting for him to respond.

The color had drained from Cody's face. "Of course, I'll lend you the money, Riley. But I don't have that much in my account. I can probably only give you seven or eight thousand by tomorrow." He worked his jaw from side to side. "I could probably get you a few hundred more from my other savings account by Wednesday, but I just made a big purchase, and my balance is low."

"Wednesday will be too late." My heels dug into the floor. "What did you buy?"

Cody tugged at his collar, looking a bit guilty. "Nothing. Something stupid."

"Oh." His vague response increased my curiosity, but I reminded myself it was none of my business. I was relieved he was helping me at all.

He continued, "The bank is closed now, and tomorrow is Sunday. I'm not sure what the ATM withdrawal limit is." He checked his phone and scrolled through his bank website. "The limit is three thousand per day. So, six thousand by tomorrow, which is about all I have. But I also have a small emergency stash of cash at my house. Will eight thousand be enough to get this guy off your back?"

I nodded as tears welled in my eyes. It wouldn't be enough, but I was grateful to Cody nonetheless. "Yeah. That's a huge help. Thank you."

"Maybe the Eckharts can lend you the rest?"

I instinctively glanced in the direction of their house. "I don't want to ask them. I still haven't paid back the other money I took from them."

Cody made a strange grunting noise as he cracked his knuckles.

"What?" I asked.

"I'm really confused about something."

"About what?"

Cody cleared his throat. "I guess it's time to come clean." He closed his eyes dramatically and then opened them as if bracing for something. "I know you didn't steal that thousand dollars from the Eckharts before you ran away."

I froze. What was he saying? Had he figured out I was an imposter? "How do you know I didn't take it?" My voice sounded meek as I forced out the question, afraid of the answer.

He made a face like he'd swallowed a gulp of vinegar. "Because I stole it."

It took a second to register his words. I pulled away from him, wondering if I'd heard him correctly. "What?"

"When you'd been missing for about a day, and people were just starting to turn frantic, I broke into that secret drawer in Wendy's desk and took their cash. A thousand dollars. It was terrible of me, but I knew everyone would think you'd stolen the money." He squared his shoulder toward me, touching his chest. "I was the one who broke into their house when they were out. I used the money to move out a few weeks later. I've felt so guilty all these years, especially for letting everyone believe you did it."

Dread pinned me down as I took in the full weight of his confession. I'd trapped myself in my own web of lies and was unsure what to say next without giving too much away. "You took the money?"

"Yes. I'm incredibly ashamed of it. You're the first person I've ever told."

I placed my hand on his back, feeling the heat radiating off his body. I softened my voice. "Sometimes good people make bad decisions." It was a phrase I often told myself so I could fall asleep at night.

His eyes were red when he turned toward me. "But why haven't you denied stealing the money? Why are you taking the blame for something you didn't do? It doesn't make any sense."

I rocked from side to side, thinking fast. "I don't know. I caused George and Wendy enough problems, and the money wasn't worth making a big deal about."

"Really?" He looked at me, measuring the truth of my words.

"Yeah. Plus, I didn't think anyone would believe me. But I probably made a mistake. I should have told the truth and denied stealing the money. It's too late now in any case." A sharp pain tightened inside my skull, along with a new understanding. Cody had stolen the money I'd always assumed Riley had taken with her when she'd run away. The money had been there after she left. Why hadn't she taken it as she'd planned? I wasn't sure what it meant, if anything.

"Maybe we can keep this between us," he said.

I nodded. "I won't tell anyone your secret."

Cody laced his fingers in mine. Lucky for him, I was good at keeping secrets.

TWENTY-FIVE

Cody handed me an envelope bulging with cash. "Here's another three thousand. It's pretty much all I have." He'd taken out the maximum last night and again today, plus the money he kept at home. "That's eight thousand in total. I wish I had more."

"No. This is great. Thank you." My fingers clutched the envelope, but my heart sank. I was two thousand dollars short. I had three hours until the deadline.

"You shouldn't be meeting this guy alone." His eyes creased with concern. "Let me come with you."

"No. He won't like that. It will only make things worse."

"I'm worried about you." Cody had insisted on sleeping on the couch last night, refusing to leave me and Noah alone in the apartment.

"How about you stay here with Noah while I meet him in the alley? It would put my mind at ease to know you're with him."

"Okay. Yeah. I can do that."

"Can you come back at three thirty? I'm going over to Harper's to see if she can lend me the rest."

"Yeah. I'll be here."

I thanked Cody, hugging him before he left and wondering what I'd done to deserve him.

With Noah buckled into his car seat and a piece of medical tape wrapped around my finger, I drove toward Harper's house.

Harper flashed her white teeth when she opened her front door. "Come on in, guys."

Noah darted ahead and found April near the living room shelves where the toys were kept while Harper and I sat at her kitchen table.

Nervous energy coursed through me, and my fidgeting fingers picked at the edge of a plastic-coated tablecloth. "Sorry to invite ourselves over like this."

"I was having a lazy afternoon, anyway."

The doorbell rang just as I prepared to explain my financial predicament. She tipped her head back with a groan. "Shoot. That's my neighbor. She wants to talk about the annual neighborhood picnic. Before I knew you were coming over I told her I was available for a quick chat."

"No worries. I'll wait." I forced a stiff smile. The delay was tortuous—my time was running out.

Harper headed toward the door. "We'll talk outside if you don't mind staying with the kids. I promise to be back in ten minutes or less." The front door opened, and Harper's voice went up an octave as she greeted her neighbor. "Hi, Jenny! Let's go sit on the bench." The door closed behind them.

"Mommy, April needs a Band-Aid." Noah's voice pulled me toward the living room, where April crouched forward, tears leaking beneath her thick eyelashes. She straightened out her leg, revealing a scrape on her knee, droplets of blood poking through. "I hit my knee on that plastic thing," she said through heaving sobs.

"Oh, no. Let me get you a Band-Aid. Where does your mom keep them?"

"In her bathroom."

I gave April a wet paper towel to hold on her knee, then found my way upstairs to the primary bedroom and the attached bathroom. A linen closet stood just inside the door, and I opened it, scanning for bandages but not seeing any. A white plastic box sat on a high shelf, and I pulled it down, thinking it was a first-aid kit. But when I peeled back the lid, something entirely different stared back at me.

A newspaper clipping from fifteen years earlier lay on top, reading, "Still No Sign of Runaway Teen." Riley's sixteen-year-old face smiled beside the words. I lifted the paper and found another similar article behind it. Flipping through the stack revealed dozens more articles about Riley's disappearance and the related police investigation. Harper had collected these and saved them. My eyes hovered over one article with some of the words highlighted in yellow marker. It was entitled "Foster Girl's Friends Questioned in Disappearance." I had only just skimmed the first paragraph, which mentioned Harper and Jacob, when a door slammed downstairs. The box slipped from my hand, paper squares fluttering to the floor. I crouched down, fumbling to scoop them up and put everything away. Most of the headlines involved Riley's disappearance and the following investigation. Others were unrelated and spread across many years: wedding and graduation announcements, suspected arson at a downtown restaurant, a black-tie charity event in a nearby suburb, a boy charged with vandalism at the high school, and an announcement congratulating Harper's mom, Lydia, for winning the Berkley raffle at the summer street fair. I wanted to pore over all the articles concerning Riley, maybe find a new clue about where she'd gone, but there wasn't the time. I'd stumbled over Harper's private box of papers she deemed important for one reason or another, and I didn't want to be caught snooping. My hand shook as I replaced the lid and returned the box to the top shelf. After another quick scan of the shelves, I spotted the Band-Aids, swiped the box, and jogged downstairs.

"I found the Band-Aids," I yelled.

Harper looked mildly stunned to see me coming down the stairs. "Everything okay?"

"Just a little scrape." I nodded toward April, smiling to disguise my invasion of Harper's privacy. "April told me where to find the Band-Aids."

Harper took the box and put a bandage on April's knee without looking up.

I met her at the kitchen table, where she sat across from me. "Sorry about the disruption. So, was there a reason you wanted to stop by? Other than a surprise visit, I mean."

"Yeah." I stopped myself from speaking for a moment before wrangling my nerves and spitting it out. "Honestly, I'm in a little bit of a bind."

Harper cocked her head. "In what way?"

"I owe a lot of money to someone." I picked at my nails while I decided exactly how much to share. "I stole from someone I worked for out in California. I'm not proud of it, but that's the truth. The guy has tracked me down and is demanding I pay him by four o'clock today. He could be violent, so I need to come up with it."

The whites of Harper's eyes expanded. "My God! Are you serious?"

"Unfortunately, yes."

"That's scary. How much?"

"I'm two thousand dollars short."

"What are you going to do?"

My mouth went dry at her question. I assumed she would put two and two together and figure out why I was there. "Well, I was hoping you could lend it to me. I promise to pay you back as soon as I can."

Harper let out a low whistle. "That's a lot of money. I don't have much savings. I'm sorry."

"Please, Harper. I'm desperate." I pressed my fingers to my temples, shaking my head. "I hate being a burden on anyone, but I wouldn't be asking if I had any other options."

She rubbed the back of her neck, avoiding my pleading eyes. "I'm not rich. April and I live paycheck to paycheck, even with the little bit of child support we get. And Mom lives off her social security payments. She might have to move in with us soon." Harper lifted her phone and scrolled to something I couldn't see but guessed was her bank account. "Yeah. My mortgage payment just got taken out, and I don't get paid until a week from Thursday."

I chewed on my lip, hating the position I was putting Harper in. She had done so much for me, and I'd only made her life more difficult.

Harper sighed as she set her phone face-down on the table. "I have some cash I keep in a safe in my closet. I can lend you that. But I'll need you to repay me within three months. It's only a couple thousand dollars, but it's my entire safety net."

Despite the guilt trickling through me, my body practically levitated off the chair. I was so grateful to Harper. She had no obligation to give me anything, but she was pulling through. "Thank you so much. You have no idea how much this means to me. I'll pay you back within three months. I'll figure something out."

"Okay. Give me a minute." Harper disappeared up the stairs, where I heard a closet opening and shuffling noises. Two minutes later, she reappeared with a stack of bills ranging from twenties to hundreds. "Here it is. Danny wiped me clean during the divorce and left me with a mortgage I can barely pay. That's all I have."

"Thank you. I really owe you now."

"Yeah. You do." Her words carried an edge that I hadn't expected, something nasty gleaming in her eyes.

I turned away from her icy stare and stood up, fearing I'd landed on Harper's bad side. It was the place where Cody had warned me not to go. But maybe I'd been overly influenced by his stories. Harper was more likely annoyed to be handing over her safety net to the friend who had abandoned her fifteen years earlier. I couldn't say I blamed her. Hopefully, she'd come around once I repaid her the money.

At 3:58 p.m., I descended the wooden stairs on weak legs and entered the alley through the back gate. A canvas bag was slung over my shoulder with $10,000 bundled inside. Drew hadn't arrived yet. Only the trash and recycling bins stood nearby.

Closing my eyes, I leaned against the gate and waited. My eyelids opened when the sound of a motor reached my ears. The black BMW approached with my former boss behind the wheel. The engine cut when he was a few feet away, and he exited the car, looking more like he was dressed for a golf outing in his khaki shorts and polo shirt.

"We meet again." A crooked smile spread across his thin lips.

"Here is your money." I handed the bag to him, aware of the pepper spray in my back pocket. "Now we're even."

He reached inside the bag and flipped through the bills, mumbling numbers as he counted. "That's the right amount. But we're not even. You stabbed me." He looked up, making sure his words landed.

A knot formed in my gut. I was dumb to think the money would be enough. "I only stabbed you because you were assaulting me. I acted in self-defense. I called 911 so you could get help as soon as possible." I hoped Drew could hear the conviction in my voice.

"Ha. Right." He rolled back his shoulders as if preparing for a fight.

My knees wobbled beneath me, my vision blurring at the edges at the thought of whatever he might do next. I reached toward my back pocket. "Please. I have a son—"

He held a palm in my direction, signaling me to stop talking. "Save it. Lucky for you, I don't have time for this today." Before I could protest further, he was inside his SUV, zooming past me.

I doubled over with relief, resting my hands on my legs and sucking in as much of the exhaust-filled air as I could handle. I'd escaped immediate danger and hoped that would be the last time I'd ever see anyone related to Toven Brothers. But events in my life had rarely gone my way, and I worried Drew Toven wasn't done punishing me for my deception. Hopefully, the identification documents I'd ordered from Bea would arrive soon, giving me an emergency out if I needed it.

Cody and Noah were waiting for me inside the apartment. I liked the life I was building here and didn't want to leave. Not only was I falling for Cody, but in a strange way, living among Riley's former friends and foster family had allowed me to feel closer to my sister than I had since the night I'd slept in her bedroom and planned our escape. I'd found a new way of keeping Riley's memory alive if she had died out on the streets as I'd long suspected. Before returning to the apartment, I straightened my shoulders, bolstering myself. I would watch for trouble from my past, but I would do whatever it took to stay here in Berkley, living as my sister.

TWENTY-SIX

I set down a plate of scrambled eggs and hashbrowns, asking a woman eating alone if I could refill her coffee. She declined, and I returned to the kitchen, more grateful than ever for my shift at the diner. Even the sticky syrup jugs and the occasional difficult customer didn't bother me. The routine tasks of taking orders and serving food kept me occupied and my mind off my recent encounter with Drew Toven. With my former boss paid in full and out of town, I could breathe again and not constantly look over my shoulder. But Drew was unpredictable, and there was always a chance he could blow my cover just for the fun of watching my life implode.

My mind was restless, and my thoughts wandered whenever there was a lull between customers. The table where Jacob and McKenzie had dined a couple of weeks ago stood empty in the middle of the restaurant. Jacob's suspicious death lingered in my consciousness, refusing to leave. A heaviness in my gut told me his death hadn't been an accident. Drew had insisted he hadn't killed Jacob, and I felt inclined to believe him. I'd spent enough time with him to recognize that his confusion had been genuine when I'd asked him about the hit-and-run. Although

Drew was a first-class slimeball, I wasn't sure murder was in his nature. I wondered if the police had narrowed in on a list of suspects with black cars and a motive to kill Jacob. My suspicions circled back to McKenzie.

My shift ended at 2 p.m. I had an hour before picking up Noah from preschool. Instead of veering left to go home, I turned right, reaching the downtown area and continuing past it. The route took me through an older neighborhood with small brick houses and even smaller yards. It was where Jacob had been living with McKenzie before they'd broken up. Curiosity had gotten the better of me after our first encounter, and I'd looked up her address. Ignoring my second thoughts, I entered the subdivision and followed the road until I located the property. My foot hit the brake pedal before I reached the house to avoid being spotted. An electric blue Honda CRV sat in the driveway. Blue, not black. I wondered if it was McKenzie's car.

As if to answer my question, the front door burst open, and McKenzie hurried outside, digging in her purse. I ducked down, hoping she hadn't seen me. She unlocked the car and slipped inside, backing down the driveway and turning in my direction. My body slumped forward as I peeked above the steering wheel, horrified to find her looking directly at me. Her car jerked to a halt. The door slammed, and loud footsteps marched toward me. I sat up, shaking my head at the idiotic risk I'd taken.

McKenzie stood outside my window, arms crossed and fury practically steaming from her nostrils. She wore no makeup, and puffy bags beneath her eyes accentuated her jaundiced skin. Her highlighted hair was matted to her head as if she'd just rolled out of bed. I lowered my window, preparing for a firestorm.

"Hi," I said in a meek voice. "I'm sorry. I didn't realize this was your house."

"Bullshit." Her stare pinned me to my seat. "Why would you come here?" She tightened her lips. "Haven't you done enough?"

"I didn't do anything. I wasn't even interested in Jacob. That's what I told him during our dinner. I'm sorry he broke up with you."

McKenzie rolled her head back and laughed, leaving me confused. When she finished cackling, she turned her sallow face toward me. "You believed that?"

I didn't answer, assuming it was a rhetorical question.

She placed her hands on her hips. "Jacob never broke up with me."

"He didn't?"

"No. He said he wanted to have one dinner with you to learn what really happened to you back then, and then he'd never see you again. But he was worried you were too scared of me to agree to it, so he told you we broke up. It sounded like a good deal to me. And I'll admit, I was curious to hear your story too, so I agreed."

The landscape tilted around me. He'd duped me. "Wow."

"Jacob came home early from your dinner and was acting all quiet. He said you hadn't told him anything more than you'd already told that reporter. I was secretly happy because I knew it hadn't gone well between the two of you, that there was no lingering spark there. He said he wanted to go to the bar down the street to shoot some pool. Let off some steam. He came home about an hour or two later and we went to bed. The next morning, he went for his run like he did every Saturday..." McKenzie's face crumpled as her fingers covered her mouth, revealing her chipped blue nail polish. "I had no idea that would be the last time I'd see him."

All at once, my emotions warmed toward McKenzie, something in my chest shattering on her behalf.

"I'm so sorry, McKenzie. Jacob was such a good friend to me back then. This is devastating."

She offered a slight nod, maybe recognizing I was another victim in all of this.

"Do the police think someone hit him on purpose?" I asked.

"I don't think so. They questioned everyone who'd seen him recently and talked to the guys who'd been at the bar where he was playing pool. Everyone said he seemed fine. No one could identify anything out of the ordinary. Jacob didn't have any enemies."

I closed my eyes, realizing Jacob must have gone to shoot pool after he confronted me at my apartment. The story he'd told McKenzie held up, so no one would know I'd seen him again. As long as Brenda Harwood kept her mouth shut.

"Why did you come here?" McKenzie's question snapped me back to the present.

"I—I don't know. I guess I was looking for my own answers."

She followed my line of vision toward her car. "Yeah." She rubbed her chin as the hint of a smile formed on her lips. "I checked out your car too."

I couldn't help chuckling at that.

McKenzie bit back her smile, replacing it with a frown. She glanced toward her car. "I've got to go."

"I'm sorry again," I said as I raised my window.

McKenzie walked back to her car, zooming past me a few seconds later. I followed at a distance, losing sight of her as she turned at the next corner. It had probably been stupid of me to come here, but at least I'd answered some questions. McKenzie drove a blue car, not a black one. Her emotion, both here and at the funeral, felt authentic. Although she made an obvious suspect, I was certain McKenzie wasn't the one who'd hit Jacob. More importantly, Jacob hadn't told her what he suspected about me—that I wasn't Riley. He'd taken my secret to the grave.

.   .   .

The following afternoon, my feet ached as I pushed Noah on the swing at the park. Harper stood next to me, pushing April. She'd texted while I'd been at the café and asked if we wanted to meet for a playdate after I picked up Jacob from preschool. I was on time, but she was already there when I arrived.

I pulled in a breath of summer air through my nose. "It's nice to be outside, away from the smell of bacon grease and burnt coffee."

Harper giggled. "That must get old."

"It's temporary. Just a couple more months until I finish my real estate class."

"Exciting." Harper stepped back from the swings and faced me, her smile morphing into something more sinister. "When can I get my money back?"

The question came out of nowhere, and something in the air shifted between us Confused, I stopped pushing and looked at her. "I mean, not yet. It's only been three days."

She pursed her lips, clearly unhappy. "Mom said I made a mistake by giving it to you. I want it back now."

"I told you it might take three months." I spoke gently, reminding her of our agreement.

She rolled her eyes and huffed out a breath of annoyance. "What exactly did you do, anyway?"

I folded my arms across my chest, preparing to share a version of the truth. "When I was working a temp job in California, I helped myself to some money from my employer's safe. I shouldn't have done it, but I was desperate, and they were bad people. That's how I justified it." I left out the part about the sexual harassment and how I'd stabbed Drew.

"Sounds like another bad decision by Riley Wakefield." Harper's stone-cold voice sent another chill through my veins.

Her hostility toward me was palpable, and I took a step

away. My mind traveled over the comments I'd heard about her past with Riley and the preserved newspaper clippings in her bathroom closet. It occurred to me again that she still harbored resentment against Riley for skipping town without warning or contact.

I waved her over to a nearby bench. She followed, sitting next to me with a questioning look. "There's something I need to say, and I'm sorry I didn't say it sooner."

Harper raised an eyebrow, waiting for me to speak.

"Back in high school, we were best friends, but I ran away without any warning. I never called or sent you a text. All those years, you didn't know what happened to me or if I was even alive. That must have been so hard on you."

"Yeah. You were a pretty shitty friend in the end." Harper touched her neck, her skin pink with emotion.

"I'm sorry."

"Everyone at school thought you were dead. It felt like the whole town suspected me of killing you at one time or another. And don't get me wrong. I wanted to murder you that night of the dance. I really did. You were going to clear your conscience and ruin my chances of getting into college."

"I don't blame you," I said, although I didn't know what she was referring to. I didn't know that she and Riley had argued the night of the dance or what would have ruined Harper's college prospects.

"You just had to do whatever was best for you, no matter the impact on everyone else. You take and take and take. You take until there's nothing left." Harper turned toward me with a sneer that made my fingers tighten around the edge of the bench.

I dipped my face downward, realizing she was probably talking about the money I'd borrowed. "I'm going to pay you back."

"Yeah. I know."

Noah and April jumped from the swings and ran to a giant play structure with colorful bars and a wobbly bridge. We stood and followed them. Harper gave me the silent treatment for a few minutes, and I focused on entertaining the kids.

"How's your job going?" I asked.

Harper's demeanor shifted with the wind as she smiled and filled me in on the latest happenings at work. It seemed almost as if our previous conversation had never happened. She even encouraged me to join the company happy hour at a local tavern a week from Friday.

A black minivan rolled past at the edge of the grass and began to turn around.

Harper's head jerked toward it. "Oh, I've got to go. My mom's here already."

"You didn't drive?"

"No. She dropped us. My Jeep is on the fritz again."

"I can drive you home."

"That's okay. I told her we'd go to her house for an hour or two before dinner."

We said goodbye, and I assured Noah we could stay at the park for another half an hour. I watched Harper and April walk up the grassy incline. The car circled back around and stopped a few feet away. Harper's mom waved to me from behind the windshield, and I smiled and waved back. That's when something alarming caught my eye: a basketball-sized dent marring the front bumper. A cold sweat gathered on my skin, my limbs suddenly heavy. I stepped forward to get a better look, but Noah pulled me toward the slide. I went with him, unease lifting the fine hairs on the back of my neck as I tried not to imagine what—or who—she might have hit.

TWENTY-SEVEN

I fumbled around the apartment, searching for enough odds and ends to create a decent dinner. Three leftover slices of pizza and a few baby carrots would have to do. Noah clutched his stuffed monkey as he asked me a series of questions about the planets in our solar system, and I tried to answer them, but worries over the dent in the front of Harper's mom's car blurred my focus. I couldn't imagine Harper's mom had done anything to Jacob unless it had been purely accidental. Mrs. Parsons had been warm and welcoming toward me at the barbecue. While she was overly involved in Harper's life, she didn't strike me as someone who would leave Jacob in the alley to die. But I wasn't so certain about Harper. I'd glimpsed a disturbing side of her more than once, and I wondered what really lived behind her pearly smile.

My thoughts veered back to the morning Jacob died. I'd dropped Noah off with Harper the night before, making up the story about cutting my finger so I could go to Lucky's Bar. Harper mentioned that her mom was coming over to help with the kids for a while. She could have left April and Noah with her mom and borrowed the minivan, especially if her car had broken down. But she still would have had to explain away the dent when she returned.

The oven beeped, yanking my spiraling thoughts. I placed our pizza on two plates and sat across from Noah, recognizing a gaping hole in my half-formed theory. There was no motive for her to harm Jacob. At least not that I could identify. Harper and Jacob were casual friends, people who had both been extremely close to Riley at one time but not as close with each other. I wanted to ask her about the car damage and find out what had caused it, but things were already tense between us. I'd have to wait until the time was right, and I didn't want her to think I was accusing her or her mom of killing someone. There was probably an innocent explanation for the damaged bumper, nothing more than a run-in with a streetlight or a shopping cart.

Noah held up his carrots and pretended they were two people talking to each other. I laughed, putting the brakes on my imagination and focusing on what was most important: creating a better life for me and Noah. I'd stay out of things I couldn't control, and when it came to Jacob's death, I'd let the police do their job.

I wiped down a table at Songbird Café the next day, preparing for the lunch rush. The bells on the door jingled, and I did a double take at the person entering. McKenzie paused in the entryway, locking eyes with me. She had a skeletal look about her, and the puffy half-moons beneath her eyes had grown darker in the two days since I'd seen her. But she looked more put together today, with her hair combed and a hint of color on her lips. My boss, who usually greeted the customers, was back in the kitchen, so I forced my feet toward her, unsure what to expect. "Hello."

She squared her narrow shoulders toward me. "I'd like a table. In your section."

My hand touched a stack of plastic-coated menus. "Will anyone else be joining you?" I asked, reciting the line we'd been taught to ask people who showed up alone.

McKenzie's lower lip trembled, and I immediately realized my mistake.

"It's just me," she said, glancing at the floor.

I grabbed one menu, eager to turn away from her and unclear why she had come here. The look in her eyes was flat and indiscernible, like staring into two murky puddles. By the look of her, I got the feeling she'd come to the café because of me, not to eat a hearty brunch. I led her to a secluded table in the corner and placed a menu in front of her keeping my distance and half expecting her to swipe a knife from the table and hold it to my throat.

"Thank you." She barely looked at the menu. "I'll have the Greek salad, please."

With a nod, I took the menu and returned to the kitchen to put in her order. It struck me how differently McKenzie was acting compared to the last time she'd been here with Jacob. She was calm today. Almost too calm, like the eye of a hurricane. Or maybe my surprise visit to her house had warmed her toward me. I checked in on a few other tables and brought her food to her a few minutes later.

"I'm glad to see your appetite is back." I nodded toward the salad as I set it in front of her.

McKenzie did not acknowledge my comment but tapped her fingernail on the edge of her plate. She pushed the salad away and looked up at me. "Can you meet me at my house after work?" Her voice was barely above a whisper, but it cracked with desperation. "We need to talk. In private."

A warning twisted through me, and I had the feeling of being set up. Glancing over my shoulder, I checked for a co-conspirator, but no one was there.

She leaned toward me. "I need to ask you about a few things."

I wiped my hands on my apron, wondering if she had figured out my massive secret. Did she know I wasn't Riley? "I have to pick up my son from preschool at three."

"It will only take five minutes."

"Miss, can we get our bill?" A man's voice floated over from a table by the window.

"Please," McKenzie said more forcefully.

I gave the man a half-hearted wave and turned to face McKenzie. "Okay. My shift ends at two. I'll stop by for a few minutes."

McKenzie nodded almost imperceptibly, apparently satisfied, as I went to the computer to print the bill for my other table.

Tabitha caught me on my way back to the kitchen. "Hey. Want to grab dinner with me at Mack's tonight? I have to go on the late side, but I thought it would be fun to hang out," she paused, smirking. "You know, away from this place."

The invitation caused a tangle of anxiety to tighten inside me, but I told myself it could be enjoyable to do something social with someone who had no previous connection to Riley. I wouldn't have to watch my every word, and Mack's was a short walk from Marigold Street. "Yeah. I'll need to find a babysitter, but it should be fine. I'll text you later."

When I turned toward McKenzie's table, she was pushing back her chair and walking toward the exit. She'd left a twenty-dollar bill near her water and hadn't touched her salad.

TWENTY-EIGHT

At 2:15, my car idled near the curb a few doors down from McKenzie's address. Every cell in my body screamed at me to bail on the plan to meet with her and hightail it in the opposite direction. Jacob's girlfriend could be dangerous if she knew too much. But McKenzie had been less threatening toward me during our brief encounters the past two days, and I needed to uncover how much Jacob had told her, as uncomfortable as it might be. So I tucked my phone into my purse and continued driving along the suburban street, pulling into McKenzie's driveway and parking behind her car.

A bead of sweat rolled down my back as I approached the door and knocked. McKenzie answered immediately, waving me inside, a faint floral scent meeting me. I scanned the front room and the open doorways, checking for a possible ambush, but only a clock ticked from the wall. It seemed the two of us were alone in the house. A collage of framed black-and-white photos adorned the wall near the entryway. They were images of McKenzie and Jacob in various settings—heads pressed together at an outdoor concert, holding hands in a field of wild-flowers, perched on a boat in the middle of a picturesque lake, and raising wine glasses at a restaurant. A gulp formed in my throat. They'd had a good life, a vibrant life filled with adventures. Now McKenzie was on her own.

She caught me studying the photos. "We had fun together. At least, most of the time."

"I'm glad he found you." I kept my voice steady to let her know I wasn't bullshitting her. By all accounts, Riley's sudden departure had done a number on Jacob. He hadn't deserved the heartbreak.

McKenzie motioned me over to a couch fitted with a denim slipcover. She sat in a chair opposite me, her body rigid. "The detective called me yesterday. He said they're not closing the investigation yet, but it's looking more and more like Jacob's death was a tragic accident. The collision most likely freaked out a negligent driver who bolted to avoid being charged with anything."

"Wow. I guess that makes sense."

"It makes sense, but I don't believe it." McKenzie's stare pierced through me, and I squirmed in my seat like a worm on a hook. "I'm not saying you killed him," she said. "I've seen your car. But the timing is just so odd. He took you to dinner and lied about us having broken up."

I shifted my legs with a jerky movement. "I didn't know it was a lie."

She held up her hand. "It doesn't matter. He was upset when he got home. Unusually quiet. He goes out to play pool. The next morning, he gets run down by a car." She closed her eyelids for a second before opening them again. "Can you help me fill in the blanks? There must be something I'm missing."

"I wish I could, but I don't know any more than you do." I trained my eyes on the window to camouflage my lie. "During our dinner, Jacob wanted me to tell him all the sordid details about my time on the streets. I wasn't comfortable sharing that part of my life. He got frustrated and cut the date short.

Dropped me off at the Eckharts' so I could pick up my son. It seemed like he was still angry at me for taking off fifteen years ago."

McKenzie twisted her lips to the side. "There was that. But he'd said you guys had gotten into some kind of argument at your prom the last time he ever saw you."

"Yeah. It was stupid. I was jealous of another girl who I thought he liked." I spoke cautiously, repeating what I'd heard from Harper and others.

"No. Not that. He said earlier that night—or maybe the day before—you were going to confess something to him, something really bad that you and Harper had done. You had to get it off your chest. That's what Jacob told me. But then you changed your mind when he asked about it before the dance. You refused to tell him and acted like you'd never mentioned confessing anything. He said he was annoyed with you for lying, and that's why he started talking to that other girl."

"Oh." My tongue suddenly felt thick in my mouth. This must have been what Harper had been talking about at the playground, but she hadn't mentioned any specifics. "I'm not sure I remember that part."

"Hmm." McKenzie responded as if calling my bluff. "Anyway, I was a sophomore at Dondero High when you disappeared."

I nodded. Dondero was a high school in a neighboring suburb.

"But I remember how it was around here. There were so many whispers around town about this person or that person having killed you. But just as many people insisted you had run away. They said some guy at the mall had lured you out to California. Jacob looked everywhere for you, even flew out to L.A. a couple of years after high school to ask around. He couldn't find any trace of you. At some point, years after the police stopped looking for you, Jacob decided that Harper must have done something to you that night."

I inhaled in a sharp breath, remembering the box of newspaper clippings in Harper's bathroom and wondering if Jacob had known something I didn't.

"Jacob wasn't sure if she'd killed you on purpose or accidentally, and of course, he had no proof either way. But he thought Harper must have attacked you or something to stop you from confessing whatever you guys did. He repeated his hunch occasionally over the last few years, but I always told him he was letting his imagination run away. He stayed in touch with Harper, posing as her friend. Or at least an acquaintance. He was convinced she'd slip up and say something to reveal what she'd done. But she never did. And then you came back." McKenzie chuckled, but it sounded sad. "I think he felt a little like an idiot."

"Oh." I swallowed, but it didn't ease my dry throat. "He shouldn't have felt that way. He couldn't have known where I was."

"Here's the thing. I don't know what other conversations went on between Harper and Jacob. She and I weren't friends. But when the detective returned Jacob's phone to me last night, I noticed something odd." She pulled an iPhone out of her pocket and scrolled through it. "I was looking through his texts. This was one of the last messages he received besides the ones I sent him." McKenzie extended her arm, and I took the phone, reading the open message.

How did the dinner go?

It was from Harper. Jacob hadn't responded.

I sat up straighter. Harper had sent me an identical message at about the same time. What had she been doing? Comparing notes? I tore my gaze from the phone and looked at McKenzie. "What does this mean?"

"I don't know. Maybe nothing." McKenzie placed her hands on top of her twiggy legs. "But what if Jacob didn't respond to her because he confronted her in person? What if he said something that made her angry?"

"Like what?" I asked, but the knot in my gut already had an idea. Jacob could have told Harper that he knew I wasn't Riley. He could have accused her of having killed Riley. Maybe he'd demanded answers the same way he'd demanded action from me. Harper, desperate to keep him quiet, could have taken her mom's car the next morning and hit him as he jogged his usual route. I steadied myself against the couch cushion, knowing I couldn't share my theory with McKenzie. Or anyone.

McKenzie spoke again. "I don't know. It doesn't make sense. I guess I saw this text, and I just thought..." She rested her head against the back of the chair, closing her eyes. "I just thought there must be more to the story. I have no proof. Nothing to take to the police. I thought you might know something because you saw Jacob that night and you're friends with Harper."

"I'm sorry. I don't have much to add." A sour taste formed in the back of my mouth at my lie as the memory of the dent in Harper's mom's black car clouded my brain. I could mention the bumper damage to McKenzie, but that would only lead to more questions, which could put me and Noah in jeopardy. And it was just as likely that Jacob had ignored Harper's text. Besides, Stacy, the woman in L.A., had spotted my sister multiple times, so Harper couldn't have murdered her. It was more likely that Harper's mom had damaged her car months ago and hadn't gotten around to fixing it. There was no need to put my massive secret at risk of exposure. I offered a sad smile. "We all want answers, McKenzie. But you might be grasping at straws here. I'm not sure this text means anything sinister happened between Jacob and Harper."

McKenzie stared straight ahead as if in a trance. "Yeah. Maybe not. I feel like I'm losing my mind."

"I'm sorry, but I need to go. I have to pick up my son from preschool. You should eat something healthy and get some rest."

McKenzie nodded but remained motionless on the chair.

I stood and let myself out, closing the door gently behind me. Unease expanded in my stomach as I started my car and drove away. I hadn't been aware of Jacob's suspicions over Harper, but Harper had been acting strangely toward me. The stories Cody had told me about how she'd stalked her ex to the point he needed a restraining order replayed in my mind. I'd witnessed Harper's moodiness, but did she also have a violent and explosive side I hadn't seen? Was she being so nice to me because she knew I wasn't Riley, an admission that would reveal her own guilt? I couldn't wrap my brain around it; I didn't know what was true and what were wild stories I'd concocted.

I parked in the church lot and waited outside the preschool door, returning friendly nods to a few other parents. The doors opened, and we filed into the room. Noah looked up from a game, his face brightening at seeing me. I wrapped my arms around him, certain of one thing: protecting our new identity and building a stable life for my son was more important than discovering the truth about who had killed Jacob. Noah clutched a stack of art projects as I loaded him into the car and drove back to the apartment. But as much as I tried to contain them, my thoughts strayed back to what McKenzie had said. Jacob had suspected Harper of murdering Riley.

My searches for Riley, both online and in person, had always come up empty. In fifteen years, there'd been no sign of her using bank accounts, applying for a driver's license, or checking into any hospital. I often wondered if Lee Clavey was somewhere across the country conducting similar searches for Gina Holland, the woman who'd killed his sister, and I suspected his searches came up empty too.

But I'd had a promising lead with Stacy, although she'd been consistently vague about my sister's whereabouts and sometimes confused. Then, Stacy had stopped returning my calls. When there'd been no trace of Riley for years, I'd accepted the likelihood that Riley had succumbed to a similar drug-addicted fate as our mother. Nameless women disappeared in the shadowy corners of big cities all the time, and their bodies were often never recovered. Still, I'd held on to a sliver of hope that Riley was alive under a new identity, living on a grand estate in the Parisian countryside or sailing around the world on a yacht, secretly laughing at everyone.

But now, a more troubling theory blackened my thoughts. Cody's confession that he'd stolen the Eckharts' secret stash of money churned through my memory. Riley wouldn't have left without the money. We'd discussed it at length the night I slept over. The cash would have been easy to access and was her only safety net. What if Stacy was mistaken about having seen Riley in L.A.? Jacob had been suspicious of Harper all these years. Now, he was dead. My intuition gnawed inside me, screaming for attention. I could no longer blindly blame my sister's disappearance on a series of reckless decisions I believed she'd made. I realized maybe Riley hadn't lost her way on the streets, a victim of her own rash choices combined with the poor hand life had dealt her. Perhaps she had been a different kind of victim, one who'd died at the hands of someone she'd known and trusted. For the first time, I faced the possibility that Riley had never made it out of this town alive.

TWENTY-NINE

Later that afternoon, Cody called to see what I was doing. I wasn't used to having someone who cared enough to call and check in on me, and I wished I could be completely honest about everything. Instead, I glossed over the most troubling parts of my day, mentioning my dinner plans with Tabitha and then redirecting the conversation back toward him. Just as we ended the call, a text popped on my screen.

> *Can you watch April for a few hours tonight? I have a date with a guy I met online!*

My jaw tightened as I read Harper's text. A day or two ago, I would have bent over backward to repay her for the times she'd watched Noah, but the conversation with McKenzie zipped through me like a warning. Harper could be dangerous, and it was safer to keep my distance. And tonight wasn't good in any case because I had plans. Wendy had confirmed that Noah could stay with them until I returned from dinner with Tabitha, but I didn't want to dump an extra child on them.

I'm so sorry. I wish I could but I'm going to Mack's tonight with a co-worker. I don't think George and Wendy can handle more than one kid.

A few minutes later, she wrote back.

Okay. I'll check with mom.

I sent another message in reply, hoping to stay on her good side.

Can't wait to hear about your date.

I paced the living room, shaking off my worries over Harper. But the dark question lurking in my thoughts refused to leave as I entered the bedroom. I crouched on the floor beside my bed, pulling my knees to my chest. My hand trembled as I stared at the worn scrap of paper I'd saved for nearly fifteen years: Stacy's phone number.

I gritted my teeth and pressed the numbers on my phone, hearing the ring. Once. Twice. Three times. This probably wasn't Stacy's number anymore if she was even alive. I closed my eyes, my conviction fading with each ring. *Please. Please.*

"Hello?"

My eyes popped open, a sharp breath lodging in my windpipe. I thought I recognized the throaty voice. "Stacy?"

"Yes."

"Hi. This is Sheri," I said, using the name I'd given her. "I met you many years ago in L.A. Over by the Days Inn."

Only heavy breathing met my ears. A dog barked somewhere in the background.

I continued. "I was looking for my sister, Riley. You said you'd seen her over the years, but she went by a different name.

I gave you a few envelopes to pass on to her, which you said you did."

She coughed, but it was muffled.

"Do you remember any of this?"

"Yes."

I waited, but she said nothing further, so I kept prodding. "I was just wondering, how sure are you that the person you saw was my sister?"

Stacy let out a prolonged sigh from the other end of the phone. "Aw shit. I had a feeling this day would come."

My fingers tightened on the phone. I wasn't sure what she was getting at. "What day?"

"I remember you, sweetheart. I was in a bad place for so many years with the drugs. A really bad place. But I'm in recovery now and need to make amends to the people I've wronged."

"What do you mean?"

She sniffled. "I lied to you. I never saw your sister. I'm sorry, hon."

My mouth was parched. I couldn't speak.

She continued. "I knew Max, though. All of us did. He had a group of three or four girls with him. Your sister wasn't one of them." She paused as if to let her words sink in. "After you showed me the photo of Riley the first time, I saw that envelope in your bag. I spotted it even before you offered it up. It was stuffed with something. I thought there was a chance there might be money in there, so I told you I'd seen Riley, and I'd give it to her. Same with all the other times. I spent the money on drugs."

My head suddenly weighed a thousand pounds. What an idiot I'd been. I should have known better. My entire adult life had been spent defrauding people, living on the run, and pretending to be someone I was not. Meanwhile, I'd been so blinded by the desire to find my sister that I'd become easy prey myself. I'd been duped. Stacy had never met Riley, had never seen her, and had definitely not given her the envelopes.

I moved the phone away from my ear.

"I'm really sor—"

I hung up. Hot tears stung my eyes, and my body trembled with a horrific understanding. Riley had never made it to L.A. She must have kept her word to me and not gone with Max. I dug my fingernails into my palms at Stacy's betrayal, at my own stupidity. The story I'd believed for so many years had never been true. A dagger of grief and fear speared through my chest, along with a dark knowing that I'd never see my baby sister again. Someone in this town must have done something horrible to prevent Riley from leaving. And I wondered again if that person could have been Harper.

A light wind tousled Wendy's hair as she sat in a lawn chair on the patio, touching the screen of her phone. Noah scurried down the steps, eager to kick a soccer ball around the backyard, and I reminded him to be careful of the native grasses Wendy had planted near the fence. The new plantings were attractive, and it was clear Wendy had a knack for gardening. But there was something other than gardening tips on my mind.

"Mind if I sit with you for a few minutes?" I asked as I approached.

"Of course." Wendy motioned to a nearby chair. "I'm only looking for a new dress to wear to that charity event I told you about. I'm happy to have the company."

I took a seat. "Thanks again for watching Noah tonight."

"It's my pleasure."

Noah busied himself, arranging sticks on either side of the yard to form two lopsided goals. I buried the shock of my recent revelation as I listened to Wendy talk about the weather and a new healthy recipe she planned to make for dinner.

When there was a lull in the conversation, I addressed the worry lodged in my brain. "I was thinking about the people I used to hang out with in high school—Jacob and Harper."

Wendy shook her head slowly. "It's a shame about Jacob. It really is. He was much too young."

"Yeah." I angled my chair more toward Wendy, leaning closer. "When I came back, you mentioned that you'd always thought Jacob and Harper had somehow been involved in my disappearance."

She waved a hand to dismiss me as she chuckled. "Oh, lordy. That shows how much I know. Good thing I'm not a detective."

"Yeah. But why did you think that? You must have had a reason."

Wendy's lips pulled back as if she was struggling to come up with an answer. "No real reason, really. It was just a hunch based on how much time the three of you spent together. And they were the last ones seen with you. At least, Harper was. But you would know better than me."

"Right." I paused, realizing this was a tricky conversation. "It's just that..." I stopped again, choking on my words. "Was there anything Jacob or Harper said to make you think they'd harmed me?"

"Not that I can remember. But people talked, you know. I heard that you and Jacob had argued that night. And Harper was always mad at you for one thing or another. Every day you didn't come home, my panic grew, and I guess my imagination did too. After a while, I couldn't help wondering if one or the other of them had whacked you over the head with a tire iron or something like that. Teenagers act impulsively. Something about their brain not being fully developed. They don't always think things through." She crossed her legs, blinking against the sun that had reappeared from behind a cloud. "It probably would have taken more than one person to hide a body, so that's the only reason I thought maybe they'd done something terrible together. But then the police said you ran away. So, I had to believe the authorities knew what they were talking about. It was a more likely explanation than murder in any event, and it explained why you helped yourself to our stash of money."

"Yeah." I tightened my fingers into fists, knowing that wasn't what Riley had done. She hadn't left with Max and hadn't stolen the Eckharts' money.

"And it turns out the police were correct because here you are, alive and well. And with an adorable son, no less."

I forced a smile and a nod. "Right. Usually, the simplest explanation is the correct one."

"Very true." Wendy knitted her brows together. "Why are you asking about it, anyway?"

"I don't know." I touched my chest, thinking of how to backpedal. "Obviously, my friends didn't harm me. But the other day, Cody told me some unsettling stories about Harper. I guess she went through a pretty ugly divorce and acted violently toward her ex to the point he had to get a restraining order. Maybe you got the same unpredictable vibe from her back then. Not that it really matters."

"Huh. I hadn't heard about that." Wendy tapped her fingers on the metal arm of the chair. "Have you felt threatened by Harper since you've been back?"

"No. She's been a good friend and a big help with Noah." I glanced away, swallowing the information about the money she lent me and the hot resentment that came with it, not to mention the box of newspaper clippings in her bathroom that now seemed disturbing, like trophies a serial killer would keep.

"I see. Sounds like it's best to let it slide, then. A lot of people's lives were upended after you left. The rumor mill convicted everyone close to you of murder at one point or another. Even George and I felt like we had to hide out for a few months until things settled down. The neighbors love to gossip, especially that busybody next door." Wendy's eyes held a dazed look, and she suddenly appeared older than her years.

"I'm sorry for the trouble I caused." I glanced toward Brenda's house. The neighbors had an even more contentious history than I'd realized.

Wendy swatted a mosquito off her arm. "There's no need to apologize. I'm only saying that Harper has been forgiving toward you. That counts for something."

"That's good advice."

I sat with Wendy until the sun moved lower in the sky and the trees cast long shadows over the patio. At last, she stretched her arms in the air and said she needed to start on dinner, so I told her I'd drop off Noah at eight. I took Noah back up to the apartment, thinking about our conversation. Wendy probably thought she'd dissuaded me from suspecting Harper of anything, but her words only supported my suspicions. Wendy had made a good point about a single person not having the strength to hide a dead body. If Harper had killed Riley, it would have been nearly impossible for her to cover it up on her own. I couldn't help wondering who would have helped her. Jacob's face flashed in my mind, but the theory didn't fit. He'd been intent on turning me in and exposing my true identity. He was the only one in this town I was certain I hadn't fooled.

But another person often lingered in Harper's shadow, always at her daughter's beck and call: her mom, Lydia, with her matching clothes and haircut and weekly visits to Harper in college. She acted more like a best friend than a mom; according to others I'd talked to, that had always been the case. I wondered if she'd helped Harper cover up an unspeakable crime. That was the type of thing a desperate parent might do to protect a child.

The theory rearranged all the facts that hadn't made sense previously. But there was a lingering question. What was the shameful secret that Riley and Harper shared? What had Riley threatened to tell? It must have been something bad enough that Harper believed it would prevent her from going to college if it were exposed.

Sharing my thoughts and theories with anyone was too risky. I would have to dig for answers on my own.

THIRTY

Dinner at Mack's, a local dive restaurant and bar, was just what I needed. Time passed quickly as Tabitha and I commiserated about our low wages and difficult customers over a few shared appetizers. She ordered vodka and tonics while I stuck to water. I could have used a drink, but I had to keep up my appearance as a successfully recovering drug addict, and I assumed that meant avoiding alcohol too. Even without a stiff drink, it was a relief to escape the swirling suspicions in my head for a couple of hours and hang out with someone who had never known Riley. Tabitha's boyfriend was arriving late to meet her for a nightcap, but it was already close to eleven, and I needed to get on my way to pick up Noah.

It was dark when I left and headed down the sidewalk, the night air balmy against my face. My apartment was only seven blocks away. I'd walked to the restaurant but hadn't fully considered the return trip in the dark. Thankfully, a line of streetlamps shone overhead as I shoved my hands in my pockets and forged toward home. The shops and most restaurants were closed, with only an occasional car passing on the road, and the usually vibrant strip felt desolate. I turned off the main road into the neighborhood, where it was darker without the glow of the streetlamps. My foot hit an uneven section of sidewalk, and I stumbled forward, catching my balance and continuing on my poorly lit path. I reached a barricade of orange barrels and plastic tape where workers were redoing the sidewalk, forcing me onto the street.

A motor sounded behind me, growling louder as it approached. I flipped around to look. The vehicle's high beams glared against the black night, burning my retinas. I expected the driver to slow down after catching me in the bright lights. Instead, the motor revved, and the driver accelerated toward me.

Bright spots floated before me, along with Jacob's recent fate. I tried to scream, but fear strangled my throat. My feet moved on their own, one in front of the other, racing to get around the barricade. I dove face-first into the narrow strip of grass along the sidewalk, feeling a gust of wind as the vehicle zoomed past and squealed around a turn at the next corner. I buried my face in my hands, remaining on the ground for a minute or two to catch my breath and calm my pounding heart. The driver had been aiming for me. I was sure of it. It must have been someone who'd known about my plans with Tabitha and had waited for their chance to catch me alone and off guard. I hadn't gotten a good look at the car because the headlights blinded my eyes. I couldn't even say what color it was, but nothing white or silver had stood out against the night, so the vehicle must have been dark. Of course, George and Wendy knew about my dinner plans, but I'd also mentioned the same details to Cody. And McKenzie had been at the diner when Tabitha invited me out. But Harper was the one who worried me the most.

"Are you okay?" The silhouette of a man jogged toward me, his flashlight bouncing as he pulled his dog behind him.

"Yeah. I'm okay." I got on all fours before standing on

shaking legs. "A car almost hit me when I was going around that barricade. Did you see it?"

"No. I heard it but was too far down the street." He nodded behind him. "People speed through here all the time. There's so many bad drivers out there." He looked me up and down, glancing toward the sidewalk under construction. "It's hard to see people at night when they're wearing all black." He shook his head. "I'm not saying it's your fault; I only know I sometimes can't see people in dark clothes until I'm almost on top of them. That's probably what happened."

I looked down at my clothes—the black pants and shirt with the dark denim jacket I'd worn in case the restaurant's air conditioning was too cold. It was possible I'd merely encountered a reckless driver who was going too fast and hadn't seen me until the last minute, but it felt like too much of a coincidence.

After reassuring the man that I wasn't injured, I brushed the grass clippings from my clothes and walked the remaining three blocks to the Eckharts' house, staying safely on the sidewalk. Noah was asleep on a blanket when I entered through the back sliding door. Wendy said everything had gone smoothly, but she and George never moved from the couch, fixated on an old movie starring Audrey Hepburn. I slipped Wendy a few bills, deciding not to mention the near-miss on my walk home for fear she'd make a big deal of it and draw more unwanted attention to me.

"Thank you, dear," she said. "We're happy to watch him anytime."

I said good night and carried Noah and his blue stuffed monkey up to the apartment. My mind and body reeled with paranoia. I needed time to think.

THIRTY-ONE

The following days passed in a blur of tangled thoughts and unchecked suspicions. I wasn't sure about any of the facts surrounding whatever fate my sister had met. I wavered on whether I believed that Harper could have harmed Riley and attempted to run me down or whether I'd merely created a fantastic story in my head. But I kept my distance from her to be safe. Thankfully, McKenzie did not show up at the diner or try to contact me again. Guilt nibbled at my conscience for misleading her about my interactions with Jacob the night before he died. She'd already been in so much pain and had unwittingly helped lead me closer to the truth.

On Friday evening, I drove ten minutes to Cody's address in Birmingham with a pre-made salad, and Noah buckled into his car seat. He had invited us over to his place for a barbecue. Initially, I'd suggested we eat in the Eckharts' backyard, confident that George and Wendy wouldn't mind if we used their grill, but Cody had grunted and said he preferred not to. He liked having his private space where he wasn't reminded of being a teenager who might be grounded for inadvertently breaking a rule. "You know how it was with them."

"Of course," I said, reminding myself I wasn't merely a desperate woman who'd been taken in by the friendly older couple. I was Riley, who had lived with the Eckharts for a year as a teenager and had been just as annoyed as Cody by their rules. "It'll be nice to see your place."

Now, I held Noah's hand with the salad balanced in the crook of my arm. The sand-colored stones and metal and glass balconies of Cody's condo building rose above us, casting a shadow as I pushed the doorbell for unit three. The building was much nicer than expected for someone who worked at a computer repair business, and I realized he must have been doing even better than I thought, financially speaking. Maybe I shouldn't have felt bad about borrowing so much money. A buzzing noise unlocked the door, and Noah and I followed the stairs up three flights, where Cody waited for us in an open doorway.

"Welcome," he said, ushering us into a bright, high-ceilinged living room lined with oversized windows and a spacious balcony that jutted off the side. The aroma of roasting food met us, along with an acoustic guitar playing quietly through a speaker. The vibe was calm and inviting.

I gazed from wall to wall, taking it all in, before handing the salad to Cody. The place looked like it had been decorated by a professional designer, in stark contrast to the garage apartment. "I love your place."

"Thanks. I bought it four years ago." He set my bowl on the counter and nodded toward the oven. "I thought I'd get the potatoes done ahead of time."

"It smells good in here." Noah hopped on one foot in a zigzag pattern, a new trick he must have picked up at preschool. I trailed a few inches behind him, worried one wrong bounce might send him crashing through the glass.

I placed my hand on Noah's shoulder. "Be careful near the windows."

Cody slipped in front of us and opened the door to the balcony, letting in a rush of warm air and the traffic noise from the street below. "We can sit outside. I'll get us some lemonade."

"Can I help?" I asked.

"Nah." He waved toward the chairs. "Go ahead and make yourself at home."

I stepped outside with Noah, who hugged my leg as he peered through the metal slats. "Look! Cool!" He pointed to the cars three stories below and a woman walking a black-and-white dog. Cody's condo was in a bustling neighborhood near a popular shopping and dining area.

A black BMW SUV with tinted windows swung around the bend, idling at the stop sign below. I tightened my fingers on the railing. Was Drew Toven still in town and following me? Panic rose in me, clogging my throat and making it difficult to breathe. The SUV pulled forward, revealing a bright yellow license plate holder. My eyelids lowered. It wasn't the same car; it was only someone else going about their day.

"Everything okay?" Cody stood next to me, holding out a drink. "You look like you've seen a ghost."

I gripped the sweating glass and took a swig, feeling the cold liquid seep through me. "Yes. I'm fine. Thank you." I focused on relaxing my voice as I motioned toward the rows of stately townhomes and mature maple trees across the way. "What a great view."

"It's not Manhattan, but it beats the Eckharts' backyard."

"Yeah, because it's yours."

Cody offered a knowing smile, and it was clear we were both grateful to be far away from the group homes of our youth. My heart rate returned to normal as we took our seats and chatted about the neighborhood, our workdays, and other harmless topics. Cody busied himself at the grill, basting the barbecued chicken. Eventually, our plates were full of food, and we dined al fresco around the little table on the balcony.

Occasionally, a motor rumbled, or a man's voice sounded from below, causing me to peer through the railings. The earlier sight of the SUV had set me on edge, along with the recent realization that Harper might have known all along that I wasn't Riley. A conversation from days earlier suddenly popped into my memory. I'd thanked her again for the money she'd lent me and then said, "I owe you." She'd responded, "Yeah. You do." It wasn't her words but the way she'd spoken them, as if she was aware of my massive fraud and had done her part to help me protect it. But what was her end game?

"Can I use the potty?" Noah's voice brought me back to my surroundings.

"Yes. Do you know where it is?"

Cody motioned to the living room. "It's right around the corner, big guy."

Noah nodded, pulled the slider open, and disappeared toward the bathroom.

A car sputtered, and I flinched, eyeing the street.

Cody leaned back in his chair, a mixture of amusement and confusion on his face. "You keep looking out there. Are you expecting someone?"

"No. Sorry." I slid deeper into my chair, focusing on him. "When you were in the kitchen, I thought I saw my former boss again. It wasn't him, but it made me remember that he could return anytime."

"Did he say he was coming back?"

"Not necessarily."

"You paid him back. He lives on the other side of the country and would be stupid to waste any more energy on you."

"I hope you're right." I rubbed my forehead, finding it slick with sweat. "Even if he's gone, Harper has been so weird about the money she lent me. She really wants her two thousand dollars returned right away."

"Didn't she just lend it to you?"

"Yeah. It's strange. She said her mom told her it was a mistake to give it to me. She's so angry about it."

A gust of wind held a piece of Cody's hair in the air. "I moved some money around in the last few days. I can give you the money right now to pay her back. You don't want to be on her bad side. Trust me."

"Are you sure?"

"Positive." He reached for my hand, our fingers intertwining as a shadow passed over his face. "Things aren't so easy for people like us. We never had a safety net like our friends did. Maybe we made more mistakes than most to find our way, but we did our best. I want to help you stay on the right path. I trust you. You can add this amount to what you already owe me. Pay it back whenever you can."

I gave his hand an extra squeeze, astounded by my good fortune. Cody understood me in a way no one had before. "Thank you. I'll give you back every penny as soon as possible. I promise."

He dipped his head and pulled out his phone, pressing the screen a few times. "You have Venmo?"

"Yes." I gave him my Venmo handle.

Noah returned from the bathroom, his pudgy hand patting my leg. "I'm bored."

He'd been on good behavior for nearly three hours and was reaching his limit. As much as I felt for him, I didn't want my time with Cody to end. "How about we turn on a show for you?" I faced our host. "Is that okay?"

"Of course."

We moved to the living room, where I turned on the TV and flipped through the guide, finding the Cartoon Network.

We didn't have that channel at the apartment, and Noah was instantly in heaven.

Cody leaned against his granite kitchen counter, scrolling on his phone. "Holy crap." His face fell as his eyes flicked from his screen to me and back again.

"What's wrong?"

He pointed to his phone, his skin taking on the color of the ceiling paint. "I subscribe to the daily headlines. This is you."

"What are you talking about?" I asked, although by the shock and anger that stretched across his face, I had a pretty good idea. The cartoons droned in the background, and my head felt like it might explode. He'd found me out.

Cody set his jaw, reading aloud from whatever email he'd received. "Authorities are still on the hunt for a thirty-one-year-old woman who stabbed the co-owner of a construction company in Las Vegas after stealing fifteen thousand dollars from the company safe."

He stepped toward me, flipping the phone in my direction. To my horror, a close-up of my face appeared on the screen, my hair long and blonde, my makeup overdone. But that was me staring at the camera. Those were my lips curved into a fake smile.

My panicked eyes shot toward Cody, who aimed a death stare at me. It felt like the floor had opened beneath me, and I was falling.

Cody returned to reading. "The woman, who lived under the stolen identity of Sandra Matthews, has likely altered her appearance and is using a different name."

I eyed the door, planning an escape route. Or I could talk my way out of it. "That's not me."

"She has a son who is approximately four years old, likely with her." Cody was speaking too loudly now and clearly didn't believe a word I said. "If you have any information, please contact authorities." When he raised his head, his pupils had grown wide. "What the hell? That's you! Did you stab someone?"

"It's not what you think." But I had stabbed someone. And I'd caused someone else's death years earlier. I'd spent my life running. I'd escaped the authorities, but karma always caught up with me. The urge to flee overtook me, and I pivoted on my heel, grabbing Noah's arm and pulling him off the couch. He began crying as I snatched my purse from the counter and hustled toward the door. "We've got to go, Noah."

But Cody sprinted ahead, stretching out his arms to block our exit. "You're not leaving until you tell me what's going on." A tendon stretched along his neck as he spat words through his teeth. "I can't believe I didn't see it. You're a con artist!" He slammed his hand against the door. "Did you scam me out of all that money?"

Noah whimpered. I lowered my head, releasing my son's hand and wrapping my arm around him. Cody had caught me, and there was nowhere else to go. He knew where to find me even if I fled to the apartment. He'd tell the Eckharts.

I covered my mouth, feeling nauseous. Then I patted Noah on the head, guiding him back to the couch. "You can go back to your cartoons."

I lowered my voice, addressing Cody. "Let's talk outside."

His fingers gripped my arm more tightly than necessary as he pulled me out to the balcony. Once the door was closed, he removed his hand and sneered at me. "I thought our connection was real."

I scanned the neighboring balconies, finding them empty. Even so, I lowered my voice to a whisper, hating myself and my bad decisions for leading me to this point. There was no other option but to come clean with him. "What we have is real, Cody. I lied to you about a few things, but our connection isn't a lie. Everything I told you about growing up in the group homes was true." I blinked, hot tears stinging my eyes.

"I'm in a bad situation. It's really bad. Worse than I told you before."

"Riley, why didn't—"

I held up a hand. "I have to tell you something important. You'll want to call the police, but I need you to hear me out until the end."

He studied my face, indecision flitting through his eyes.

"Promise?" I asked.

He threw his hands up. "Yeah. Go ahead."

"I am not Riley. I'm Gina Holland. Riley was my younger sister. Just like her, I grew up in group homes and foster care. We were separated at a young age. She was three, and I was six. Riley and I only met once since being removed from our mother's care—two weeks before she supposedly ran away."

Cody leaned against the railing, his eyes traveling over every millimeter of my face. "What the—"

I kept my voice even as I told Cody the rest of the story, not always getting things in the correct order. I told him how I'd agreed to run away with Riley to prevent her from leaving with the creepy guy named Max, how I'd accidentally killed the bully from the group home a couple of days before we'd planned to leave and had to flee, how I'd changed my identity and searched the streets of L.A. for Riley, never seeing her. I told him about the woman named Stacy, who'd assured me she'd seen Riley on the streets over the years. I explained how I'd spent years living on the run, trying to make a fresh start in each place. But my luck always ran out eventually, causing me to make reckless decisions. Sometimes, I'd done illegal things out of desperation, like stealing money and valuables. But ever since what happened with Marianne Clavey, I'd tried to avoid detection. Once I got pregnant and Noah's father left, I put all of myself into being the best mother for my son, no matter what it took. Everything I'd done since getting pregnant with Noah was for him.

I told Cody how I'd attempted to set down roots in Vegas, living as Sandra Matthews until things turned dangerous with Drew Toven. I'd stolen Drew's money, stabbing him in self-defense in the process. Out of desperation, I'd resorted to becoming my sister, the foster child who had run away so many years earlier. The one whom I guessed barely anyone had missed but with whom I shared a strong resemblance.

Cody lifted his head, a stunned look in his eyes. "You're Riley's sister?"

I bit my lip, giving a nod.

A long stream of air blew from his lips as he ran his fingers through his hair. His gaze traveled toward a distant spot on the horizon, but when he refocused on me, a hint of admiration gleamed in his eyes. "That's incredible. It explains why you seem so different from the girl I knew back then."

"Yes. Because I'm not her." I paused, giving him the chance to say something else, but he continued staring as if caught in a daydream. "Anyway," I continued, "when Drew Toven found me, I told you as much as I could. I needed to borrow money so I could pay back what I'd stolen, just like I told you."

Cody nodded.

"I'm not scamming you, Cody. You're the first person I've met in so long who understands me. You're so kind, smart, and handsome. Generous too." I gave him a sheepish smile and was relieved when a dry laugh escaped his mouth. "I may have lied about my past, but my feelings about you are true." I watched his face, waiting for him to either wrap me in a hug or push me over the railing.

He did neither. Instead, he crossed his arms in front of himself. "I'm not judging you. I've hardly lived my life on the straight and narrow. But I'm going to need some time to take this all in. I mean, you can't live under a fake identity for the rest of your life."

I shrugged, silently disagreeing with him.

He gave his head a little shake. "Is that everything?"

"I wish it were, but there's something else."

Cody's eyebrows raised. "What is it?"

"Since I've been back here, I've realized I was wrong about what happened to Riley. She didn't run away. I discovered that Stacy had lied to me for years about seeing Riley out there. Riley was never with Max. I'm pretty sure she never went to L.A."

The creases around Cody's mouth deepened. "Where did she go?"

I paused, gathering the courage to say what came next. "I don't think she ever made it out of this town. I'm starting to believe that someone here killed her. And I have an awful feeling I might be next."

THIRTY-TWO

Car brakes squealed from the intersection below the balcony. A motor revved and faded in the distance. A slack-jawed Cody shook his head at my murderous theory. "Why would you think someone killed Riley?"

The volume of his voice had increased, and I put a finger to my lips, peering toward the street to make sure no one had heard. "I know it sounds crazy, but I've learned important facts since I've been here, posing as my sister." I motioned toward Cody. "Like the Eckharts' money. She had planned to take it with her, but she didn't. You took it."

Cody swallowed, giving half a nod. "Maybe she was in a rush and didn't have time to get it."

"Maybe. But that's not the only thing that doesn't add up. Jacob figured out I wasn't Riley. After we went out to dinner that night, he confronted me and said I had one day to leave town, or he'd tell everyone who I really was. The next morning, he was plowed down in a hit-and-run. It couldn't have been a coincidence."

Something changed on Cody's face, his features tightening

slightly. "You've got my attention." I heard a mild tremble in his voice.

"At first, I thought Drew Toven had killed Jacob to scare me or something. But after talking to Drew, I'm sure he didn't do it. He didn't know who Jacob was, much less that Jacob was about to expose my identity."

Cody paced back and forth across the balcony. "Okay. You're probably right that it wasn't him."

"Jacob must have told someone what he knew about me, someone who knows I'm lying but wanted to keep my true identity a secret."

Cody's chest rose and fell a few times as he seemed to process the information I'd thrown at him. "What else do you have?"

I told him more about my recent phone call with Stacy, who'd admitted she'd lied about having seen Riley in L.A., the strange text message from Harper on Jacob's phone from the night before he died, and the dent in Harper's mom's black car. I paused, leaning closer to his ear as I dropped my theory in his lap. "What if Harper killed Riley? Her mom could have helped her cover it up."

Cody hitched up his pants, coupled with a slight shake of his head. "It tracks with everything I know about Harper, but I'm not sure I can make that leap. She and Riley were good friends, weren't they? What motive would she have?"

"I'm not completely sure about that yet, but they were keeping a secret about something bad they'd done a few weeks earlier, something that Harper worried would prevent her from getting into college if exposed." I continued telling him about Jacob's long-held belief that Harper was responsible for Riley's disappearance and how, on the night of junior prom, Riley had told Jacob she needed to confess something to him but later changed her mind, causing an argument between them. She'd left the dance with Harper.

"Huh."

"Maybe later that night, Riley told Harper that she couldn't keep their secret any longer and needed to clear her conscience. Harper could have snapped and done something drastic the next day or night to prevent Riley from talking."

Something flickered in Cody's eyes. "Oh my God. It actually makes sense."

"And Harper could have killed Jacob too. After confirming I wasn't Riley, Jacob might have gone to Harper's house. He was angry and could have accused her of having done something. Maybe he was too close to the truth. It makes sense that she would run over Jacob to keep him quiet."

Cody flattened his palms against his eye sockets. "It sounds crazy, but Harper is capable of it. Danny told me so many stories about her. He was convinced she tried to kill him once by running him off the road." He pulled in a deep breath, his eyes wide with worry. "But that means that Harper knows you're not really Riley."

My chest seized as I wondered if Riley had mentioned my existence to Harper. The night I'd slept in her room, Riley had sworn not to tell anyone about me and our plan. She understood there could be serious consequences otherwise. Still, it was possible Riley had let the information slip. My mind raced back over the time I'd spent with Harper and the occasions I'd left Noah in her care. She'd been sugary sweet to me, almost too nice. Until she wasn't. Harper was easily unhinged by all accounts. Little things seemed to set her off. Perhaps she was keeping me close until deciding what to do with me.

Cody moved toward me and gave me a tight hug. "I'm glad you told me the truth. It's not pretty, but everything makes much more sense now."

"I'm sorry I didn't tell you everything sooner. I wanted to, but I didn't know how you'd react, and I have so much to lose." I leaned into his warm body, grateful to have him on my side. I no longer had to lie to him; it felt like a thousand bricks had toppled from my shoulders. Beyond the glass sliding door, Noah still sat on the couch, watching TV.

Cody rested his chin on my head. "You need to watch out for Harper. She could be dangerous."

"Yeah, but I can't stay away from her just yet."

"Why not?"

"I need to know for sure if Harper killed my sister. I have to find out what terrible thing Harper and Riley did, and whether the secret was so big it was worth a sixteen-year-old murdering her best friend to protect it."

THIRTY-THREE

After debating for several minutes about what to do next, Cody insisted that Noah and I stay the night at his place. Darkness tinged the sky, and nothing outside the walls of Cody's condo felt safe, so I agreed. I didn't want to scare Noah, so I told him in an animated voice that we were having a sleepover as Cody helped us set up a sleeping bag, pillows, and blankets on the couch.

Cody and I holed up in his bedroom, talking late into the night. I told him more about my life over the past fifteen years, how I'd changed my appearance, name, and occupation from place to place, and how I always had an escape plan ready in case things got dicey, which they usually did.

Cody took the information in stride, telling me he understood because he'd broken the law too. He'd crossed paths with some awful people in the course of his computer repairs. He often opened untitled and misnamed folders, or files that had been recently deleted, leading him to disturbing discoveries. He had stumbled across an independent financial broker skimming large sums of money from his clients and keeping detailed records of his fraud. There was also a gym owner who collected compromising photos of women so that he could extort them later. The recently deleted files showed a playbook of the gym owner's crimes. In both cases, Cody had secretly installed ransomware. A few weeks after completing the repairs, he activated the ransomware, routing it through a server in Eastern Europe and holding the perpetrators' computers hostage until they each paid him over $100,000. Then, he anonymously tipped off the police. Suddenly, his fancy condo made a lot more sense.

"I shouldn't have done what I did, but that was five years ago." His voice wobbled. "I've changed since then. I don't steal things anymore, even when it seems justified."

I lay my arm atop his, letting him know his secret was safe, and I didn't judge him for taking matters into his own hands. "I'm waiting for a new identity to arrive, but I like it here. The documents are only a safety net; I don't want to use them."

Cody blinked, giving a nod. "Hopefully, we're wrong about Harper. Maybe she doesn't know you're not really Riley, and it won't come to that."

I agreed, but a heaviness settled in my gut. It felt like time was running out.

Cody returned to his apartment the next morning with drinks and muffins. "I did it," he said, kissing me on the cheek. "I told a guy I forgot my phone at home and needed to make an emergency call." Cody handed Noah a muffin and pulled me to the side, lowering his voice. "I called the police station and asked them to look into the dent on Lydia Parsons' black minivan."

I nodded in acknowledgment. The night before, we'd decided he would call in an anonymous tip about Jacob's hit-and-run without compromising my secret.

"Perfect," I whispered. "And I sent Harper the money I

owed her. That should get me back on her good side, at least for now."

"Let's hope that's the end of it."

I still had trouble comprehending how Harper might have committed such horrible acts against someone who had been her best friend, not to mention Jacob. And then there was Lydia Parsons. Would a mother go that far to protect her daughter? Harper and her mom getting arrested for Jacob's death would be a bitter outcome. On the other hand, they couldn't harm me from behind bars.

"Maybe the dent was from something else," I said, hoping to convince myself as much as Cody.

"Maybe." He looped his arm around me. "At the very least, the police attention might prevent Harper from doing anything stupid."

I leaned into him, hoping our tip to the police wouldn't make my precarious situation even more dangerous.

THIRTY-FOUR

That afternoon, I was back in my small apartment, opening my laptop as Noah napped. Despite not having Cody near me, my body felt lighter at the relief of sharing the truth with him. He'd remained loyal, even after the bombshell I'd dropped on him. But fears of Harper entangled my thoughts. A knowing spread through me, ugly and dark like a bruise. It seemed more and more possible that Harper had killed my sister. However, I needed to find a motive before I could be certain.

I wasn't sure exactly what I was searching for, which made my research more difficult. Thinking of all the possible crimes that teenagers might commit, I typed in "teen shoplifting Berkley Michigan," along with "April May" and the year of Riley's junior prom. When the first search produced irrelevant results, I tried "bullying" instead of shoplifting. Then, "cheating school," "drunk driving accident," and "arson." None of the results appeared to be anything Harper or Riley could have done. Unwilling to give up, I searched "vandalism." Several headlines appeared on my screen, but one in particular caught my attention, sparking my memory. "Teen Charged in Vandalism of Berkley High School Classroom." It was dated

April 22nd— about three weeks before the junior prom and a week before I'd followed Riley home from school and spent the night.

The headline was familiar because I'd seen the same article inside the box hidden in Harper's bathroom closet. At the time, I hadn't thought it had anything to do with Riley.

I leaned closer, my eyes swimming over the article. "After four days searching for a person who broke into a Berkley High School chemistry classroom the night of April 17th, police have arrested Zach Crenshaw, an eighteen-year-old senior at the high school. Crenshaw allegedly broke into the classroom through a window, destroying supplies such as beakers and microscopes with a baseball bat and spray-painting profanities on the wall. When questioned the day after the incident, the teacher of the trashed classroom did not identify any potential suspects but conceded that she'd failed an entire class on a recent exam after discovering a cheat sheet being passed around the room during the test. 'You never know how a student will react to a grade he or she perceived as unfair, but I never expected this,' said the teacher. An anonymous tip pointed investigators in the direction of Crenshaw, who had fresh cuts on his hands and had been suspended by the school three times previously for unruly behavior. His whereabouts on the night of the incident could not be verified. But the night before the vandalism occurred, a security camera at a restaurant next door recorded him walking toward the school at 11 p.m. Crenshaw was among the students who received a failing grade four days earlier. The suspect denies having anything to do with the damage and claims he cut his finger fixing his skateboard ramp. When asked for a comment, he said, 'I don't care about my grades that much and must have been set up.' A hearing has been set for May 10th."

I swallowed against my scratchy throat, making sense of the information. By all accounts, Harper had yearned to make her mom proud and be the first person in her family to go to college despite her lackluster grades. I could only imagine how a failing grade in chemistry might have set her off, especially if she'd deemed it unfair. It was more than feasible that she was responsible for the vandalism. Maybe she had recruited Riley to help her. Harper must have identified an easy scapegoat in Zach Crenshaw.

From what little I'd known of my sister, I sensed that sitting back and watching the wrong person take the blame for their crime wouldn't have been acceptable to her. Riley had wanted to tell someone the truth. She'd been close to telling Jacob the night of junior prom but had left with Harper instead. By the following night, Riley had vanished.

I searched for more articles about the vandalism, discovering Zach Crenshaw never admitted guilt but was expelled from school and ordered to complete a hundred hours of community service.

The newly discovered information clamored through me, enraging me on behalf of the troubled teen boy who had been wrongly accused and sentenced. I wished I could show up at Harper's door and scream at her, but I couldn't because she likely knew I wasn't Riley. Getting too close to her was perilous, like a bomb that could explode any second. My knees buckled as I stood before I righted myself and crossed the room. I called Cody and told him what I'd found and how the vandalism article had matched the one Harper had preserved in her creepy little box.

"I remember when that happened," he said, breathless. "Everyone thought it was Zach, but I guess it could have been them. It must have been. Why else would Harper have that article?" Cody seemed to be talking to himself more than me.

"Maybe she still feels guilty. Or else she's a sociopath and proud of everything she's gotten away with. People like that save mementos."

"I wish I didn't have to go to that conference in New York tomorrow."

I touched my cheek, finding my fingers cold. Cody had mentioned the tech conference in New York City yesterday—something required by his employer—but I'd put it to the back of my mind.

"I'm sorry I'm leaving, but it's only for a couple of nights. Promise me you'll stay away from Harper until I get back."

"I promise." I kept my promise and didn't wander outside the confines of the Eckharts' backyard for the rest of the day.

Noah was excited about his Sunday trip to the zoo with George and Wendy. Wendy met us on the patio with a bottle of sunscreen and a beach bag packed with drinks and snacks, eager to get to their destination before the crowds. I tugged at my waitressing uniform, feeling a little depressed that I couldn't join them for the outing, but I had a shift waiting for me at the café, and I was thankful for childcare that didn't involve Harper.

Despite looking over my shoulder and jumping at every loud noise, work passed quickly due to the neverending stream of diners. When I left the café six hours later, my back hurt, and my clothes smelled like sauteed onions. I was eager to see Noah and hear about his day at the zoo, to flop on the couch and watch a movie with him while I envisioned the police arresting Harper or her mom for Jacob's murder. I parked out front and made my way into the backyard, expecting to see them on the patio or inside the glass slider, sitting on the couch. But the patio was empty, and the living room was dark. I checked my phone to see if I'd missed a text message, but there weren't any, other than the one I'd received from Cody telling me he'd landed at LaGuardia. I decided to text Wendy.

Will you be back soon?

After a minute with no reply, I cupped my hands around my eyes and peered through the glass. A light shone from deeper within the house. Maybe they were home. I rapped my knuckles against the glass, but no one came to the door. Panic jolted through me, terrible thoughts swarming my head. What if Harper had come here? What if she'd done something? I gripped the door handle and pulled it open, only half surprised to find it unlocked. "Wendy?" I projected my voice, hoping for a response. Only a silent house surrounded me. The door slid closed with a thud, and I walked toward the hallway light, poking my head into the kitchen. No one was in there either. I jogged upstairs, checking the bedrooms, including the home office that used to be Riley's bedroom. Each room was silent.

I headed back downstairs, certain no one was home and my imagination had run away with me again. The Eckharts had likely hit traffic on the way home or stopped for ice cream with Noah. As I was about to head back to the patio, the door to the basement caught my eye. I'd seen George disappear down there to retrieve old toys from storage for Noah, but I'd never seen the space. Curiosity getting the better of me, I gripped the handle and turned, the hinges creaking as the door opened to a darkened stairwell. I flipped on the light. Cool, musty air surrounded me as I descended the steps.

A storage area opened up at the base of the stairs. Boxes, plastic bins, extra cleaning products, and a few smaller kitchen appliances sat on metal shelves lining the walls. There was nothing out of the ordinary here. I almost turned to go back up when I noticed another door beyond the far wall of shelves. I strode toward the door and opened it, once again met with darkness. A string hanging from a bulb dangled near my head. I pulled it, illuminating the space.

The unexpected décor caused me to draw in a sharp breath.

A beige carpet remnant covered the floor, and the light-green walls were adorned with large, framed photos. More pictures sat on tables around the perimeter. Dozens of kids—boys and girls of different ethnicities and ages—smiled back at me. My gaze paused on a small frame containing Riley's photo, and I picked it up, cradling it in my hands. It was an image I had never seen before. She leaned against the fence in the Eckharts' backyard, sunlight creasing her eyes. My fingers trembled as I set the picture back down, my eyes landing on another face I recognized: a younger, skinnier version of Cody. His head tilted in an unnatural position against a marbled gray background, his face frozen in a somber expression. It must have been his senior picture from high school, likely taken around the time Riley disappeared.

I studied a few more faces before coming to a framed poem written in caligraphy about the blessings of being foster parents. Taped around the poem were a few crayon drawings of happy families, sunshine, and rainbows signed with children's uneven handwriting. Two newspaper articles in silver frames formed book ends on each side of the wall, the first reading "Local Couple Offers Hope to Foster Kids." It was dated four years before Riley arrived at the Eckharts' house. The second, "Foster Parents Open Their Home to Teens," was from about a year before she moved in. I skimmed over the articles praising the Eckharts for their role as stand-in parents and quoting a few of the grateful children who had lived with them. My gaze returned to the poem, the drawings, and the photos. These must have been all the foster kids Wendy and George had taken in at one point or another. Two candles sat on the tables, giving the space a shrine-like feel. I wondered how often the Eckharts came down here. It must have been a bigger blow to them than they'd let on when the agency had revoked their foster care license.

Several thuds sounded from upstairs, causing my arms to

drop to my sides. Noah's familiar footsteps skittered across the ceiling above my head. They were back.

"Someone's down here," George said, feet tramping down the steps.

"It's only me," I yelled, pulling the cord and rushing from the little room into the storage area.

George's face changed when he spotted me from a few steps down. It was clear I'd stumbled into what was meant to be a private room, and I hadn't had permission to enter their house in the first place. Heat rose through my core, burning my face. He'd caught me snooping, and I couldn't give any valid reason for being down here. "I'm sorry," I said. "I shouldn't be down here, but I was worried when you weren't here and—"

"It's okay." George frowned, his voice cold. "That's our memory room. We've got the little guy upstairs, all safe and sound."

"Of course. Thank you." I hoped I hadn't embarrassed him by stumbling across the room, which likely held tremendous emotional significance. I looked at my feet as I followed him up the stairs, feeling like a common burglar.

"Mommy! I saw the polar bear!" Noah skipped toward me with rosy cheeks.

"How fun!"

"What on earth were you doing down there?" Wendy glowered at me beneath her oversized sunhat.

"Sorry. I was worried about Noah when I couldn't find anyone. I thought you'd be home by now, so I texted you." I pushed a few stray hairs away from my face, aware my reasoning didn't make much sense.

Wendy clucked, pursing her lips.

George placed a hand on his hip as he addressed his wife. "She was looking at our memory room."

"Oh." Wendy scratched her elbow. "It probably looked strange to you, but it's too painful to keep all the children's photos where we see them all the time. I just miss them so much, so I go down there when I need to remember the good times. Time went by so fast." She forced a sad smile.

My heart pulled for Wendy and what she and George had lost.

She motioned at me. "But at least now I can visit you and Noah anytime in the backyard."

"You're probably seeing too much of us," I said with a nervous chuckle.

No one spoke for a moment, but Wendy finally removed her hat and set it on a nearby chair. "We're wiped out, Riley. You can take Noah back to your place. We need to rest."

"I want to go back to the zoo!" Noah's face crumpled as he let out a prolonged squeal. He arched his back, flopping to the ground. "I want to see the polar bear again," he said between sobs.

Before I could comfort Noah, Wendy grabbed his arm and yanked him from the floor, anger brewing in her eyes. "That's enough." Her palm delivered two sharp swats to his bottom.

Noah howled. The thwacking sound made me flinch. Traumatic memories from the supervisors at the group homes punched through me, forcing my mother-bear instincts to the surface. I had suffered at the hands of too many people who'd wielded their little bit of power over me, and that was even before Marianne Clavey had entered my life. I had never laid a violent hand on my son.

"Don't hit him!" I scooped Noah up, glaring at Wendy. "That's not how I do things. We don't hit each other."

Wendy stepped back, a mixture of surprise and hurt on her face. She flattened her lips. "I'm sorry, Riley. But sometimes, a little discipline is necessary."

"A spanking or two never hurt any kid." George raised his chin. "Our society has gone soft."

I gritted my teeth, staring them down. "It's not okay with me. He's my son. Never do that again."

Wendy inched toward me, a palm held in the air. "You know what? You're right, dear. You're the mom. I overstepped, and I apologize."

George nodded. "She didn't mean anything by it, Riley. It was hot out there. Everyone's tired and hungry."

I pulled Noah closer, gathering my composure. Because of my past, I was highly sensitive to adults hitting children, even a quick spank. While I would never approve of Wendy's actions, perhaps I'd overreacted to her misstep. She was of a different generation and had likely been brought up with a stricter way of parenting. I took a calming breath so that we could exit the situation. "Thank you for giving him a fun day." Roping my arm around my son, I guided him out the door, no longer feeling embarrassed for snooping in their basement. Wendy and I had both made mistakes this afternoon. And the last thing I needed was to ruin my relationship with the Eckharts.

THIRTY-FIVE

Despite major distractions, I made it through my real estate class on Sunday night, safely locked inside my apartment with Noah. A few weeks ago, I'd hoped to live happily ever after under my sister's name and build a legitimate career and a stable life for Noah. But now, my plan was precarious, balancing on the edge of a knife. My focus had shifted to uncovering the truth about Riley, even if it meant I had to eventually flee in the night once again.

I kept a close watch on my surroundings all night and the following day as I dropped Noah at preschool and reported to my waitressing job. My September rent was due in six days, and I needed to scrape together as much money as possible. I hoped Wendy had grown fond enough of Noah that she'd let me stay as long as I needed, even with the shortage.

Nothing seemed unusual as I went about my day, taking orders and wiping down tables. But I'd never received an acknowledgment from Harper that I'd repaid her money. I wondered, again, if the police were questioning her or her mom at this very moment and whether the dent in the car would lead them to Jacob's killer. I hadn't noticed anything out of place in my apartment in over two weeks and couldn't help but question the details of my memory. With Drew Toven paid off and gone, maybe the lingering threat to my well-being was in my head.

Cody texted me every few hours from New York to ensure I was safe. Even so time crept slowly, and I couldn't wait for him to return, to have someone else in my corner after surviving alone for nearly my entire life.

At last, the lunch rush thinned out, and the café closed. The clouds thickened in the sky as I picked up Noah and pulled toward my usual parking spot on Marigold Street. My heart lurched at a familiar vehicle. Harper's red Jeep was parked at the curb. She hadn't mentioned she was coming over, and I was scared to learn the reason for her visit. My head swung in all directions as I scanned the street, searching for a sign of Harper hiding behind the bushes with a knife, ready to attack. But only the wind rustled through the boxwood and forsythia branches. I debated pressing the accelerator and driving away, but that was a temporary solution. We had nowhere else to go. As much as I didn't want to, I needed to confront Harper. For Noah's sake, I stayed calm as I helped him out of the car, keeping my phone ready in case of emergency.

"Take my hand," I said to Noah. "We're going to go straight up to the apartment, okay?"

"Can I have a granola bar?"

"Yes." I pulled him behind me through the gate, senses on high alert. I halted, my feet tripping over themselves when I spotted her. Harper sat on a low step of the stairway leading up to the apartment, her posture board-straight.

"Hi," I managed to spit out.

Her sunglasses were perched on her head, and bright red lipstick added a deranged look to her smile. "I thought you'd be back soon." She stood up, the smile vanishing.

"I didn't know you were coming over. We could have met you and April at the park." The air felt charged between us. I struggled to keep my voice light, hoping she couldn't hear the note of panic. I searched her features for any telltale signs that she was a murderer and that she'd been playing me this entire time, but her face showed no expression.

"I was just passing through. Thought I'd stop by to chat." Harper paused, lifting her chin. "You know, the way friends do."

"Yes. Of course."

"Thanks for giving me my money back." Her voice was flat, and she didn't sound much like someone grateful. Nonetheless, I acknowledged her with a nod.

A light rain began to fall, pelting my forehead and then my arm. Harper and I locked eyes, both of us standing tall. We squared off at the base of the stairway, seemingly testing each other to see how far the other one would push. Again, I studied the flecks in her eyes and the twitch of her lips to discern how much she knew. But her face gave nothing away as she crossed her arms over her chest.

The rain grew heavier. "Do you want to come inside?" I asked, gesturing toward the apartment.

"Yes. Thanks."

The last person I wanted in my apartment was Harper, and I immediately wished I could bite back the words. I should have dug deeper into the reason for her visit or asked whether she felt guilty about what she'd done to Zach Crenshaw while we were outside, within sight and earshot of the neighbors.

But Harper was already taking the steps in a quick and jerky motion like someone wired a little too tightly.

Alarm bells rang in my head as I chased after her. This was a person who may have murdered my sister. And Jacob. She may have tried to run me down the other night. She was a live wire who acted impulsively. I silently took inventory of possible weapons in the apartment that I could use to defend myself and Noah if necessary: a butcher knife in the kitchen drawer and pepper spray in a backpack on the back of my bedroom door. I glanced at the Eckharts' house before unlocking the entry to the apartment. Their windows sat dark with no visible movement, and it appeared no one was home.

I opened the door, flipping on the light as we ducked out of the rain. Harper brushed some droplets from her spikey hair as she scanned the mismatched kitchen and the threadbare furniture, making a face. "Nice place."

"Thanks," I said, although I hadn't missed the sarcasm lacing her voice.

"It must feel weird to live in the same space as Creepy Cody."

"His name's just Cody." I glared at her, feeling the need to defend my boyfriend.

Harper ran her fingers over the back of a kitchen chair, showing no reaction to my statement. "You've lived here for how long? Over a month, I think, and you've never invited me over. Me, your former best friend."

"Yeah. Because I'm not exactly proud of living here."

Noah weaved around my legs, pulling at my sleeve and asking for a granola bar. I got him one from the cupboard and asked him to eat in the bedroom while he looked at his books, adding, "Harper and I need to talk with just grown-ups for a couple of minutes."

Noah pouted but followed my request, stomping into the bedroom and closing the door behind him.

I waved toward the couch. "Want to sit?"

"No, thanks." She placed her hands on her hips, looking at the floor. An uncomfortable beat of silence passed between us. When she raised her eyes, they had transformed into those of a shark—cold and flat—and I feared whatever was coming next. "I got a visit from Detective Brinmore today. So did my mom."

I cocked my head as if surprised. "Really?"

"Yes. Someone tipped him off about Mom's minivan having a dent."

"Did they say who?"

"No."

I shrugged. "That could have been anyone, I guess. Maybe a neighbor."

Harper pursed her lips before speaking again. "Mom doesn't go out much, barely at all, except to see me and April or get groceries. Her neighbors know the dent is months old. I saw you staring at her bumper the other day when she picked us up at the park."

"I noticed it, but I didn't think—"

Harper stomped her foot, causing me to jump. "It was you! You called the police."

"No."

"I know it was you."

"It wasn't." I averted my eyes toward the rain hitting the window. Technically, Cody had called in the tip, although it had been my idea.

"You were always such a tattletale. You haven't changed at all."

I swallowed, unable to speak. She must have been referring to the vandalism incident and Riley's desire to confess. But unless she'd been taking some high-level acting classes, her vitriol toward me was real. She still seemed to genuinely believe I was Riley.

The next words flew from my mouth unfiltered. "Do you ever feel guilty about letting Zach take the blame?" I stood motionless, aware I was holding a flame to a stick of dynamite.

Harper's eyes bulged, her gaze darting in all directions before landing on me. "You shut up right now. We promised to never talk about it again."

"I never agreed to that."

Harper yanked at her cropped hair. "What? Yes, you did.

We swore ourselves to secrecy." She stepped toward me, jabbing her finger at my face. "I think you lie a lot. I think you're a liar."

"I'm not," I said, although that was another lie. I'd built my life on lies and was good at it.

Her eyes narrowed as she caught sight of my hand. "How's your finger?"

I swung my hands behind my back and laced my fingers together, feeling my blood drain out of me. I'd forgotten to wear the bandage the last few days. I'd gotten sloppy. There was no scar, and she'd noticed.

"It healed quickly," I said, mumbling.

A terrifying laugh erupted from her lungs before the room returned to silence. "My mom reported her fender bender to the insurance company nearly four months ago. A car ran a stop sign, and they smashed into each other. That's how her minivan was damaged. Not in a hit-and-run that killed Jacob. She was at my house the morning Jacob died, helping me take care of *your* son. My next-door neighbor saw us out on the patio at the exact time Jacob was hit. The police verified the facts in a matter of minutes."

The balls of my feet pressed into the floor as I steadied myself. "That's good that they know she wasn't involved." The cadence of my voice was upbeat, but I could see by Harper's sour expression that she wasn't buying my act. My hunch that she had hit Jacob with her mom's minivan crumbled beneath this new set of facts. I'd drawn lines between dots that may have never existed. A sickening feeling pooled in my stomach because I'd clearly fallen deeper into Harper's bad side. I wanted to curl up into a ball and disappear.

Harper spoke again, releasing her ire on me. "You're the same crappy friend you used to be. I thought you changed, but you didn't. Riley Wakefield can't be trusted. I guess it's my fault for giving you another chance. Fool me once, shame on you, and all that."

Harper thought she was hurting me, but my shoulders lifted at her venomous words, confirming that she still believed I was Riley. Jacob must not have told her the truth. But now I needed to do some damage control.

"I'm really sorry, Harper. There's no excuse for what I did back then. And I'm so grateful for all you've done to help me since I returned. I paid back your money like I promised. And I can watch April anytime you need a break."

She bit her lip, shaking her head. "Save it, Riley. We're not friends anymore."

"I'll make it up to you. I'm sorry if you felt like I accused you of something."

"There's no making up this time. And if you want to accuse anyone of anything, you should probably start with your new boyfriend. He's still Creepy Cody, as far as I'm concerned—the same guy who used to stare at you at night through the window."

"What?"

"Jacob takes you on a date to rekindle your high school romance just before he dies in a suspicious accident. Days later, Cody swoops in and makes a move." Harper made a face as she gave a dramatic shrug. "I'm only saying maybe it wasn't a coincidence."

I gripped my hands together. "That's not what—"

"I said everything I had to say. Good luck with your life." Harper turned on her heel and left the apartment.

I stared at the door as rain battered the roof. Everything I thought I knew had tilted on its side, shifting the facts and forming a distorted picture. It was an image I couldn't decipher. I made my way to the couch, falling onto the scratchy fabric. My mind churned, processing the new information. I didn't give any credence to the idea that Cody had been responsible for

Jacob's death. Cody had no reason to do something like that. Our mutual attraction would have developed naturally, even if Jacob was still alive. But the name Harper had called Cody bothered me. *Creepy Cody.* She'd mentioned the nickname a few weeks earlier, but I'd dismissed it as teenage girls being mean. Cody had never mentioned it to me, but then again, he probably hadn't been aware of it.

THIRTY-SIX

I hunkered down in the apartment with Noah, sheltered from the rain and whatever dangers lurked outside. It was after 8 p.m. when Cody's name flashed on my phone. I hurried into the bedroom to answer it, the bed creaking beneath me as I sat.

"Hey. Everything okay?" he asked immediately.

I hesitated as the encounter with Harper pulsed through my memory. "Harper came to my apartment after work today."

"Seriously? You let her in?"

"Yeah. I didn't really have a choice."

"What did she say?"

I slid to the edge of the mattress, telling him how Harper had figured out I'd tipped off the detective, how the dent in her mom's car was from a months-old accident, and how the neighbor had provided an alibi for them at the time of Jacob's death.

A sigh heaved from Cody's end. "Man. I can't believe we were so wrong. I'd really convinced myself."

"Me too." My fingers gripped the blanket, balling the fabric in my hand. "But we were right about the vandalism. You should have seen her face when I mentioned Zach Crenshaw.

She was terrified and angry, said we'd promised never to talk about it."

Cody gasped. "Wow. Harper and Riley were behind that all along, just like you thought."

"Harper believes I'm Riley. She couldn't have been the one who killed her."

"Are you sure?"

"One hundred percent. It was clear by her reaction and the things she said to me. It wasn't an act."

"I hope you're right."

"She also said I'm not her friend anymore and can't be trusted."

Cody's pained groan sounded through my phone. "I hate to say it, but it's probably for the best."

I rubbed my knuckles, knowing he was right.

Cody fumbled with something on the other end of the line. "That's really good news, though. I was so worried you would have to leave. And right when I was just getting to know you."

"I don't want to leave. Trust me." I said, thankful for more time together.

I steered the conversation to safer topics, asking Cody about his conference. He said it was boring but not all bad. His hotel window overlooked the Empire State Building, and he got to eat at a fancy French restaurant for free.

"That sounds amazing." I leaned into the pillow behind my back, wishing I could be there with him. But the nickname Harper had mentioned hovered near my thoughts like a blood-thirsty mosquito refusing to leave. I had to ask him about it. "Harper said something else kind of funny."

"What's that?"

"She said Riley used to call you Creepy Cody."

He snorted. "What? Why?"

"I guess she caught you spying on her once through the window."

Cody grunted, clearly put off by the accusation. "I don't remember that, but I was a teenage boy filled with raging hormones, so I probably did stare at her—and dozens of other girls who crossed my path—once or twice. I wasn't trying to be creepy."

"Of course. I didn't mean—"

"And, as you know, there's a clear view from one of the apartment windows to the house. Sometimes, I looked out at night just to see the lights and activity over there. Riley's bedroom faced the backyard, so it was kind of hard not to see it."

I recalled all the times I'd stared out the window toward the house just to see the lights. His explanation rang true. "I remember looking across at the apartment the night I stayed in Riley's bedroom," I said. "I saw you through the window. It never occurred to me I'd be living here fifteen years later."

After we agreed that the world worked in mysterious ways, I promised Cody I wouldn't let anyone else inside the apartment. We said good night, and I returned to the living room to watch TV with Noah before bed.

A creak woke me, followed by a noise like a branch hitting a window or a wall. My body bolted upright as I stared through the darkness. The bedside clock glowed with the time—3:07 a.m. I kept myself still, listening. Another thump disrupted the silence. It could have been a cupboard or a door clicking shut. A shiver crawled up my spine. Was someone in my apartment? I fumbled for my phone but realized it wouldn't do any good. I couldn't call 911 without drawing unwanted attention to myself. Instead, I crept out of bed and removed the pepper spray from the bag hanging on the back of my door. Holding my breath, I cracked the door and peered into the living room and kitchen, unable to see anything through the blackness. I lunged through the opening and flipped on the light, ready to spray someone in the face if necessary, but the room was empty. I lowered the pepper spray, finding my breath. Nerves still rattled through me as I entered the kitchen to get a glass of water before returning to bed. That's when I noticed something on the counter. It was a scrap of paper that hadn't been there before. I forced myself closer to it, slowly picking it up and reading the thick black letters printed across it.

KEEP YOUR MOUTH SHUT OR YOU ARE NEXT!

THIRTY-SEVEN

I read the words again, convinced my eyes were playing tricks on me. But the same warning stared back at me.

KEEP YOUR MOUTH SHUT OR YOU ARE NEXT!

I sprinted to the window. The backyard lay in darkness, except for a tiny light that shone from the corner of an outdoor air conditioning unit beyond the Eckharts' patio. I could barely see more than a couple of feet beyond the windowsill. I checked the windows and doors, which were closed and locked. Whoever entered must have had a key. My feet stumbled backward as I found my way to the couch, perching on it. Who would have done this? Harper's face instantly flashed in my mind. Could she have swiped a key from the Eckharts' laundry room when she'd gone inside to use the bathroom at the barbecue? She'd been so angry when I'd found her on my steps yesterday afternoon. But I already knew that too many of the pieces related to Harper didn't fit. My thoughts pulled in a hundred directions, trying to make sense of it.

Who else could have known my secret? Who could have harmed Jacob and attempted to run me over the other night? My suspicions circled back to McKenzie. Maybe she'd been the one who'd fooled me. Perhaps she'd been more jealous of my dinner with Jacob than she'd let on. Maybe Harper's initial hunch that McKenzie had offed her boyfriend had been correct. But McKenzie had never even known Riley, so why would she care about not revealing my true identity? It didn't make sense.

I returned to the window, looking toward George and Wendy's house but barely able to discern its shadowy outline. They had a key to my apartment in case of emergencies or for occasional repairs. Riley and Cody had both complained about how strict they'd been. I'd witnessed Wendy's anger at Noah after the trip to the zoo, the way she'd yanked him off the floor and swatted his bottom without a second thought. Maybe George and Wendy weren't the kind, forgiving foster parents they'd made themselves out to be. But the idea didn't sit right as I looked around the rent-free apartment. Wendy had been over-joyed to see me when I'd shown up at her doorstep, believing Riley had returned. George and Wendy loved Noah, practically acting as his grandparents. Wendy had been fond of Jacob too. She'd tried to protect him from getting his heart broken again. It didn't make sense that she'd go to the trouble of shielding his feelings only to kill him the following morning. Besides, the Eckharts' matching silver cars didn't fit with whoever had hit Jacob. I was sure the car that had aimed for me had been a dark color too, and George and Wendy had been at their house watching Noah when I'd nearly been run down.

I turned my thoughts away from the Eckharts, but there was one name I couldn't shake from my head. Cody. He might have saved a key to the apartment from when he'd lived here. Or he could have easily swiped one during one of his visits to George and Wendy's house. Had he been playing me all along, using our mutual attraction against me? He'd recovered quickly after

I'd confessed my true identity to him. Maybe too quickly. Perhaps Cody had been more infatuated with my sister than he'd let on. Maybe he was the one who'd ended Riley's life, stealing the Eckharts' money to make it look like she'd taken it before running away. And Wendy had mentioned she'd accused Cody of doing something to Riley after she'd disappeared. She must have had a reason for pointing a finger at him. What if Wendy had been correct, and that was the real reason Cody had kept his distance from the Eckharts until I arrived in Berkley?

Cody was supposedly in New York City at a work convention but could have lied to throw me off his scent. It was a tactic I'd used more than once to get others off my trail. I'd never seen his car, which he told me was black. Was that because it had damage from hitting Jacob? Was a major car repair the secretive purchase that had drained his savings account? Maybe the note on my counter was a scare tactic to get me to stop poking into things, to get me to leave town—the sooner, the better. I gritted my teeth, hoping I was wrong. My theories didn't match the Cody I knew, and I wondered if I was self-sabotaging my first chance at a real relationship in years.

My body anchored to the couch, and I remained in place for several minutes. Finally, I hoisted myself up and retrieved a glass of water before returning to the darkness of my bedroom. Noah's soft breath repeated in a steady rhythm from his mattress on the floor as I slipped back under the covers and closed my eyes. But sleep was no longer a possibility.

Two pots of coffee brewed beside me as I ducked into a corner at Songbird Café, scrolling through my phone. My section of tables sat empty, which wouldn't last. This was my chance to make the call, the one I'd been debating for several hours. Self-hatred tunneled through me for what I was about to do, but I had to know if Cody was lying. He and I had been raised without parents to guide us. We were cut from the same cloth—the kind of cloth that charmed people and kissed them on the cheek while simultaneously picking their pockets. We'd had no other choice.

I dialed the number for his office and waited for an answer. "Hello," a man's dull voice said. "This is InterTech. How can I help you?"

"Hi, this is Mary Maples." I paused, cringing at the name I'd made up on the spot. "I spoke with a man a few weeks ago about my laptop freezing up and had a follow-up question. Cody Beck. Is he available for a second?"

The man cleared his throat. "Cody is out of the office for a couple of days. Can I send you to his voicemail?"

"Oh. Is this the day of that tech conference in New York he told me about?"

"Yes."

My forehead dipped, my grip loosening. I was wrong again. Cody hadn't been lying. The way I'd lived my life had scarred me and made me incapable of trusting anyone who got too close.

The man spoke again. "But Cody didn't go to the conference. Only Miles went from our office. Cody's off on personal time."

"What?" I placed a palm against the wall to keep myself upright. Four people entered the café and sat in my section.

"Cody is not at the conference," the man repeated. "We only sent one person. I'll put you through to Cody's voicemail, and he'll get back to you."

I ended the call before it went any further. The truth surrounded me like a cloud of noxious gas, making it difficult to breathe. Cody had lied about being in New York. I'd let my guard down, falling for his story. He knew too much about me, and it was dangerous.

I stumbled through the remainder of my workday, my mind trapped in a confused and terrified state as I combed through all the possibilities of who else could have left the note on my counter, but the facts continued pointing to one person. The phone call to InterTech convinced me it had been Cody—or Creepy Cody as Harper and Riley used to call him.

When I exited the café at the end of my shift, I was surprised by the bright day outside. Two women walked past me, laughing, but I existed in a different dimension. My tunnel vision was only for discovering the truth and keeping Noah safe.

I drove home, unsure what to do next. Confronting Cody was the most direct route to discovering the truth. There was an hour before I had to pick up Noah from preschool, and I could make the call to Cody when I got back to the apartment. I parked out front and cut through the gate to the backyard when I glimpsed a familiar figure standing on the Eckharts' patio. His back was to me, but I recognized his shaggy hair. Sweat darkened the armpits of his collared shirt. I ducked down behind the bushes, my heart pounding in my ears. Drew Toven had returned to punish me. I peeked through the branches as he knocked on their back door. The slider opened a second later.

"Yes?" It was Wendy, clearly surprised by the sight of a strange man in her backyard.

"Hi, ma'am. My name is Tom. I'm here about someone living in your apartment back there." He thumbed toward the garage.

"What? You mean Riley?"

"Whatever name she gave you, it's not real."

Wendy placed a hand on her chest. "I'm sorry. Who are you?"

"I'm a concerned citizen who fell prey to one of her schemes. She's a con artist and an imposter. She has hurt a lot of

people. I'd hate to see her victimize anyone else, so I just
wanted to put you on alert."

I sucked in my lips, holding back the scream that burned in
my lungs. He couldn't let things end. Drew was blowing my
cover before I had a foolproof escape plan.

Wendy huffed. "Well, I think I know what my own foster
daughter looks like."

"You're supposed foster daughter is probably a look-alike.
Maybe a sister."

Wendy's face was a picture of confusion. "A sister? No.
There was no mention of a sister in her records."

"Even so, the woman in the apartment is dangerous. I'd call
the police if I were you."

Wendy made a muffled noise, not quite a yes or a no. "You
can be on your way now."

"No problem. Stay safe."

My back ached as I crouched lower, trying my best not to
breathe. The glass door slid shut, followed by a click. Drew
traipsed leisurely across the patio and onto the grass until the
back gate opened and shut. A car engine started, quickly fading
into the distance.

He was gone. I rested my face in my hands, unable to stop
the tears from leaking. My secret was out. My cover completely
blown. Even after finding the threatening note on my kitchen
counter, I believed I still had a chance of outsmarting whoever
was after me and continuing as Riley. But now I was certain
that the perfect suburban life I'd been creating for me and
Noah was over. Once the police investigated, they would eventually discover that I was, in fact, Riley's sister, Gina Holland, a
wanted fugitive. I should have known my plan was too risky, my
dream of a stable life too big. It had always been out of reach,
and this was how it would end. I'd justified my actions in one
way or another, but I'd forgotten that I was a criminal. I'd stolen
identities, including the name and likeness of my dead sister. I'd

stolen money. I'd stabbed a man and accidentally caused the death of a woman. Now karma had caught up with me. I would go to jail and lose Noah. The cycle of foster care would continue. I'd failed as a mother. And that was the thing that hurt the most of all.

THIRTY-EIGHT

In a last-ditch effort to save myself, I sped to the post office, locating my P.O. box. My hand shook so violently that it took three tries to slide the key into the slot. There'd been nothing besides a bill when I'd checked the box a few days earlier, and I hoped today would be a different story. But only a couple of envelopes sat at the bottom. No packet from Bea's contact. No new identities for me and Noah. The walls closed in on me. There was no chance of escaping now.

My body seemed to move by itself as I returned to the parking lot and got into my car. My instinct was to call Cody, but I couldn't trust him. It would be reckless to confide in him. I had to stay calm, for Noah's sake. Surviving one second—one breath—at a time, I drove to the preschool to pick up my son for what I feared would be the last time. I stood in the sunshine for a moment too long, taking in the sound of laughing children and eager parents and memorizing the light breeze across my cheeks. These were the little things I would yearn for when I lived in a musty cinderblock cell.

Noah ran toward me, and I gasped at his wide smile and tousled hair. I thanked the teacher a little too profusely as we left. Noah grabbed my hand and yelled, "See you tomorrow!" to a girl standing nearby. My heart split inside my chest, oozing grief, love, and regret, preparing itself for the loss that was to come. I wondered if Wendy was calling the police right now.

"I love you, buddy."

"Love you too," he said while waving a piece of construction paper with a crayon drawing in the air.

I hoped to have one nice, normal night before the hammer fell and shattered our lives. My anxiety grew as we neared our address, so I made a pitstop at the playground, which thrilled Noah. I savored each minute with him, afraid of what awaited us at the apartment. After the park, we stopped for ice cream. It was something out of the ordinary that he could remember when I was gone, eating ice cream for dinner. Noah became antsy once we'd finished the treat. There was nowhere else to go, so we finally headed to the apartment. We cut through the backyard a few minutes later, and I half expected police officers to jump out of the bushes and put me in handcuffs. But only a sprinkler swung back and forth, spraying a freshly weeded flower bed.

We hurried up the wooden stairs, and I locked the door behind us, digging through my brain for any idea of how to escape the mess I'd created.

A clip from the movie *Titanic* reeled through my mind: a group of musicians playing a final hymn on their stringed instruments as the ship went down. It was best to go out doing what you love, and what I loved the most were the quiet moments with my son. I pulled out Noah's Legos and suggested we build something together. Noah scampered over and joined me at the living room table.

Nearly an hour passed before a loud knock at the door ripped away our storybook evening. I covered my mouth with my hand, feeling like I might vomit. This was it. My life as a free woman was over.

"Riley! It's me, Wendy."

It was Wendy. Not the police. Or were they waiting behind her? Maybe I could explain my way out of the situation if she hadn't called them yet. I forced myself toward the door, pulling it open.

"Hi!" She glanced up toward the dwindling daylight. "It was such a beautiful day, wasn't it?"

I looked at the pink sky beyond her shoulder, wondering if her question was some kind of trick. But no one was out there, and she continued smiling at me.

"Yes. It looks like it's still nice out."

"George and I were wondering if you and Noah would like to come over for pizza tomorrow night. It's nothing fancy, just a little get-together."

"Oh." It wasn't what I'd expected her to say. I centered myself, finding my voice. "Yes. Thank you."

Wendy clapped her hands together, eyes sparkling with delight. "Perfect! We'll see you around six."

"Okay." *What the hell was going on?* Just as I had the thought, something on Wendy's face shifted, and I knew what was coming next.

"Say, you don't have a sister, do you? I always thought you were an only child."

"I don't. You're right. I'm an only child." I kept my voice steady as I lied.

"That's what I remembered." An uneasy smile pulled at Wendy's lips but quickly vanished. She scratched her head, staring into the distance before turning back to me. "I had the strangest encounter today. A man showed up on our patio claiming you were an imposter."

My stomach folded. I had to think fast. Something to explain him away. "Was his name Tom? About fifty years old with hazel eyes and messy hair?"

"Well, yes. That was his name, and that's exactly what he looked like."

I feigned surprise, widening my eyes. "Oh, no. He found me again. He's a sleazy man. A drug dealer."

Wendy gasped. "That's the sense I got from him, that he wasn't honest."

"When I was at my lowest point, he gave me some drugs for free. I was never able to pay him back. He's been popping up every year or two, saying I owe him money. I went by a different name then. That must be why he called me an imposter. He must have seen my face on the news when Melissa Miner interviewed me."

"Oh boy. I bet you're right." Her foot tapped nervously as she glanced over her shoulder. "He sounds like he could be dangerous."

"I'm really sorry for leading him here, but he's more bark than bite. He never stays in one place too long in case the police catch up with him."

Wendy placed a hand on her hip. "Even so, you should call the police if you see him again. And keep your door locked."

"I definitely will."

"I could tell he was trying to cause trouble. I wanted to make you aware so you could protect yourself."

"Thanks. I appreciate you looking out for me. And I'm sorry again."

"It's not your fault. Take care, and we'll see you and Noah tomorrow night." She turned toward the stairs but then paused and faced me again. "By the way, George doesn't know about any of this." She was whispering now. "He can be overprotective sometimes, and I don't want to give him any reason to kick you out of the apartment."

"I understand. We'll keep it between us."

Wendy gave a nod. "And don't forget that your rent is due in a few days."

"I'm getting it together." I gave her a reassuring grin, although I was a few hundred dollars short.

She hobbled down the stairs as I closed the door.

My body practically floated above the floor as I returned to Noah, letting him lead the way with the Legos. Wendy had been gullible, readily accepting my explanation. She clearly wanted to see the best in her former foster daughter and easily believed my story over Drew's. But I wasn't convinced I was safe. I had no idea if Drew had confronted anyone else.

Before I had more time to weigh the odds of the police showing up, a text from Cody buzzed on my phone.

Mind if I stop by to say hello when I get home later?

I read the words, frozen with indecision. Cody already knew the truth about my past and could help me figure out what to do next. Still, a warning darted through me. Cody had lied about being in New York the same night someone left a threatening note in my kitchen.

I wrote back.

I'll have to see how I'm feeling. My throat's a little scratchy.

Oh no! I hope you feel better. I'll call you tomorrow.

And so he wouldn't suspect anything, I added:

Can't wait for you to come back

The night passed with me lying close to Noah and a chair shoved beneath my front door handle. No police showed up, and no intruders broke in either. The extra time was a gift; I would use it to my advantage. I needed to check with Bea to see what was taking so long for the documents to arrive.

When morning came, I called in sick to work but dropped Noah at preschool as usual, still on edge. I spent the day hiding in the apartment, brainstorming my next move. I spied through the windows every few minutes, searching for any sign of Drew Toven. I only saw Wendy tinkering in her garden again, directing a man on a small backhoe to dig the holes for the two saplings she was planting. Brenda Harwood paced along the fenceline, eyeing the commotion with a scowl.

At 1 p.m., I called Lucky's Bar, but no one answered. I worried Bea might not be in until later, so I called again after picking up Noah. When no one answered, I loaded him in the car and told him Mommy had to run an errand.

Noah whined and cried for most of the car ride to Detroit, and when I parked in the gravel lot outside the run-down establishment, pulling my son kicking and screaming from the car to enter the smoky bar, I knew for sure I'd failed as a mother.

I spoke calmly in his ear. "We're going to a pizza party tonight with Wendy and George, but you have to be good now, okay?"

He sucked in a few jagged breaths, sniffling. The idea of the upcoming get-together calmed him down as I carried him into the dimly lit room. Bea's back was to me, and a skeleton-like man stared at us from a table in the corner.

"Bea."

My voice startled her, and she jumped, turning toward me. Her gaze traveled over me and a bleary-eyed Noah as she shook her head. "You've got to be kidding me."

"Please. I'm desperate. I need those documents."

Bea looked down her nose at me. "I told you not to come back here. Twice. But here you are again. With your kid."

"I don't have another choice." My fingers closed around a

cardboard coaster on the counter. "Do you have the paperwork?"

"No. Like I told you before, my contact will mail it directly to the P.O. box you gave me."

"When will it be there?"

Bea threw up her arms. "How should I know? My part is done. Thanks to you, I'm on bad terms with the guy now."

"Can you call him? Can you ask if it's on the way?"

"I'd prefer not to."

"Please." I pulled Noah closer to me. "You don't have to do it for me. Do it for my son."

Bea closed her eyes in dramatic fashion, seemingly taking a moment to weigh her options. "Wait here." She disappeared into the little room in the back. I helped Noah climb onto one of the barstools and swivel back and forth, overly aware of the inebriated man watching us from the shadows.

Bea returned about five minutes later, placing her hands on the counter and speaking in a whisper. "Okay. He sent it yesterday. It should be there soon."

"Thank you." I wanted to hug her, but her body language indicated I shouldn't get any closer. "Thank you." I repeated the words, my voice cracking with emotion.

Bea gave a slight nod, then looked at the door. "Don't come back again."

We left the bar, my hand pushing Noah in front of me toward our car. A flicker of hope sparked in my chest as I backed out of the spot.

It had been too risky to return to my sister's former home and pose as her. I'd overplayed my hand and should have known better. It was time to accept I might never know what had happened to Riley. Noah and I would head to Canada under our new identities as soon as the envelope arrived. I only hoped no one would get to me first.

THIRTY-NINE

Noah and I arrived on the patio, finding Wendy and George
already there. In a dangerous move, I'd called Wendy a few
hours earlier to ask if Cody could join us, and she'd simply said,
"The more, the merrier." I'd told Cody I was feeling better and
invited him to the dinner because being alone with him felt
unsafe. Still, getting answers to my questions about his whereabouts was vital. Before supposedly leaving for New York,
Cody had been nothing but good to me. He'd lent me thousands
of dollars, been a fun companion to Noah, and offered me
constant support. For my own sanity, I wanted another chance
to judge the authenticity of his words and actions and decide if
he was the trustworthy person I'd believed him to be or a grown-
up version of a troubled teen who'd been so infatuated with my
sister that he'd murdered her. I hoped my suspicions were
unfounded and that he'd take the gathering as an opportunity to
come clean about where he'd really been the last few days.

"There they are!" George shielded his eyes from the sun.
"Glad you could make it."

I gave him my best smile, pretending I wasn't planning an

imminent undercover getaway. "Of course. We'd never turn down free pizza."

Noah skipped toward the table. "I love pizza."

Wendy tucked a thick bundle of hair behind her ear and gave me a conspiratorial wink. She seemed to enjoy sharing our secret about the man who'd visited her doorstep. As we took our seats on the patio, gratitude rushed through me but dried up just as quickly as the memory of the threatening note scraped through my consciousness. *KEEP YOUR MOUTH SHUT OR YOU ARE NEXT!* Surely, the "you are next" referred to the previous deaths of Riley and Jacob. And there was a possibility that Cody was responsible for both.

George brought out glasses and a pitcher of lemonade, eyeing the pile of dirt next to the patio. "Sorry about the mess. Wendy and her gardening projects never end."

"The saplings will be here tomorrow, and then I'll have it all cleaned up. It will be a relief to have more shade out here," Wendy said, and the rest of us agreed. But I suddenly worried about her constant presence in the yard making our escape more difficult.

Cody arrived a few minutes later, greeting me with a hug and a kiss on the cheek, which I did my best to return. The gesture raised George's eyebrows.

Wendy folded her hands together. "It's nice to see you two getting along so well."

"I never realized how awesome Riley was back then." Cody shrugged as he shot me a sheepish glance. "Teenagers aren't always on top of their game, I guess."

Everyone giggled at that, even me, despite my nerves. George went inside, returning with two boxes of pizza. We helped ourselves to a piece or two and began to eat while George recounted his busy day cataloging a new load of used cars that had arrived and complaining about the condition of some clunkers that weren't selling.

When he stopped talking, I butted in. "Cody just returned from a work conference in New York City."

"Oh! How exciting." Wendy said, clearly eager to hear more.

I turned to face him. "Do you have any fun pictures to share?"

Cody dug his phone from his pocket and produced an image of the Empire State Building against a cloudy sky. "My hotel was so close to it." He pointed to the image, doubling down on his lie.

"Cool," I said. "Any photos of you with your co-workers?" I kept my voice light, asking an innocent question.

"Nah. We don't really do that. This was the only photo I took."

"Shoot. I would have loved to see more." The image of the iconic skyscraper was the kind anyone could grab off the internet. I wanted to probe further to let him know I knew he'd lied, but it seemed awkward and risky to do it with our hosts sitting around the table.

I tried to stay in the moment for the remainder of the gathering, reminding myself that the Eckharts had been good to me, and this was probably one of the last nights I'd spend with them. Even though the immediate threat of Drew Toven exposing me had been moved to the back burner, the note made it clear that it was unsafe for me and Noah to remain here. Our only option was to start over again, someplace where no one had any ties to my past. My breath hitched at the realization that I was running out of time to learn what really happened to Riley.

I studied Cody's face when he wasn't looking at me, wondering again if he could have been the one who murdered my sister. She must have called him Creepy Cody for a reason. Why lie about going to New York unless it was to cover up something else? Like breaking into my apartment in the middle of the night.

George got up to take away an empty pizza box, and Wendy excused herself to the restroom, leaving me and Cody as the only two adults at the table. A chill traveled through me as he scooted his chair closer. "How about I stick around tonight? I missed you."

"I missed you too," I said as my jaw tightened. "But I can't tonight. Too much work for my real estate class."

His body sagged, but he didn't say anything.

"Let's make plans for the weekend instead," I said, hoping Noah and I would be long gone by then.

"Sure." His voice was flat as he tightened his arms across his chest. "I have an early-morning meeting, anyway."

Once Noah was asleep, I organized our important things into piles so they'd be ready to throw into a couple of suitcases and go. I would explain everything to him once we'd driven across the Ambassador Bridge and far into Canada. He was only four and couldn't be trusted not to get upset and blurt out the secret before we were safe.

I stuffed a carton of old food into my overflowing kitchen trash, gagging at the foul odor. Removing and tying the bag, I carried it through the kitchen not wanting to leave too much extra work for George and Wendy once I was gone. I would not be paying the September rent they were expecting, and I hoped it wouldn't take them long to find a new tenant. Noah was out cold in the bedroom. He'd be fine for two minutes while I ran the smelly trash down to the larger bin in the alley.

I tiptoed out the door, closing it gently behind me. Moving swiftly, I exited the back gate and tossed the bag into the bin, thankful no one lurked in the shadows. I headed back through the gate and toward the stairs, eager to return to Noah.

"Out and about, I see."

The unexpected voice startled me, but my eyes followed the

sound, quickly landing on Brenda Harwood, peering over the fence at me. A bulb glowing from her porch backlit her shock of hair, giving her the appearance of an electrocuted corpse.

"Oh. You scared me." I continued on my way.

"You have a smart mouth."

"Yeah. Sorry about that." I took another step, feeling a tinge of remorse over the aggressive way I'd spoken to the older woman during our last encounter.

"That man was in your apartment." Brenda kept talking. "I saw him."

My feet stopped moving, my blood reversing course as I registered her words. Had she seen the intruder the other night? I spun toward her. "What did you say?"

"I remembered when I saw an update on the news today. His big white pickup truck always made such a racket. He was always lurking around here."

A big white pickup truck. I froze. "Jacob?"

"That was the name they gave on the news. Yes."

"He's dead."

"I know."

"When did you see him?"

Brenda huffed. "The night before he died. You should know better than anyone. He was up there with you late at night. Then he stormed down the steps and headed to the front yard. I thought he would speed away in that big truck of his."

"Didn't he?"

"No. He sat there idling in his truck for a few minutes. Then he marched right up to their front door." She nodded toward the Eckharts' house. "George and Wendy invited him in. I saw it all through my bedroom window."

I couldn't speak as I processed Brenda's words. A surge of terror filled my body, seeping to the tips of my fingers and toes.

Brenda shook her head. "Then, on the news today, I came to

learn that the same young man died in an accident the very next morning. I thought, what in the world is going on?"

I clutched my elbow, goosebumps erupting over my skin. "Jacob went into George and Wendy's house after he left my apartment?"

"Yes. Those two are always so friendly with everyone. Too friendly if you ask me. It's fake."

My mind tumbled back to the night Jacob confronted me after dinner. He'd figured out I wasn't who I'd said I was. He was supposed to give me twenty-four hours to leave with Noah. But what if he had gone to the Eckharts with his information instead? Maybe he believed he was protecting them from my fraud by telling them about my true identity. It felt as if someone had yanked my legs from beneath me, and I stumbled toward the fence, grasping on to the metal post. Jacob had known too much. Could George and Wendy be the ones who killed him? I could only think of one awful reason they wouldn't want him telling people I wasn't Riley.

My bones shifted beneath my skin as I stood across from Brenda, but I couldn't let her see me freaking out. I had to stay calm and dig for information. "Do you remember anything unusual from when I lived here before? From around the time I ran away?"

"Huh." Brenda shook her head. "It's been a while. Let me think." She touched her face, peering around the darkened backyard. "I was angry with them over the patio." She tipped her wild hair toward where we'd been eating pizza hours earlier. "That patio didn't used to be there, as you know. They had the cement poured just before the start of summer, but they didn't get a permit. That's illegal. A permit is required!" Brenda's voice had turned frantic, and it seemed the lack of a permit still caused her a great deal of distress.

I ground my molars together. "What was there before? I can't remember."

"Just grass. Then, a backhoe arrived out of the blue and dug up a big pile of dirt. Before I could attend the next city council meeting to complain, a contractor showed up, leveled it off, and poured the cement. But they didn't get away with it. I convinced the council to send them a hefty fine a few weeks later." She lifted her chin defiantly, clearly proud she'd gotten the last word on the patio dispute.

I remembered that night I'd spent in Riley's bedroom. It was early May, only a couple of weeks before she disappeared. I didn't recall any signs of a patio being added. Then again, I'd gone in and out through the front door, and it had been dark outside when I'd peeked through her bedroom window toward the garage apartment. Still, something sour turned in my stomach. I was sure Riley had never made it to L.A. It now seemed possible that George and Wendy could have done something terrible to stop her from running away. The ground beneath a cement slab would have provided an undetectable hiding place for a body. I looked toward the patio, viewing it through a darker lens. Had Riley been this close to me the whole time, encased in a patio-shaped tomb?

A soft light glowed somewhere inside the second floor of the Eckharts' house. I didn't want to believe they had harmed Riley or Jacob or that they were the ones who'd left the note telling me to keep my mouth shut, but I couldn't discount what Brenda had seen.

My senses were suddenly amplified. Brenda's porchlight burned my eyes, blurring my vision. I uttered a flustered good night and raced up to the apartment, locking myself inside and trying to make sense of the disturbing discoveries. The pieces were coming together, creating a terrifying picture. I thought I'd been the one scamming Riley's former foster parents, but I was mistaken. They had been one step ahead of me the entire time.

FORTY

I collapsed to the floor, hugging my knees to my chest. A rush of memories clogged my head, and I struggled to arrange them in a sensible order. More red flags appeared, and I scolded myself for missing them. Wendy had received so many signs that I wasn't Riley, and she'd played dumb, ignoring them all. She'd never flinched at the TV news reports about Sandra Matthews with my face on the screen or the mention of my potato salad, the same one I'd brought to her barbecue. She'd disregarded another report describing a woman on the run with a four-year-old son, never connecting the dots that hovered so clearly before her. And when Drew Toven had knocked on her door, intending to blow up my life, Wendy had accepted my side of things much too easily. She and George must have known all along I wasn't Riley. There was only one reason I could think of for them to go along with my lies; they needed my story to stay intact because they had killed my sister. They could never be guilty in the court of public opinion—much less charged with murder—if everyone believed Riley was still alive.

The shock of their betrayal sent a chill crawling across my skin. My mind flipped back to how Wendy had greeted me when I'd first arrived at her door. She'd been surprised, which was expected. But her confusion had quickly morphed into delight. She'd taken pity on me and offered me the apartment free of rent. She had even thrown a party to let everyone know I was back. What I'd interpreted at the time as thoughtful gestures now appeared calculated and self-serving. Before the party, Wendy had made a point to bring photo albums to me and review each picture, reminding me of names and funny anecdotes. In retrospect, she had likely been coaching me to ensure my act was believable, that I didn't get the names of former friends wrong, like Aunt Leslie, and that I remembered specific details about Jacob, including the truck he used to drive and our night at the junior prom. The gossip that had swirled around town for so long about Riley's foster parents' potential involvement in her disappearance would cease as long as I didn't screw up. Everyone would finally know the Eckharts were innocent of any wrongdoing, and the agency had acted unjustly in prohibiting them from taking in any other kids. My reappearance as Riley had completely exonerated them and restored their once-stellar reputation in the community.

But Jacob must have threatened the Eckharts' plan when he shared what he knew with them. They silenced him before it was too late.

I forced myself to stand, moving toward the window. Light from the second story of the Eckharts' house illuminated the patio. An unexpected sadness pulled through me, anchoring my arms to my sides. The side of the house bordering the McKneelys' yard sat in darkness. They hadn't returned from their vacation yet, but I knew what waited in the shadows—a giant hole for the saplings Wendy had supposedly ordered, the trees I still hadn't seen. A terrifying understanding grabbed hold of my bones. The hole wasn't for saplings. George and Wendy were preparing a hiding spot for another body. I thought of the near miss as I'd walked home from my late night out with

Tabitha and the threatening note in my apartment. I was their obvious next target.

I had become too much of a wildcard for them. George had caught me snooping in the basement. The secret room enshrined with photos now felt more like a creepy memorial rather than a private place to remember former foster kids. I'd gotten too close to Cody, a relationship George and Wendy probably hadn't anticipated. Maybe they'd realized I'd come back as Riley not only to hide from my crimes but also to investigate my sister's death. It made sense for them to get rid of me. My worries turned toward Noah. What would become of him? He wouldn't survive a group home. The Eckharts acted more like his grandparents, and I wondered if they would move to gain custody. The notion catapulted through me, and I wanted to scream and throw something at the wall, but Noah was sleeping. Instead, I clenched my fists and paced across the living room. Cody was the only other person who knew my secret. He could be at risk too.

I fought the urge to call him, to find out any detail he could remember from when Riley had disappeared or when the cement had been poured for the patio. But Cody had lied about his whereabouts the same night I received the note, and I didn't know why. And one piece of my theory about the Eckharts didn't fit. Wendy and George drove silver cars, the ones I'd seen them driving nearly every day since I'd moved in, the cars they parked in the garage below me. Neither of them drove a black car. But Cody did. I wasn't sure who to trust.

Noah and I needed to leave town quickly, but we couldn't without the documents. And now, another obligation kept me in place. My sister deserved justice. The entire truth swung like a wrecking ball near the edge of my psyche, trying to break through. But some questions remained unanswered. As long as I had to wait for our papers to arrive, I would watch my back and turn over a few more stones.

As I stepped toward the outlet to plug in my laptop cord, a shadow darkened the front window, a board creaking outside. Terror seized my body, my blood ice-cold. I couldn't move. I couldn't breathe.

Someone was out there.

FORTY-ONE

I ducked down, but hiding was pointless. The lights were on, and my car was out front. It was obvious I was home. I envisioned George and Wendy stationed outside, holding a knife or a gun, ready to take me down and bury me in the hole. They'd tell people I'd run off again, this time without my son.

"Hey. It's me. Cody." His voice sounded through the door, followed by a few soft knocks. "Are you awake?"

I slunk toward the counter, slipping a knife into my back pocket just in case. Then, I peeked through the window, confirming he was alone. He held a small box wrapped in red gift wrap in one hand. I couldn't let my guard down. He'd lied to me, and I needed to confront him. My fingers touched the knife handle. I was prepared to defend myself if necessary, the same way I'd done with Drew.

I cracked the door, wedging my face in the opening. "What are you doing here?"

"Sorry. I thought you seemed a little upset at dinner. Or distant or something. I just wanted to make sure you were okay." He held the box out to me. "I got you something."

"In New York?" I asked, struggling to hide my eye roll.

"Yeah."

I huffed out a puff of air. "Cut the crap, Cody. I know you didn't go to the conference. I called your office."

His head dropped, but not before I saw the flash of shame on his face, the look of someone who'd been caught. "Shit. I'm an idiot. I should have just told you."

"Told me what?"

"Can I come in?"

My arms moved stiffly as I motioned for him to enter. I squared my shoulders to block him from moving any further, one hand touching the knife handle behind my back. "Where were you? I don't have time for bullshit. Tell me the truth, or I'm done."

Cody ran his fingers through his hair, his other hand lowering the present. "I've been seeing someone else for about six months. Her name is Liz. She lives about an hour away near Lansing."

"Oh." It wasn't what I thought he'd say, and an unexpected ball of jealousy tumbled through me.

He continued talking. "After I met you, I realized the thing between me and Liz wasn't real. We met online. Before her, I'd been on so many bad dates. I thought she was the best I was going to get. But then you showed up. Things were so different and easy with you." He let out a prolonged breath. "I went to her house to break up with her in person. I thought I owed her that. Then I took an extra night to visit a friend who lives near there."

"I see." Heat flushed my cheeks, a strange mixture of anger, jealousy, and flattery.

He tugged at the hem of his shirt, a pained look on his face. "It was stupid of me to lie. I just thought you'd be mad I'd never mentioned Liz after we'd already been dating for a while, and I knew a co-worker was going to the conference in New York. I wanted to end things with Liz without you knowing."

I stepped closer to him, smelling a hint of his aftershave. It was the best reason for lying he could have offered. "Yeah. You should have told me." My fingers released the knife handle, leaving it in my pocket. "But I'm probably going to have to disappear soon. Then you'll still be alone."

He gave a nod. "You might need to run, but I want you to be safe. You taught me that I don't have to settle, and I'm grateful for that."

I leaned into him, inhaling his scent as he wrapped an arm around me. Cody was the type of man I'd never let myself dream of when I'd been on the run. I'd never been in one place long enough. I'd never been allowed to be myself. My connection with him felt different because it was real. There was so much I needed to tell him about the Eckharts. Before I could say anything, he pushed the tiny box into my hands.

"This is for you. Open it."

"For what?"

"Just open it."

I ripped off the paper and removed the lid, finding a baby-blue Tiffany box and a pair of earrings sparkling inside. "Oh my gosh. They're beautiful!"

"Diamonds and sapphires. And because we're being completely honest with each other, I should tell you I bought them for Liz a couple of weeks before I met you." His eyelids lowered as he offered a sheepish grin. "I realized almost immediately that I'd made a mistake. I shouldn't have spent so much of my savings on a gift. I was going to return the earrings and get my money back, but now I want you to have them."

The earrings weighed in my palm as I recalled the secretive purchase that had drained Cody's liquid savings. This must have been it, not car repairs as I'd imagined. Of course, he wouldn't have wanted to tell me about the expensive jewelry he bought for his other girlfriend.

He gestured toward the box. "Take them with you if you need to run. You can sell them and live off the money for a while. They're still in the box; you should be able to get eight or nine grand."

Tears welled in my eyes. Cody had pulled through for me again, but our time together was running out. "Thank you." I hugged him and led him toward the couch. "Noah and I may need to leave sooner than we thought."

"What does that mean?"

I walked him through the harrowing events of the last few days, starting with Drew showing up at Wendy's door and blowing my cover—with Wendy accepting my explanation, no questions asked—and the intruder who'd left the threatening note in my kitchen in the middle of the night.

Cody let out an incredulous gasp. "I had no idea this was going on. You should have told me."

"You lied about where you were. I couldn't help thinking it might have been you."

"I screwed up." Cody winced, shaking his head. "I shouldn't have lied to you."

I continued before he could apologize again. "There's more. I just spoke to Brenda Harwood."

"The mean woman next door?"

"Yeah. She said the Eckharts poured a cement patio without a permit shortly after Riley disappeared. There was a pile of dirt there." I widened my eyes at Cody. "I think George and Wendy killed my sister and buried her beneath their patio. I think they've known I'm not Riley since I arrived. They went along with my story to exonerate themselves from all the rumors people said about them back then."

Cody grew unnaturally quiet, a strange look flickering through his dark eyes as he stared at nothing in particular.

"Did you hear me?" I asked.

He squeezed his eyes closed, still saying nothing.

"Cody. What's wrong?"

He snapped out of whatever trance he'd been in and faced me. "It all makes sense now."

FORTY-TWO

"What makes sense, Cody?" I leaned closer, willing him to speak, but he had traveled somewhere else in his mind. "Do you remember anything else from back then?"

His gaze crawled across the walls before he refocused on me. "When I first moved into this apartment, I was so happy. It felt like I'd won the lottery, especially after having zero privacy in the group home."

"Yeah. I'm sure it did."

He picked at his cuticle, taking a breath. "George and Wendy had a lot of rules, though. Some of them weren't bad, like I had to do yard work every Saturday or be home by nine on weeknights and eleven on weekends. Normal parenting stuff."

"Okay." I leaned in, hanging on every word.

"Before Riley moved in, another kid lived in that bedroom." Cody's eyes flicked in the direction of the Eckharts' house and Riley's former window.

I gasped, never having contemplated who had lived in Riley's bedroom before her.

"His name was Pete. He only stayed there for three or four months before returning to the group home. At first, I thought the Eckharts sent him back, but then I found out later that Pete had requested the move. It didn't make sense because the group homes I'd lived in had been terrible compared to this."

I nodded, silently agreeing that the years spent living in the group homes were some of the worst of my life.

"But I'll never forget Pete's face before he left, the look of hatred in his eyes. He was happy to leave. When I asked him what happened, he only said he couldn't wait to get away from George and Wendy."

Something sour churned in my stomach as I listened to Cody's story, noticing the glint of terror in his eyes.

"And here's the thing." Cody swiveled his knees toward mine, pausing to take a breath. "A social worker came here the next day and interviewed me, asking about George and Wendy and their fitness as foster parents. It wasn't the same social worker who did the monthly check-ins. It was obvious the woman was there because of Pete. He must have said some really bad things about them. I told her that the Eckharts were strict but that they provided a good home. I didn't mention that we ate buttered noodles or ramen practically every night for dinner and peanut butter sandwiches every day for lunch, while George and Wendy made themselves much better food. Some-times, I smelled steaks or barbecue chicken on the grill and noticed fresh fruit and salads in the fridge, but it was for them, not us. When I questioned George about the food one time, he told me I could buy expensive food when I had a job someday. He made me feel like I was a freeloader for even asking, and I never mentioned it again."

"Are you serious?" Cody's description of George and Wendy seemed at odds with the couple who had welcomed me into their home over the last several weeks. They'd been generous to a fault.

"Yeah. In retrospect, I can see that they didn't really care about us. It was more like they were in love with the control they had and the way people praised them for taking in foster kids. I don't know what George and Wendy did with our monthly stipends, but they weren't spending it on our food or clothing. Our clothes were hand-me-downs. I overheard George telling someone on the phone that they got a couple hundred more per month for taking in kids over fourteen. Still, I didn't make a big deal about it because things weren't too bad, and I didn't want to risk losing the apartment and getting sent back to the group home."

"I can understand that."

"But, maybe two weeks after he moved out, that kid, Pete, died."

My mouth fell open as Cody's statement ripped through me. I shook my head, not wanting to believe it. "Are you serious? What happened?"

"Some business owner found him in an alley one morning. Pete had overdosed on pills. Or at least that's what it was made to look like. No one ever questioned his cause of death, not even me." Cody's face turned ghostly white as he looked at me. "But all of a sudden, I'm not so sure."

My insides felt hollow as I processed his words, my heart twisting for the boy named Pete, whom I'd never known. Had he and Riley met similar fates?

Cody clutched his head before lowering his arms back to his lap. "I never put the pieces together then. No one did. George and Wendy had everyone fooled, acting like gracious foster parents who rescued kids from horrible situations. Everyone in this town showered them with praise like they were saints or something. They must have thought their goodwill gave them a license to do whatever they wanted to us. And I started noticing some weird stuff after Pete died."

"Like what?"

"Things in my apartment moved to a different spot than where I'd left them."

My blood dripped through my veins as I scanned the apartment walls, remembering the off-kilter rug and the open closet door. "That's been happening to me too."

"You should have told me." Cody fidgeted, something indiscernible brewing behind his eyes. "There's more, though."

I nodded, encouraging him to continue, even as I was afraid to hear whatever he would say next.

"One time, I wanted to go out with some friends to the arcade. Wendy asked if I'd finished the yard work. I hadn't gotten to it yet but didn't want to miss the fun, so I told her I'd done it. When Wendy discovered my lie the next day, she was so pissed. But then her demeanor completely changed, like someone had flipped a switch. She acted all sweet, telling me about the lasagna she was making with garlic bread and Caesar salad and asking me to help. It was a better meal than she usually made, and I was relieved because I thought she'd forgiven me. So when she asked me to stir the sauce, I went to the stove to help. Wendy bumped a pot of boiling water with her elbow, and it dumped all over me."

A sharp breath caught in my throat. "She spilled boiling water on you?"

Cody nodded, a deadened look in his eyes. "She acted like it was an accident, but I had a feeling she'd done it on purpose to get back at me for lying about the yard work."

"Did you report it?"

"No. Wendy kept insisting it was a mishap. She said she'd been clumsy lately, always tripping and knocking things over. The burns on my arm were severe, but George and Wendy wouldn't let me go to the emergency room. They said we had to treat the burns at home because my health insurance wouldn't cover it. Wendy spent the next several days doting on me and making sure I had all the painkillers and bandages I needed. She apologized so many times that she convinced me it must have been an accident. Again, it wasn't worth getting

sent back to the group home, especially if I was wrong."
Cody's body seemed to shrink into itself as he relived the
memory. "It took months for my arm to heal. Riley probably
wondered why I wore long-sleeved shirts even when it was
warm outside."

"I'm sorry," I said, but my mouth was so dry I could barely
get the words out. "I didn't realize they physically abused you."

"They never did it directly. Even now, I'm not sure Wendy
spilled that water on purpose. It was always in a way that made
me question myself and wonder if I'd misinterpreted the situation. Another time, I had a follow-up appointment with the
same social worker who talked to me after Pete left. I was
changing my clothes in the bedroom before meeting with her.
When I came out of the room, George stood outside my door
holding a hammer. It totally freaked me out. He said he'd let
himself in to take care of some nails that had popped out around
the doorframe, but the tone of his voice wasn't right. It was more
like he was threatening me without saying the words. I dressed
as fast as I could and got the hell out of there."

"Did you tell the social worker?"

"No. I was too scared. And just like the boiling water, I
wasn't sure if I was making something out of nothing. As an
adult, I can see that what he did was wrong. But I was only a kid
then. I'd never had a real family and didn't know how parents
were supposed to act."

"I'm so sorry."

"That's why I didn't feel bad about stealing their money
and moving out. I realize now that I only helped support their
story that Riley had run away, but I didn't think about that at
the time. I was always grateful to the Eckharts for getting me
out of the group home and letting me live in my own apartment.
But somewhere deep inside, George and Wendy scared me.
And when they started accusing me of having done something
to Riley, I kept my distance from them. Riley lived in the house

with them, though. It must have been even worse for her. I really thought she'd bolted. It made sense to me."

I sat up straight. "Maybe they found out she was planning to leave."

"They must have flipped out and gone too far."

I couldn't breathe for a second, my vision sharpening in a moment of clarity. It all made sense, just like Cody said. But one piece still didn't fit. "What about the black car that hit Jacob? George and Wendy both drive silver cars."

Cody shook his head. "I don't know. But George works at a car dealership. He could have taken a used car for a test drive. Maybe he chose one that already had some damage to the front. He could have run it through the company car wash to eliminate evidence."

I dug my fingers into the couch, remembering George talking about the shipment of clunkers that had arrived, which sounded like a regular occurrence. "He can probably drive any of the cars on the lot whenever he wants."

"I'm sure he moves cars between lots all the time."

I held my breath, the complete and horrible picture imprinted in my mind.

Cody grasped my hands, forcing me to lock eyes with him. "Are you okay?"

I nodded, but I felt sick. I had done dishonest things to get by, but the Eckharts were different. They were the worst kind of con artists. They preyed on kids who were desperate for parents. They were pure evil. I gripped Cody's hands tighter, knowing he was correct. Brenda Harwood from next door had seen it too, but I'd disregarded her rantings. I hadn't realized the extent of the Eckharts' ongoing fraud until today. They had beaten me at my own game.

My head turned toward the window, where a faint light still glowed from the room that used to belong to Riley. She'd been so desperate to run away. She must have seen through George and Wendy's façade, although she'd never told me the whole story. As much as I wanted to get as far away from them as possible, my body was now fueled by the need to get justice for my sister.

My voice hardened into something sharp and venomous as I released Cody's hands and spoke the next words. "We have to make them pay."

FORTY-THREE

Cody and I stayed up all night, brainstorming a plan to expose the Eckharts. We had a dilemma, though. Sharing our suspicion that Riley's body was buried beneath the patio with the police would expose my true identity and put me in danger of being arrested. No action could be taken until I had the documents for me and Noah in hand and one foot out the door. Noah zoomed around the apartment, fully rested and ready for preschool. He'd been especially excited about a visit from a local aquarium today to learn about sea creatures and look at some fish. But it wouldn't be safe for him to go.

I caught up with him and crouched to eye level. "I'm sorry, buddy. You're not going to school today. We're doing something different."

Noah let out an ear-piercing whine and collapsed on the floor. "I want to go to preschool. Today is the fish day!"

I looked at my watch, wanting to get to the post office as soon as it opened. Noah let loose another prolonged and pained cry. I couldn't bring him with me in this state. It would draw too much attention.

Cody ran a hand across his forehead, taking in the scene. "Should I take Noah to my place?"

"No. Wendy or George might see you. It's better if we don't alert them that anything out of the ordinary is happening."

"Okay. I can stay here with him. I'll call in sick."

"Are you sure?"

"Yeah. George and Wendy likely know who you are and what you've done. They could do something at any moment." He stepped toward me, lowering his voice so only I could hear him. "We need to get you out of here as soon as possible. Once you're safe, I'll call the police to report the Eckharts. I'll suggest they dig up the patio."

"You're right. Thank you. I'll be as quick as I can." I nodded toward the two suitcases packed with important belongings and my backpack containing the valuable earrings. "I've got our bags ready to go."

"Good. Don't worry about us. Just watch your back."

I told Noah I'd return soon, and then I darted down the steps and across the backyard, thankfully avoiding any encounters. Striding past the far side of the house and the giant hole in the ground, I tried my best not to envision my lifeless body buried inside.

I opened my P.O. box with trembling fingers. A large envelope was curled inside, and I nearly screamed. Hugging the envelope close, I hurried back to my car and hunched over, tearing it open and flipping through the birth certificates—one each for Noah and me—and a matching Minnesota driver's license for me, the enhanced kind that allowed passage to Canada. My name was Kathleen Hardy, age thirty-two. Noah was my four-year-old son, Marcus Hardy. His birth certificate showed he'd been born in Minneapolis. We had social security numbers too. It was more than enough documentation to give us a fresh start. Bea's contact had delivered.

Adrenaline coursed through my body as I drove to an abandoned warehouse several miles away and ditched my car in the corner of the overgrown parking lot. I speed-walked a half-mile to a gas station, calling for an Uber to take me to a nearby car rental, where I rented a car using my new I.D., paying extra for insurance and confirming a drop-off location near Toronto. I'd return the rental car in Toronto and purchase a used car somewhere nearby using whatever cash I could get from the earrings. Noah and I would find our way to our new home from there. Cody was to wait twenty-four hours before calling the police to give us time to disappear. Before I tossed my phone into one of the local waterways, I would text McKenzie something like, *The Eckharts killed Jacob because he knew I wasn't Riley. Look into it.* That way, the tips would come from multiple sources.

I arrived back at Marigold Street, moving with a sense of urgency and ready to grab Noah and our bags and go. Parking in the back alley, I jogged up the steps and through the front door with the envelope zipped into my purse. But no anxious boyfriend and crying son greeted me inside. I took a disoriented step as I looked around at the empty space. A cabinet above the sink was open, and a half-eaten piece of toast rested on a plate. The room held an eerie aura, as if everyone had left in a hurry.

"Cody! Noah!" I called, but there was no response as I searched the apartment. They weren't in the bedroom or bathroom. I texted him.

Where are you? Is everything okay?

A bitter taste filled my mouth as no answer came.

Maybe Cody had sensed a threat and driven somewhere or couldn't stop Noah from crying and took him to the park. Or had he tricked me into thinking he was on my side? Had I trusted him too easily and allowed him to kidnap Noah? I sprinted through the backyard and out to the street. A vehicle that matched the description Cody had given me of his car—a newer model black Ford Explorer—was parked about half a block down. He hadn't driven anywhere.

Unease expanded in my gut as I made my way back to the empty apartment. I'd seen the Eckharts' cars in the garage, but their house showed no sign of activity. The windows gawked at me, black and silent like watching eyes. It would be dangerous to venture inside, yet the thought of Noah being with them lured me toward the glass door beyond the patio. As usual, it slid open easily, a familiar noise meeting my ears as I entered the living room. Noah's giggle echoed through the hallway. He was here. I followed the sound, reminding myself to play it cool so they wouldn't suspect anything. I couldn't let them know I'd figured out the horrible thing they'd done. I needed to get my son away from them.

"Noah! Mommy's here."

"Hi!" His voice echoed from below me. They were in the basement.

I headed toward the stairs, fear pulsing through me as I took the wooden steps two at a time.

"I bet you make nice drawings like that." Wendy's voice came from inside the little room, the one with the newspaper articles and the photos of their foster kids lining the walls.

"Yeah," Noah answered her.

I realized it wasn't a room lined with happy memories but a ghastly space decorated by two monsters. I entered the room. My hand shook as I dug through my purse for the pepper spray, gripping it.

Wendy eyed me as I approached, then refocused on Noah as she pointed at one of the crayon drawings on the wall. "Some of these boys and girls were good. And some were very bad. Which kind would you be?"

Her question crawled down my spine, but I remained silent.

"Good," Noah said in a matter-of-fact tone.

"I knew you wouldn't be like the bad ones." She patted Noah's head as she trained her eyes on the framed photo of Riley. "There was one really bad girl who tried to run away in the middle of the night." Wendy clucked her disapproval. "She threatened to report us after all we'd done for her. So ungrateful."

Wendy's comment scraped a raw nerve, and it took every ounce of self-restraint not to lunge toward her and punch her in the face. I remembered the force with which she'd yanked Noah from the floor and spanked him, and I suddenly knew she must have hit Riley too.

"Noah, come here." I struggled to keep my voice even as I stood near the doorway, waving him to me. "It's time to go. We can visit Wendy later." I forced a stiff smile in her direction.

Wendy only stared back at me, apparently not buying my act. She grabbed Noah, pinning him to her side with both arms. Noah squirmed, which only made Wendy squeeze him tighter.

Her gaze lowered on me like a net. "I got the strangest call that Noah didn't show up for preschool today."

I cringed, kicking myself for forgetting to call in Noah's absence this morning and for listing Wendy as the emergency contact.

Wendy tutted. "I thought I better check on him. You can imagine my surprise when I saw your belongings packed in bags." Her eyes grew darker as she spoke. "Were you going somewhere?"

I forced my words through my teeth. "Give me my son back."

"I think he'd be happier living with us." Her matter-of-fact tone was paired with a deranged smile on her lips. Noah began to cry, but Wendy kept a firm grip. "I know who you are." Spittle flew from her mouth. "Your resemblance to Riley is uncanny, but it took me about thirty seconds to realize Riley must not have been an only child. You're obviously her sister."

I clenched my molars, considering my next move.

Wendy shook her head, smirking. "Did you think I didn't recognize you from the news reports about Sandra Matthews?"

Terror seized my throat, my neck growing hot at my own stupidity.

Wendy raised her chin. "But I still didn't understand why you couldn't live under your real name. Why pose as your missing sister? You had altered your appearance enough since you left Las Vegas. No one else in this town would have connected you to Sandra Matthews."

I wanted to strangle her, but I couldn't move, couldn't speak.

"So, I researched local unsolved crimes from fifteen years ago, and, lo and behold, I stumbled on an article about the suspicious death of a young woman fresh out of a group home in Roseville." She paused, something dangerous glittering in her eyes. "I bet the police would love to know the whereabouts of Gina Holland."

"No." I spit the word at her. "You're wrong. Give me my son."

She took a step back, dragging Noah with her. "I'll make a deal with you. Go somewhere far away and change your name and appearance. We'll say you ran away again. No one will arrest you for all the things you've done."

My muscles coiled, ready to fight the vile woman. "I am not leaving my son. And I know Riley didn't run away. You killed her. And Jacob. And you killed that other boy, Pete, too."

"Jacob was a shame. He knew too much." Wendy stared me down, refusing to blink. "But Riley and Pete brought it on themselves. They caused too much trouble for us. We should never have taken in teenagers. Those entitled brats couldn't keep their mouths shut."

Noah wriggled in her arms, but she squeezed tighter, looking down at him. "Stay still, Noah. I don't want to have to spank you again."

I found Noah's eyes, silently letting him know that I wouldn't let Wendy hurt him. Then I glared at the despicable woman. "Why did you do it?"

"I had no choice. The night after the high school dance, I caught Riley with her suitcase packed. She said she was leaving and I couldn't stop her. She was going to report me for some nonsense—slapping her and burning her with a candle—as if she didn't deserve a punishment for getting that hideous tattoo and coming home late from the dance." Wendy scoffed. "When I laughed at her, she held up a note Pete had left beneath the dresser as a warning for the next kid. It detailed all the times we'd supposedly hit him or withheld his food. Riley was going to turn that in too. We would have been ruined if she corroborated Pete's story. We'd only just gotten back on the agency's good side and convinced them Pete was a lying drug addict." Sweat glistened through the powder on Wendy's forehead.

Wendy had confirmed my worst fears. They'd been responsible for all three deaths. "You didn't have to kill them." My voice stretched with so much despair I barely recognized it as my own.

"You tried to kill your boss at the construction company. And you killed Marianne Clavey. So we're no different, really."

I righted myself, refusing to let Wendy twist things around. "I'm nothing like you. I wasn't trying to kill either of them." I spun toward the stairwell and yelled, "Cody! Help!"

Wendy shook her head. "He can't hear you. He's all tied up right now."

The floor seemed to tilt beneath me, weakening my knees. They'd done something to Cody.

"You can't turn me in without turning yourself in. I told you the truth about your sister. Now, I'm giving you one chance to get away right now and leave Noah with us."

"I'm not sure." I chewed on my lip, pretending to consider her offer. But my stomach convulsed as I feared the worst—losing my son. The pepper spray weighed in my hand, but Noah was too close to Wendy's face. I couldn't spray her without harming him too. I moved toward the nearest framed picture, the solid metal one containing an image of a teenage Riley smiling by the fence. I grabbed the hard object and lunged toward Wendy, swinging the metal frame and hitting the corner as hard as I could against her head. Her eyes widened as she fell to the ground, releasing Noah on the way down. I whacked her one more time on the back of the skull to make sure she'd stay down for at least several minutes.

Noah began to cry and I scooped him into my arms, leaving Wendy lying in a heap on the floor. "Let's go."

I ran up the stairs, fleeing to the outdoors. But as we crossed the patio, a scratching noise drew my attention to the side of the house. I peeked around the corner to find George hunched with a shovel, pushing dirt into the hole.

FORTY-FOUR

It took a second for my brain to register the scene. George scraped dirt into a hole, shielded by the Eckharts' house on one side and the out-of-town neighbors' house on the other. The gate blocked the view from the street, and a wheelbarrow sat nearby. I lowered Noah and told him to stand by the flowers on Brenda's side of the yard, not wanting to think about what George was burying. But I already knew.

Cody. My throat let loose a low howl, animal instinct taking over. I felt as if I was floating above myself, watching another person fly into action. George lowered the shovel, eyes bulging when he realized I was charging him. I shot the pepper spray toward his face as I neared. He held up his arms, which did little to shield him from the noxious chemical. He doubled over, groaning in pain. I peered into the ditch, finding a thin layer of dirt covering a long, body-shaped lump. "Oh, no. Oh, no." Frantically, I dropped to my knees and brushed away the dirt, revealing the side of Cody's face. My senses were heightened, my heart throbbing in my ears. I never should have returned here. Jacob was dead because of me. I'd put Cody in danger, and now I'd lost him too.

George fumbled around nearby, cursing me to hell. But another softer sound startled me, something like a cough. It came from beneath the dirt. Cody was still alive. I reached toward him, but his body lay at least a couple of feet down, and I couldn't lift him out.

"Cody, I'm here," I said, scooping the dirt away from his face. "Hang on. I'm going for help." When I turned around, George had disappeared, probably having gone inside to wash out his eyes and find his wife. I grabbed Noah's hand, nodding toward Brenda's house. "Come on, Noah. I'll race you next door."

When we reached Brenda's front yard, I called 911 from my phone. "George Eckhart at 1189 Marigold Street is burying someone alive. Please hurry." I gulped back a sob, altering our plan. "And George and Wendy Eckhart have murdered three people. Riley Wakefield is buried beneath their patio. They killed Jacob Fletcher in the hit-and-run. And they may have killed a boy named Pete who lived at their house fifteen or sixteen years ago." I repeated the address and hung up.

A gasp drew my attention toward the shrubs, where Brenda appeared through the branches, clinging to her hedge trimmers. "Is that true?"

"You were right about them."

"I knew it." Her eyes dimmed with a realization. "But if Riley is under the patio, then who are you?"

I ignored her question, carrying Noah back to the alley and checking to see if it was safe to grab our bags from the apartment. A faint siren sounded in the distance. George and Wendy were still inside unless they'd made a run for it. I took the opportunity to carry Noah up the stairs, collect our belongings, and race to my car. I wanted to check on Cody, but it was too risky to stick around. The police would be here momentarily, and hopefully an ambulance. My escape plan had escalated to a red alert.

.   .   .

I ditched my phone in a water reservoir and drove toward the Detroit–Windsor border crossing with Noah in the backseat. Three hours later, we were well into Canada and nearing Toronto, the first stop on our way to starting over as Kathleen and Marcus Hardy. But I would only succeed if Cody survived. Riley, Jacob, and Pete would only receive justice if George and Wendy were charged with multiple murders. Hopefully, all the broken pieces I'd left behind would somehow fall into place.

From a motel room on the outskirts of Montreal, I sat on the bed watching a U.S. news station. We'd been hunkered down in the outdated room for five days, paying in cash and hiding behind the olive-green curtains. Yesterday, I sold the Tiffany earrings to a nearby pawn shop, providing me $8,000 in cash. When enough time had passed, Noah—now Marcus—and I would get on the road again and continue to our final destination: a suburb called Dartmouth in Nova Scotia. I hoped to settle for the last time, enroll Marcus in school, and find a job. But my chest felt hollow without Cody. We had no means of contacting each other, and my internet searches hadn't revealed anything about his well-being yet. I worried he hadn't survived. I'd been watching the same station for hours every day, hoping for a glimpse of the mess I'd left behind and yearning for justice.

A woman with platinum hair and wearing a red power suit stood in front of a map of Michigan. I drew in a sharp breath and moved closer to the TV as the screen zoomed in on the Detroit area, landing on Berkley. The newscaster began her report. "A gruesome discovery was made today in a twisty murder case in a Detroit suburb. The body of sixteen-year-old Riley Wakefield was uncovered beneath a cement patio of her former foster parents' home. Riley had been missing for over fifteen years. Authorities previously believed she'd run away, a theory bolstered when a woman recently showed up at the home claiming to be her. And the imposter, who is now believed to be Riley's sister and a wanted fugitive, Gina Holland, fooled everyone. Gina tipped off police about Riley's body buried beneath the patio and, even more strangely, a man being buried alive at the same property.

"The man, now identified as Cody Beck, was rescued shortly after being discovered unconscious in a dirt hole and taken to the hospital for treatment. Meanwhile, former foster parents George and Wendy Eckhart are suspected in the hit-and-run of another local resident, Jacob Fletcher, that resulted in the death of the thirty-two-year-old man. George Eckhart allegedly used a car from the Chevy dealership where he works to commit the crime. The couple faces two murder charges in the deaths of Riley Wakefield and Jacob Fletcher and one count of attempted murder related to Cody Beck. A third count of murder may be added as authorities begin to investigate the suspicious death of another one of the Eckharts' previous foster children, Peter Zallen, whose lifeless body was discovered in an alley two weeks after he left their care sixteen years ago."

I flopped backward on the bed, feeling at peace for the first time in days. I'd been correct about Riley's tragic fate, and the truth about her death was finally known. It was a bittersweet satisfaction, but I could begin to heal. Cody was alive. He'd been rescued. My heart ached with the knowledge that I may never see him again, but at least he was safe. And it was only a matter of time before George and Wendy went to prison.

EPILOGUE
ONE YEAR LATER...

Afternoon light filtered through the kitchen as Marcus tramped past me, reciting facts about dinosaurs. I pushed the curtain aside to view the gray colonial next door, where colorful balloons tied to the fence post fluttered in the wind. Our tidy suburban home in Dartmouth was nicer than anywhere I'd ever lived, and the quarter-acre lot was big enough for us to kick a soccer ball. Affording this family home was a luxury I'd never had.

"You look nice. Ready for the party?" Michael stepped next to me and kissed my head. I'd adjusted quickly to Cody's new name, Michael Samson, but his presence still felt surreal.

I thought back to the night Cody and I had been huddled together in the garage apartment, planning my escape. The reality of losing him had been too much to bear, so I'd whispered a secret in his ear, sharing the place where Noah and I were headed. "Dartmouth, Nova Scotia." He had only blinked at me, giving an almost indiscernible nod. Revealing the vital information broke every protocol I lived by, but something in my gut knew Cody was worth the risk, and he had the street smarts to cover his tracks. While I was confident he would take my secret to the grave, I wasn't sure if he would follow through on the move. It was a lot to ask, and I'd prepared never to see him again.

But four months after Noah and I left Michigan for Canada, becoming Marcus and Kathleen, Cody disappeared in the night, leaving everything behind to join us. He sold his condo and purchased an iron-clad new identity from his contact on the dark web. He found me two weeks later, just before kindergarten pickup time, in the parking lot of Marcus's elementary school—the third school he'd checked. We used the proceeds from his condo, which had increased drastically in value since he'd purchased it, to pay for our house in cash. I did the marketing and bookkeeping for our newly formed business, which specialized in building and optimizing websites for large companies. Even though I'd had to give up my prospective real estate career, my position with the family company felt just as rewarding. The life I'd always dreamed of had become a reality. I had a loving family, a nice home, and a good career. I only wished Riley could have been a part of it.

I smoothed down my dress and retrieved a bowl from the fridge. "I'm ready to mingle with the neighbors." The family next door was hosting a neighborhood potluck today. My potato salad would have been a hit, but serving it wasn't worth the risk. I'd made a run-of-the-mill macaroni dish instead.

"It seems we're not the newest family in the neighborhood anymore." Michael nodded toward the front window, where a vacant house had been for rent across the street. A moving truck had appeared three days ago. "Hopefully, the new neighbors will be at the party."

A few minutes later, we meandered around the tables of food and drinks as a gaggle of kids played backyard games. We talked to the people who lived on our street about summer vacations, home improvements, and new restaurants.

"Kathleen!" A woman from a few doors down smiled

widely. "Meet our newest neighbor, Lance Claymore. He just moved into the rental across from you. He's from the States too."

I held out my hand instinctively before looking up. "Hi, I'm Kathleen."

"Nice to meet you." His fingers were warm as they squeezed mine. My gaze lifted, and I gasped. The man's face was familiar—so familiar it felt like a kick to my stomach. I'd seen those catlike eyes before, light green with a ring of yellow. They were the same eyes as Marianne Clavey's. The man's strawberry-blond hair was a similar shade to hers, except for the patches of gray around his sideburns. *The Detroit News* article from sixteen years ago clawed through me, one line permanently scarred on my brain: "I vow to hunt down the person who killed my sister, no matter how long it takes."

The new neighbor held a beer bottle in one hand as beads of condensation collected on the glass. "Where are you from?" he asked.

A cold sweat slicked my skin. "Minnesota." I paused, hesitant to ask the next question. "You?"

He shrugged. "All over, really. Orlando, Florida, most recently."

I exhaled—Florida, not Michigan or Indiana. However, "All over" was too ambiguous, and he could have been lying just like me.

He nodded toward our backyard. "You have a beautiful house. How long have you been there?"

"About six months. It's a nice neighborhood." I cleared my throat, avoiding his stare and keeping my panic in check. My mind conjured up a hazy memory of the only photo I'd ever located of Lee Clavey—a grainy black-and-white mugshot thumbnail taken more than a decade earlier. I searched for something familiar in the shape of my new neighbor's face but was no closer to determining if this could be the same person. "Sorry, what was your name again?"

"Lance. Lance Claymore. I'm a freelance architect. My wife and I divorced last year, and I needed a change of scenery." He threw his hand in the air. "I thought, why not Canada? She always thought it was too cold, but I love the open spaces."

"Me too." I pulled in a mouthful of air, telling myself to get a grip as Lance chatted about a trail at a nearby nature area that he couldn't wait to hike. His excitement seemed so genuine that I second-guessed my initial visceral reaction. I scanned his face again, realizing his lips weren't as thin as hers. He seemed friendly and well-adjusted. Nothing like the bully from the group home. And his name was Lance Claymore, not Lee Clavey. Not that he couldn't use a fake name. Still, it was probably only a coincidence the initials matched. Plenty of people had light green eyes and strawberry-blonde hair. There was no way anyone could have traced me here.

Another neighbor butted in and introduced himself to the newcomer. I waved goodbye and headed toward Michael, focusing on the solid ground beneath my feet and reminding myself to stay calm. My past had scarred me and left me paranoid. I couldn't allow a vague resemblance to unhinge me and the life I'd built. The new neighbor was merely a single guy making a fresh start. He was Lance Claymore, a recent divorcé from Florida, not Lee Clavey, an older brother hell-bent on revenge. I stole another glance behind me.

I was almost sure of it.

A LETTER FROM LAURA

Dear reader,

I want to say a huge thank you for choosing to read *The Foster Daughter*. If you enjoyed it and want to keep up to date with all my latest releases, just sign up at the following link. Your email address will never be shared, and you can unsubscribe at any time.

www.bookouture.com/laura-wolfe

I hope you loved *The Foster Daughter*, and if you did, I would be very grateful if you could write a review. Reviews make such a difference in helping new readers discover one of my books for the first time.

I love hearing from my readers—you can get in touch through my social media or my website.

Thanks,

Laura Wolfe

KEEP IN TOUCH WITH LAURA

www.LauraWolfeBooks.com

facebook.com/LauraWolfeBooks

instagram.com/lwolfe.writes

bookbub.com/profile/laura-wolfe

ACKNOWLEDGMENTS

Many people have supported and assisted me in various ways along the journey of writing and publishing this book. First, I'd like to thank the entire team at Bookouture, especially my editors, Jayne Osborne, Harriet Wade, and Catherine Cobain. Their insights into my story's structure, pacing, and characters made the final version so much better. Thank you to Jess Whitlum-Cooper for coordinating my editing schedule. Additional gratitude goes to copy editor DeAndra Lupu and proofreader Elaini Caruso for their keen eyes, and to Bookouture's top-notch publicity and marketing teams. Thank you to Catherine van Lent for assisting me in the final proofreading of my book. Thank you to the friends and acquaintances who continuously support my writing and provide inspiration and encouragement (you know who you are!). Thank you to the many book bloggers who have helped spread the word about my books. I'm so grateful for the authors in the Bookouture Authors' Lounge Facebook group, who are always there to prop me up, offer laughs, and answer questions. It's a joy to be a part of such a supportive group of talented writers from around the world. Thank you to my parents, Bob and Sue Peterson, my siblings, my cousin Lisa, my mother-in-law, and other family members, both near and far, who have supported my books. I appreciate everyone who has taken the time to tell me that they enjoyed reading my stories, asked me, "How's your writing going?", left a positive review, or sent me a personal message. This process would have been much less fun without my canine "writing partner," Milo, who sat by my side as I wrote every word and forced me to take occasional Frisbee breaks. Most of all, I'd like to thank my kids, Brian and Kate, for always cheering for me, and my husband, JP, for supporting my writing and reading my crappy first drafts. As always, I wouldn't have made it to the end without their steadfast love and encouragement.

PUBLISHING TEAM

Turning a manuscript into a book requires the efforts of many people. The publishing team at Bookouture would like to acknowledge everyone who contributed to this publication.

Audio
Alba Proko
Sinead O'Connor
Melissa Tran

Commercial
Lauren Morrissette
Hannah Richmond
Imogen Allport

Cover design
The Brewster Project

Data and analysis
Mark Alder
Mohamed Bussuri

Editorial
Jess Whitlum-Cooper
Imogen Allport

Copyeditor
DeAndra Lupu

Proofreader
Elaini Caruso

Marketing
Alex Crow
Melanie Price
Occy Carr
Cíara Rosney
Martyna Młynarska

Operations and distribution
Marina Valles
Stephanie Straub
Joe Morris

Production
Hannah Snetsinger
Mandy Kullar
Jen Shannon
Ria Clare

Publicity
Kim Nash
Noelle Holten
Jess Readett
Sarah Hardy

Rights and contracts
Peta Nightingale
Richard King
Saidah Graham

Made in United States
Orlando, FL
21 October 2024

52959400R00181